The Seasoning of Elizabella
A Jamestown Bride Story

by
Tamera Lynn Kraft

M Zion Ridge Press
Books Off the Beaten Path

Mt Zion Ridge Press LLC
295 Gum Springs Rd, NW
Georgetown, TN 37366
https://www.mtzionridgepress.com

ISBN 13: 978-1-955838-49-8
Published in the United States of America
Publication Date: December 1, 2022
Copyright: © Tamera Lynn Kraft 2022

Editor-In-Chief: Michelle Levigne
Executive Editor: Tamera Lynn Kraft
Cover art design by Tamera Lynn Kraft
Cover Art Copyright by Mt Zion Ridge Press LLC © 2022

DEDICATION

I dedicate this story to my loving husband who has supported me throughout this journey in life. He is my best friend, my confidant, and my biggest fan. I've never known a man as honorable or godly as him.

FOREWORD

Usually, I write my historical fiction using the same words they would use in that time period. However, in this story, I took some liberties since most of us don't speak Old English, although I tried to keep the essence of the time period. For instance, in that time period, a corset would be called a boned body, but for the reader's sake, I used the word corset.

There are many things we don't know about Jamestown. I did extensive research and visited Jamestown in researching this novel and strove to be historically accurate in a time when history is being distorted or erased. However, more information is being discovered every day from archeological digs from the Jamestown site.

Chapter One

London, England
November 1619

Elizabella Clark gave her sister the fiercest look she could conjure. "Why didn't you inform me about this earlier?"

"Because I knew you would try to stop me." Honesty didn't even offer a glance as she escorted the burly cart driver to where her trunk sat in front of the large loom in the center of the room.

"You speak truly." Elizabella shivered, but 'twas nothing to do with the cold. The main room used as their seamstress shop contained a fire blazing so exceedingly well, she sometimes longed to open a window, no matter how frigid the outside air.

She glanced at the nearest wall where unused bolts of satin, silk, and embroidered linen cloth she'd ordered from a costly weaver lined the shelves. When she first opened the shop, Honesty and she had spent more time weaving than sewing to make ends meet. Tightly woven cloth sheets and blankets went for a fine price, and she'd learned to make short work of them. Now, they had more sewing jobs than they could handle, and the loom often sat idle.

Her stomach knotted into a tight ball. Without Honesty by her side, how could she hope to fill all the orders in a timely fashion?

Two rocking chairs sat empty in front of the hearth, a sewing basket beside each chair. They'd been hired to sew at least a half dozen gowns for the royal ball, and only one was finished. They should have been laboring over the dresses instead of wasting time on this folly. If only her sister would listen to reason.

"I can't stay." Honesty's voice cracked. "After my heartbreak with Sir Robert, it would be too painful. Come with me."

"Nay, I could never leave our home." Elizabella turned so her sister wouldn't see her watery eyes. "Wounds heal. You'll see. You're so young, barely old enough to wed at fifteen. Once word is out that you no longer have a suitor, gentlemen and tradesmen will flock around here like pigeons at the marketplace. Time enough to acquire a husband more suited to your station."

"My station. I tire of hearing I'm not worthy of the mighty Weathersby family." A tear rolled down Honesty's cheek, and she swiped at it.

The carter leaned under the weight of the trunk, seemingly unsure of what to do.

"Fiddlesticks. They're not good enough for you." Elizabella desired nothing more than to give the eldest son of Lord Weathersby a scolding he'd never forget.

Asking for Honesty's hand in marriage, then retracting the offer when his father disapproved of the union, was reprehensible. If he hadn't been a nobleman, she would have had him arrested for breach of contract.

"Every one of them lives in leisure while doing nothing to help those they consider their inferiors. You're well rid of Sir Robert."

"He isn't that sort. He just... His parents are concerned about our upcoming nuptials. He desires to honor them."

"He should have upheld your honor." A lump rose in Elizabella's throat. He wouldn't defend her sister any more than her father protected her. "He lacks the courage to be a good husband."

Honesty dried her eyes with her pink embroidered handkerchief made of scraps from one of the gowns she'd sewn. "All the more reason to start a new life in a new land." She turned to the carter and handed him a coin. "I'll need it delivered to the *London Merchant* at Saint Katherine's Wharf."

The man readjusted the trunk on his back and carried it to where Elizabella blocked the door, then let out a gusty sigh. She threw up her hands and stepped to the side. He hauled her sister's belongings to his cart parked on the narrow cobblestone road in front of their brick home. It looked out of place in the affluent neighborhood near the Royal Exchange in Central London.

Elizabella stood at the door, biting her lower lip, and watched him drive away. She turned to her sister. "Consider the consequences of this foolishness. You'll move away from everyone you hold dear, and for what? You've heard the stories. Savages attacks in the middle of the night!" A shudder went through her. "What about disease and starvation? When Mary Cartier sailed back to London after her husband died, she said most who travel to Jamestown don't even survive the first year." She took hold of her sister's hand. "I won't be there to protect you."

Honesty pulled her hand away. "I'm a grown woman. I have no need of you hovering over me like a mother hen."

"We have a good life here. Don't discard it so easily."

"Without a husband and children? That's no life."

"How could you say I have no life?" Elizabella's chin trembled. Her sister couldn't have wounded her more if she had plunged a knife into her heart. "I've done everything I could to take care of you, and now that we've created a gown for Queen Anne, our shop will become even more lucrative among the rich and titled. We might even need apprentices."

"Tis your dream, not mine."

"I did this all for you."

"I never asked for any of this. I only desire a husband and a brood of offspring." Honesty draped her dark blue cloak around her shoulders, one of the matching capes Elizabella had made them for Christmas last.

This Yuletide, her sister would be in a savage land all alone. She couldn't let her leave. "Why can't you pursue matrimony here?"

Honest fiddled with tying the string at her neck into a bow, then gazed at her, brow furrowed and pity showing in her eyes. "I know what you sacrificed for me, but I'm a grown woman now. You're still young. At twenty-three, there's still time to marry and have a family."

"I do have a family. You! Only you'd rather traipse off to some unknown land and leave me here alone with all these gowns to sew. I'll never complete them in time."

"You just spoke of hiring apprentices."

"I don't want an apprentice!" Elizabella blinked to keep tears from forming. "You're the only kin I have left."

Honesty stood erect, her shoulders back, unmoving. "Please. We may never see each other again." Her tone was calm, as if she soothed a crying baby. "Do you want our parting to end in a quarrel?"

Elizabella clenched her jaw, unsure of what to do. She couldn't lose the only person in the world who didn't blame her for the fire. She could trust no one else, at least no one who loved her.

"Walk with me to the wharf so we can say a proper farewell."

Heat assaulted Elizabella's eyelids. "Nay, I won't permit this folly. I shan't let you go."

Honesty kissed her cheek and swept past her out the door.

A sob rose in her throat, but she tamped it down. She sat in her rocker and grabbed the expensive silk she was sewing into a gown for Lady Bedford.

Honesty could do whatever she like. If she wanted to travel to a distant land to marry some uncultured farmer, so be it. Elizabella certainly didn't have to approve of it by going to the wharf with her.

She poked the needle through the fabric, tears obscuring her vision. She'd tried to keep her vow to take care of Honesty. 'Twas not her doing that she'd never see her again.

Two stitches later, she tossed the bodice in the basket, wiped her eyes, and threw on her dark cloak. No matter how devastated she was, she couldn't let her only sister depart with angry words between them.

She stepped outside, and cold, crisp air burned her cheeks. Pulling up her hood, she headed toward the docks on the east side of the River Thames. She hurried through central London toward the bridge separating it from the east side. As soon as she crossed London Bridge, the air turned rancid with the stench of rubbish.

She hurried past the butchers' shops. Hog dung mixed with decaying animal carcasses, and she tried not to breathe through her nose. It did no good. The stink assaulted her.

Damp clothing hung on lines, but they never smelled fresh airing in this filthy place. Men lay drunk in the narrow alleys formed by the run-down wattle and daub buildings. Shops took up the first floors, and they crammed as many as ten families into the upper rooms.

She turned the corner onto Pudding Lane and gasped. There it was. Another house had been built to replace the one she had lived in most of her childhood – the one that had burned to the ground. She almost tripped over a man in an inebriated state and stepped over his legs to keep herself from toppling.

This was the area of the city she'd worked hard to escape after Father had died. She'd sewn gowns by candlelight long into the night and saved every halfpenny. Forgoing any comfort, she had been able to purchase a home in Central London for them.

Why couldn't her sister appreciate all she had done to keep her safe? Even though they resembled each other in appearance, they were nothing alike. Honesty cared more about adventure and romance than about the sacrifices she'd made. Her sister never considered the danger her recklessness could cause.

Elizabella swallowed at the lump in the back of her throat. Perhaps they were too much alike, after all. One careless act. One foolish moment leading to a lifetime of remorse.

She'd been overprotective since the fire, but she couldn't lose another sibling. Honesty was all she had left. She would have found her sister the right husband, given a little time, somebody to cherish and protect her, someone Elizabella could trust. Not a coward like Sir Robert Weathersby.

They were good enough to make Lady Weathersby's dresses, but the stench of Pudding Lane still hung around their necks like nooses when it came to matrimony. Sir Robert wasn't any better than his father. If it wasn't for him, Honesty would have stayed in England where she belonged.

A groan escaped her lips. 'Twas her fault. She could have stopped this romance between her sister and a titled man, but Honesty had seemed so happy.

As Elizabella turned the corner at the baker's shop, she caught a glimpse of her sister's light brown curly hair sticking out of the hood of her cloak and hastened to catch up. When she reached the corner, Honesty was nowhere in sight. She slowed her stride and watched for some sight of that blue cape.

A crash sounded near the livery. She hurried toward the noise and turned onto a narrow road.

"We want our money," a tall fellow shouted. He and a stout chap hovered over a man cowering in the corner. They both wore dirty, shapeless woolen shirts with sleeveless leather jerkins.

She drew the back of her hand over her mouth to keep from crying out.

"I know nothing of it," the third man rasped out. He had a brown woolen blanket draped around him, and he pulled it tighter as if it would protect him.

Without daring to turn around, she silently took a few steps backward. She had to get out of here before they discovered her.

The stout brute punched the man wrapped in the cover. He staggered back but remained standing.

She managed to slink back a bit more.

The tall one grabbed the cowering man's shirt. "You took it. I know you did."

"Nay, 't wasn't me."

Everything in her wanted to turn and flee, but they'd hear. She dared another footstep toward the road.

The tall man growled and stabbed him in the stomach.

She stopped, sluggish, unable to move. Everything slowed.

The stabbed man gazed at where blood stained his blanket. His mouth opened. He let out a slight gasp. His blanket dropped to the ground. Then slowly, as if somebody stood behind guiding him, he fell. Blood oozed from his middle and made a puddle in the dirt.

Elizabella screamed, then clamped her hand over her mouth. Too late to stop it from escaping.

The men jerked around and rushed toward her.

Panic rose from her gut. She hoisted up her skirts and ran down the road as fast as her legs could carry her. She heard their pounding feet chase, but she didn't dare look back. She surveyed the road ahead. Where could she hide? What store offered refuge? A cart drove in front of her and blocked her way. She almost ran straight into it but turned a corner just in time.

A small courtyard with no passageway through. She perused the area for a doorway or someplace to hide. A barrel squatted in the corner with a haystack and pitchfork nearby. Clothes hung to dry in the other corner. She ducked behind the barrel.

Footfalls rushed closer. She dared not breathe, fearing they'd find her. Her heart beat boisterously, perchance loudly enough for them to hear. Nay. Nay. Nay. They couldn't find her. They couldn't.

"Elizabella, is that you?" Honesty's voice.

She raised her head a little and glanced over the barrel.

Before she could speak, the murderers rushed in behind her sister. With dread rising in her, she stood. "Honesty!"

The stout ruffian grabbed her sister. Honesty jerked, and he tossed her to the ground, a bloodied knife in hand.

"Stop!" A weight dropped onto Elizabella's chest. "Leave her be."

"We got the wrong girl." The tall man pointed to her. "She's the one what saw us."

Rage rose out of her. Spittle formed in the corners of her mouth, and she grabbed the pitchfork.

A roar from deep inside escaped her lips, and she charged toward the men, jabbing at them, wanting to stab them as they had plunged that knife into her sister. "Get away from her!"

The men backed away to avoid the weapon.

"You crazy wench." The stout man tried to grab the handle, but she stabbed at his hand, drawing blood, and he pulled back. "What are you about with that thing?"

She tried to thrust the pitchfork into his stomach, but he brushed to the side, and she missed. Grasping the handle, she ran toward them, determined not to miss the mark again.

The tall man grabbed the stout man's arm. "Let's get out of here."

She rushed toward them until they scurried out of the courtyard. Reaching where her sister lay, Elizabella ceased the pursuit, but she kept the pitchfork firmly gripped in her hands. If they came back, she'd be ready. Footsteps faded, then scuffling noises.

Shouts. "You there. Stop in the name of the king."

All the anger drained out of her. She dropped the weapon. Her knees gave out, and she collapsed in the mud beside her sister.

Honesty moaned.

Tears welled up behind Elizabella's eyes. "You're alive."

Blood seeped from the wound in Honesty's shoulder. Elizabella's stomach roiled as she pushed her hand against the gash.

A constable entered the alley, sword drawn. He viewed the area, gazing both ways down the road, then sheathed his weapon. "Looks like you've had some trouble here. What happened? Did those two ruffians waylay you?"

"Help me." Elizabella tried to lift her sister. A flood of emotions threatened to swallow her. "She's been stabbed."

Chapter Two

Jamestown, Virginia

Miles Bonneville stood over the grave of his wife and newborn son, shovel still in his hand, at the edge of his plantation at the Neck of the Woods near Jamestown. He gazed at the foreboding sky. Storm clouds overhead mirrored the darkness inside him. His throat ached from grief.

The grove of oak trees, although barren this time of year, would provide a suitable resting place with shade from the hot Virginia sun. It had a clear view of the tobacco fields. He swiped his hand across the back of his neck. What difference did the setting make? She wasn't there to see it.

His younger brother Hugh stood beside him. "I'm sorry. She was a good woman."

A muscle in Miles' jaw twitched. He held back the retort that Hugh had never cared much for Mary. His presence at the funeral was some comfort. At least he was sober.

A drizzle started to fall, concealing the moisture escaping his eyes. Lightening lit the sky, followed a moment later by crashing thunder.

Reverend Cochran placed his hand on Miles' shoulder. "Remember the words of our Lord during this time of grief. He is the resurrection and the life. Trust in Him."

Miles nodded, afraid if he spoke, his remarks would betray him. He would see Mary again, but the loss felt too great for platitudes to offer much consolation. Another crash of thunder sounded as a deluge of rain pelted them.

"We should head toward the house." Hugh swiped his dark wet hair out of his eyes. "This approaching tempest looks fierce."

Miles didn't move. He couldn't leave Mary and the babe yet, not in this cold ground. He wasn't sure he could ever depart.

Hugh touched his arm. "We must take shelter." Another jagged lightning bolt followed by a roar of thunder confirmed his words.

Miles nodded and followed Hugh and Reverend Cochran to the home he'd built to live in with his wife. The storm came down in torrents by the time they reached his wattle and daub home of four rooms, larger than most in the area. He'd wanted the best for Mary. With Hugh's help, he'd built it within a few months of their marriage. They'd even chopped down trees and laid boards for a wood floor.

Hugh had never stayed there. Plenty of space, but he insisted they needed privacy. He stayed in their old one-room house near the servants' quarters.

Miles paused at the door, then stepped in.

The crib sat against the farthest wall next to Mary's loom and spinning wheel. He'd spent a fortnight building it. Only a week ago, they'd decided on a name for the babe. Most colonists refused to name their offspring for at least two years, to avoid heartbreak until they knew their children would survive, as if lack of a name could change that.

Mary had refused to live in fear. "His name will be James in honor of our king and our new home."

He'd laughed at her insistence. "What if it's a girl?"

"It won't be." She had a twinkle in her eye, as if she'd been given information she couldn't possibly know. "It couldn't hurt to choose a girl's name for the next babe."

He had hugged her close. "Then if it's a girl, we'll name her Joy because you've brought me so much happiness."

No longer anything to be joyful about. Yesterday, James was born dead after an arduous labor, and Mary soon followed him into eternity.

Why hadn't he taken her back to England? Jamestown was no place to raise a family. With his nearest neighbors sailing to London, there wasn't even a woman available to attend her, and he had no idea how to help.

Reverend Cochran moved toward the hearth where the fire had almost gone out and poked it a few times, then set a couple of logs on it to revive the flames. Miles braced his hands on the table in the middle of the room, exhausted from the emotions he tried to keep at bay.

"Your garments are drenched," Reverend Cochran said. "Come, sit by the fire and warm yourself."

Miles shuffled to the fireplace and collapsed into the rocker he'd made for Mary. The fire caught hold of the logs and put out enough warmth now, but it didn't warm his heart. He turned to his brother. "Sit, dry yourself."

Hugh pulled on his ear the way he always did when he was up to no good. "I must attend to important matters. I'll see you on the morrow."

Miles lifted an eyebrow. "In this rain? Stay here for the night. Your business can wait until the morn."

"Nay, these matters shan't wait."

Miles gave a curt nod, his emotions too raw to question Hugh's intent. This once, he'd let him go without a lecture.

As the door closed, the ache in Miles' chest spread throughout his body. "Reverend, thank you for coming out and saying a few words at the burial."

"Of course, Master Bonneville. I'm sorry for your loss." Reverend Cochran cleared his throat. "The General Council meets in a week. I'll let them know of your tragedy. They would surely excuse your absence."

The thought of going into town for a meeting so soon after Mary's death caused a heaviness Miles wasn't sure he could shake, but he wouldn't give in to it. There were many issues that needed resolving, including setting up laws for the new government and determining how to keep an uneasy peace with the Powhatan's new chief, Opechancanough.

Relationships with the savages had grown tense after Chief Powhatan died. He was the one who formed the alliance of tribes into the Powhatan, named after him. Things had only worsened when Captain John Rolfe returned with news that Lady Rolfe had passed away in England. Lady Rolfe, also known as Pocahontas, was the daughter of the late Chief Powhatan, the niece of the current chief.

It didn't help that Captain Rolfe already had a new wife and had left Lady Rolfe's son in England. If Rolfe had acted properly and had brought the child to Jamestown with his new wife instead of abandoning him in London for relatives to care for, the chief might not have been so angry. A man of Rolfe's status should have known better.

Miles tapped his fist against his mouth. He needed to attend that meeting. His duty to the colony surpassed any personal tragedy. "I'll be there."

"Good man." Reverend Cochran patted him on the shoulder. "The bride ship from London should arrive in a few months."

Miles' jaw twitched. How dare the reverend choose the day of his wife's funeral to bring this up? He let out a breath to keep his anger at bay. "I have no desire for another bride."

The reverend lit his pipe and sat in the chair next to Miles'. "A man of your stature requires a wife."

Miles smacked his hand down on the rocker arm harder than intended. "I have a wife. At least I did."

"Master Bonneville, matrimony shall ease your grief and provide you with more sons."

He shook his head. "Nay, nothing shall dispel my sorrow."

"Were you not the one who encouraged the bachelors to secure brides for the benefit of the colony? I believe you even wrote the letter to the Virginia Company insisting they bring more women of marrying age over here to perpetuate the settlement and to help the men abstain from vices that might overtake them if they were to remain single."

Heat flushed Miles' face "I have no such vices."

Reverend Cochran lifted his eyebrow. "I know you to be an honorable Christian man, but we are all subject to temptation."

"How dare you? Lady Bonneville was just laid in the ground, and you think I shall use it as an excuse to indulge in all sorts of revelry. I'm not my father or my brother."

"I implied no such thing." Reverend Cochran's tone was gentle. "Your greatest temptation is pride. You require someone to remind you of your need for a Savior. A good woman could do that."

Miles gripped the arms of the rocker. Staring at the fire, he clenched his jaw to hold of his tongue. Everything in him wanted to dispatch Reverend Cochran out of his house. The man had no right to chide him, a member of the Burgess and an upstanding church member. If others guarded their reputation as he had, the colony would be cleansed of the debauchery that plagued it.

The reverend gazed at him as if he could see every dark spot inside his soul. "At least consider it when the ship arrives."

Miles had never lied to a vicar before, but he would promise anything to end this conversation. "I shall give it due consideration." It wasn't exactly a lie. It deserved no further reflection.

Reverend Cochran's eyes shone with a touch of compassion. "'Tis all I ask." Thunder crashed. The torrent barraged the roof of the house with more intensity. "By your leave, I'll stay here tonight. By morrow, the storm should have moved on."

"Stay as long as you desire." Miles' voice cracked. The vicar had angered him, and he wanted nothing more than to forcibly remove the man from his home. Memories of Mary begged for his attention, but it would not be Christian to show the reverend such lack of hospitality during the storm.

Cochran stood and grabbed the kettle of water heating on the coals. "I'll make us some hot barley water."

Miles nodded and gazed at the fire. What errand was so urgent that Hugh braved this tempest? Mischief, no doubt. Hugh was too much like their father. Mary knew how to comfort his fears when his brother was off doing who knew what.

Lord, what am I to do without her? How do I go on?

Reverend Cochran filled the teapot with hot water and pulled a tin of barley and a jar of honey off the shelf. Miles ignored him, but he couldn't discount the melancholy overshadowing him. If he left Jamestown, mayhap he could escape all the memories of his wife and son.

Nay, he would never return to England. Nothing was left for him in the land where he was born but scandal and a tattered reputation he could never overcome. England was no longer his home. The only way he could establish a life worth living would be in this colony of death.

He couldn't go back.

Chapter Three

London, England

Elizabella paced the front room, waiting for the surgeon to finish treating her sister. Why hadn't she accompanied Honesty to the ship? Saint Katherine's Wharf was notorious for ruthless men accosting people and stealing their belongings.

"'Tis my fault." She'd allowed her sister to traverse these dangerous roads alone because of her own stubborn refusal to accompany her. She'd never forgive herself if Honesty died because of her.

The heavy door creaked open, and the surgeon came into the room, blood all over his apron. Honesty's blood. She swallowed, too afraid to ask.

"Your sister is weak, but she'll recover, providing infection doesn't overtake her."

"Praise be."

"She must rest and cannot be moved for at least a fortnight."

Elizabella couldn't believe her good fortune. The ship would sail for Jamestown without Honesty on board.

The surgeon wiped his hands on a bloody cloth. "I'll keep her in my back room and hire a maid to care for her." He was short, bald, and portly. "I have some potions to ease the pain, but my services are costly. I require a pound sixpence."

Elizabella reached for the coins in an inside pocket of her cloak. "I have means. Whatever you need to care for her." She paid him.

He grinned as if he'd come into his fortune and dropped the coins into a nearby wooden box. "The wound was not deep. I gave mandrake for the pain while I stitched her up. It will make her drowsy for a day or two, but the pain will return. There may be other remedies she'll need, ones even more dear."

"See to it." Elizabella placed another pound into his hand. He was probably dealing deceitfully with her, but it didn't matter. She wouldn't take a chance with her sister's life to save a few coins. "If you need more, I'll pay it. When can I see her?"

"She'll be groggy, but you can go to her now." He opened the door to the back room.

She entered. Honesty lay covered on the wooden cot, staring into the fireplace. Bloody clothes were thrown on the floor in the corner. Her sister's blood. At least her eyes were open.

Elizabella took her hand. "Thank the Lord you weren't badly

wounded."

Her sister wiped a tear from her face. "I won't be able to sail."

"You'll be in good health in no time, then we can forget this folly about going away to some savage land."

"I'm traveling to the Americas as soon as possible. Other bride ships are planning to sail at some time during the next year or two."

"We can talk about this when you've regained your strength."

Honesty closed her eyes, and for a moment Elizabella thought she'd fallen asleep. "Do me one kindness."

Elizabella leaned closer to hear.

"My letters of passage are in my purse. Take them to the *London Merchant* at the wharf and tell the men there why I'm not coming."

"Nay, I won't abandon you like this."

"Please, Elizabella, this one indulgence. If I don't board without sending word, I'll forfeit my opportunity to gain passage on another ship."

"Would that be such a tragedy? You're here with me where you belong."

Honesty tried to raise herself up off the bed. "If you won't go, I'll do it myself."

Elizabella placed a hand on her sister's shoulder. "You need to rest and take time to heal."

Honesty sank down into her pillow and closed her eyes. "Then you'll do it?" Her voice sounded so weak.

"Aye, you've given me little choice." Elizabella grabbed her sister's purse. "This isn't the end of this discussion. When you're better, I'll convince you of the foolhardiness in this if I have to sit on you to do it."

Honesty let out a soft snore. Already asleep from the mandrake she'd been given.

Elizabella kissed her on the forehead and headed to the wharf. When she arrived an hour later, a chill blew in from the ocean, and she pulled the hood of her cloak up around her head. She motioned to a sailor passing by. "Do you know where I can find the *London Merchant*?"

The man pointed to a nearby ship, its gangplank stretched to the dock. *London Merchant* was painted in white block letters on the side. A cluster of young women congregated on the deck, chattering and gazing over the railing.

"Thank you." Elizabella rummaged through her sister's purse until she found papers from the Virginia Company and headed toward the gangplank.

A tall man passed by, and her heart skipped a beat.

He was the same ruffian she'd seen murder that poor man, the one who stabbed her sister. He stopped near the gangplank and leaned against a wood beam, blocking her path away from the ship.

The stout chap who'd also taken part in the crime strode toward him.

She wasn't close enough to hear them, but their whispers to each other were animated.

Panic rose to the back of her throat. Everything in her wanted to run away from them, to escape. She forced herself to remain still despite her heart nearly exploding in her chest. If she made haste, they'd notice her.

They continued their argument. She didn't dare walk past them to get away, fearing they might see her. She turned the other way and almost tumbled into a cart filled with barrels and sacks. Wagons lined the path, making escape impossible. What was she to do? The only way was past the ruffians, unless...

If she could make it aboard the ship and present her sister's papers, they would allow her aboard as one of the brides. Even if the murderers followed her, the crew wouldn't let harm come to her. She'd be safe. As soon as the men left, she could explain and depart before they set sail.

Covering more of her face with her hood, she headed toward the gangplank.

Don't rush.

One step at a time.

As if she was out for a stroll.

As if her life wasn't in danger.

She reached the ship and dared a glance back. If the men recognized her, they didn't show it. The ocean waves crashed against the wood, making a thudding noise that matched the beat of her heart. She hastened up the narrow gangplank, almost tripping on her long skirt, recovered, and made it onto the deck.

"You there," an officer onboard called out and marched her way.

The men near the gangplank glanced toward her, but she twisted away, turning her back to them.

The muscular officer wore a black jacket with a red waistcoat and carried himself in a commanding way. A scowl twisted his lip under his bushy reddish-brown mustache. "I need your name and papers before you board my ship."

She handed the letters to him.

He read the top page. "Miss Honesty Clark. An hour has passed since you were due here."

"Pardon my delay." She kept her voice low to keep the men on the dock from hearing her. "I had to attend to a family matter."

"That doesn't concern me." He turned to another man dressed in civilian clothes. "She's the last of them."

The man nodded and climbed down the gangplank onto the dock.

The officer shouted, "Aboard, aboard the ship." He faced Elizabella and placed his hands on his hips. "Do you need a formal invitation? Report to your chaperones on the main deck."

Elizabella nodded and risked a peek toward the dock. The murderers untied the ropes holding the ship to the moorings. The back of her throat ached. If they were hired by the shipyard, she wouldn't be able to disembark in time.

The officer called to the deck. "Cast off!"

Sailors moved to raise the gangplank.

She hurried to the side and looked down. The men still stood where it was moored. If she tried to scamper down the gangplank now, they'd see her.

A voice bellowed from somewhere below deck. "Toss oars!"

Her chest couldn't have been tighter if she'd been wearing a whale bone corset. If she didn't leave now, the ship would sail. She risked another glance. They still blocked the way. She closed her eyes tight and struggled to take a breath.

The man barked another command. "Let fall."

She ran to where the gangplank had been pulled up. "Wait!"

The stout brute on the dock regarded her, his eyes widening, and a scowl crossing his features. He'd recognized her.

Another order. "Give way together!" The ship jerked away from the dock.

She took a step back.

He nudged the other man and pointed to her. They ran toward the ship and tried to grab hold of the ropes, but they slipped through their fingers.

Her legs threatened to give way. *They can't reach me here. I'm safe.* She repeated the words in her mind, even though she didn't believe them. Everything around her started swaying.

"Oars! Let Fall!"

"Miss Clark," the officer said, "are you deaf? Report to the main deck now."

She nodded but couldn't bring herself to move. The officer threw up his hands, marched to where sailors were doing something with the sails, and started shouting orders.

The ruffians on the dock yelled obscenities she could clearly hear above the bellowing of the officer. Even the women on the main deck turned toward the uproar. Water surrounded the tiny ship, and the land receded with each pull of the oars. The rogues now resembled children playing games. She could barely hear their ugly shouts.

London grew smaller as they traveled the Thames River toward the channel. When they reached the mouth, the men pulled ropes. Big white sails rose to the sky.

She needed to get off this ship now before they sailed into the Celtic Sea. After that, the Atlantic Ocean. Mayhap, she could jump overboard. She ran to the railing.

Nay, the shore was too far away, and she knew of nobody who'd been able to swim across the channel. Besides, she'd never been a strong swimmer.

Jamestown. She was headed to Jamestown. Every limb in her body grew weak. She couldn't stay aboard to be carted off to the same savage land she'd warned her sister about.

Once the sails were fully erect and caught the wind, the officer strode to her, glowering with lips pinched, and pointed toward a group of young women gathered in the center of the deck. "If you don't mind, Miss Clark, I wish to request your presence with the other women on the main deck." His voice dripped with sarcasm.

She struggled to find her voice. "Are there any other stops before the New Land?"

"Nay, our next landfall is the New World."

"Perchance you could stop in Plymouth or even Ireland? I need to get off this ship."

"Of course, my lady." The officer bowed slightly and chuckled under his breath. "First Mate Rogers, at your service. I'll go tell the captain to lower the sails and head to the nearest coastline because one of our Jamestown brides got the shakes and changed her mind?"

"Could you please?" Her voice came out squeaky like a child's.

First Mate Rogers' mouth gaped open as if he couldn't believe what she was saying. "Woman, your brain is as dry as a half-eaten biscuit after a voyage. Nay, I shan't do any such thing."

The floor beneath her dissolved away, and she grasped the railing to keep from falling.

He jerked his head toward the deck. "Off with you, Miss Clark. It's a bit too late to turn back now."

~~~~~

Jamestown, Virginia

"The Powhatan have reason to be angry." Miles rubbed his clenched jaw. "They offered us trade and assistance, and we treated them like savages."

Most of the twenty men in the General Assembly were gathered in the Jamestown Church. It had been the first meeting since many of them had taken to their beds with marsh fever. The first three days had gone well until Governor Yeardley approached the topic of Native relations. Since then, tempers had flared.

"They are savages." Master Douglas' face reddened as he gripped the wooden bench in front of him. He was the oldest of the Burgesses, and his age was only matched by his obstinacy. "Surely, Master Bonneville, you're not saying these godless brutes are our equals. They need to be shown the might of the British Kingdom. That will get their attention and respect."

"And what might is that?" Goodman John Cooper said. He was rugged and tall, a year younger than Miles at age twenty-seven, and the youngest
~~~~~

member of the assembly. "We are a small colony a long way from home, and there are close to twenty thousand of them. I pray these savages don't decide to show us their might."

Miles strove to keep his tone steady. "Master Douglas, does Scripture not say we are all deserving of God's wrath? Christ died for their redemption as well as ours."

"Look at Lady Rolfe," Governor Yeardley said. "She was a Powhatan, and she converted and was baptized into a saving faith in Christ. Surely, you consider her a fellow Christian."

"Still an Indian." Master Douglas looked at his feet. "I suppose her baptism and marriage to Lord Rolfe did give her a certain status."

"Her conversion and baptism were heartfelt, I assure you," Reverend Cochran said. "These savages are God's creatures, just as we are. If we are to convince them civilization is a better way, shouldn't we apply the golden rule?"

"The golden rule might get us slaughtered in our beds." Master Douglas stood and rubbed his thigh as he limped about. His leg had a tendency to cramp during long meetings. "You can't trust any of them."

"If for that reason alone, we must try to keep this uneasy alliance between us." Samuel Jordan was one of the earliest settlers and had married a young bride who recently gave birth to his fifth child. "Some of us have our wives and children to consider."

"Balderdash." Master Douglas stomped his foot twice before plopping onto his seat.

Miles sighed noisily. "We must do all we can to improve relations with the Natives. Can any of you soon forget that the peace we kept with the Chickahominy encouraged them to supply us with the food we needed during the starving time? Or that Chief Powhatan was a friend to the colony? His brother may not be as affable, but we should meet with him and do what we can to appease him."

"Appease him?" Captain Lawnes, a retired Naval sea captain who'd recently settled in Jamestown, beat his hand on the wooden bench in front of him. "How, when he blames the white man for Lady Rolfe's death, especially when Rolfe left her son, a member of their royal family, in London?"

"We have to try," Miles said.

"Perchance you could send your brother to converse with them." He grinned. "Or do his frequent visits to the tribe only include the squaws?"

Snickers filled the room, but when Miles glared at the men, they had the decency to blush.

"Watch your tongue, Captain Lawnes." Miles crossed his arms and moved closer to him until he felt the man's breath in his face and smelled the eggs Lawnes had for breakfast. "Hugh visits the Powhatan for the purpose of trade. His proficiency with the Powhatan language and culture make it possible for him to make agreements that not only benefit the Bonneville Plantation but every farm around here."

"And what does he trade with the Indian maidens?" Master Douglas patted his leg and let out a full belly laugh.

The rest of the Burgesses didn't bother to hide their merriment this time.

Heat shot up Miles' back. "You make a fine jester, Master Douglas. Mayhap you should use your talent in the king's court. It has no place here. Your wit cuts at the heart of my family's honor. Unless you can produce evidence of fornication and formally charge my brother, I demand an apology."

"Come now." John patted Miles on the shoulder. "Nobody's making any formal allegations." He raised an eyebrow. "Perchance this bit of humor has gone too far. I, more than most, know the consequences of an accusation like this."

Some men cleared their throats.

"I meant no harm," Captain Lawnes said as he bowed slightly.

Miles nodded. He would never admit he'd had the same suspicions about Hugh, but he would hate to see his brother whipped in the middle of the fort while a crowd watched and cheered as John had been three years earlier. Although in John's case, it had been well deserved.

"My apologies," Master Douglas said, "but you would do well to gain a sense of gaiety to go with that fastidiousness you carry like an anvil around your neck. It wouldn't hurt you to laugh on occasion."

Miles' hands formed into fists, and he took a step toward the man.

"Master Douglas." William Capps, representative from Kecoughtan, stepped in front of Miles, blocking his way. "May I remind you it's been only a fortnight since Master Bonneville lost his wife and son?"

The crotchety old Burgess turned red. "Forgive me, Master Bonneville." He cleared his throat. "I was away hunting and hadn't heard about your loss until this very moment. Mistress Bonneville was a fine lady."

Miles rubbed his jaw. Scripture commanded him to forgive, although he often found that difficult to do. "We all say things we regret. I accept your apology."

"Gentlemen, we need time to allow cooler heads to prevail," Governor Yeardley said. "Let's adjourn for now and take nourishment. We can revisit the issue in the afternoon session."

The men stood and headed outside toward the hall where women from the fort had prepared refreshments. Miles waited until they all had left. The last time he'd been in the church, Mary had been with him. She wouldn't miss a church service, no matter how close the birthing was. Now she was gone, and he was here alone.

He knelt on the pew in front of him and buried his head in his arms.

"Lord, I don't know what to do. You've brought me this far, but with the disgraceful way Hugh is acting and the Indians on the verge of war… How can I go on without her by my side?"

Reverend Cochran had suggested another wife, but how could he find a woman as honorable as Mary or one he had such great affection for?

He looked at the cross in the front of the church. Perchance he should remain a widower for the rest of his life in honor of her memory.

Chapter Four

Aboard Ship, Atlantic Ocean

Elizabella made her way to the deck where her chaperone, Goodwife Constance Wright, stood watching the waves. It had been a week since the ship had sailed. She tried to make peace with what had happened, but every time she thought she had quieted her soul, dread swept over her and made her stomach roil.

This had to be a nightmare. There was no other explanation. A little over a week ago, she was sewing gowns for the royal ball, her seamstress shop the conversation of the court. Now, she was sailing to an untamed wilderness under her sister's name.

A lump formed in her throat. She didn't even know if Honesty had recovered. The doctor said she would as long as infection didn't overtake her, but one never knew about such things. If Honesty did survive, she would never know what happened. Would she believe Elizabella deserted her?

The only way was to tell her chaperone how she ended up onboard. If she confessed the whole matter, Goodwife Wright could assist her in finding a way to journey home.

Elizabella tugged on the neckline of her blue-flowered jacket. It was implausible even to her that this could happen, and she was the one who lived through it. What if the goodwife didn't believe her?

She watched the steady waves rippling against the ship with a thud. Each wave followed by another. Each event causing another. Her life rippling out of control. Nausea swept over her. She closed her eyes and placed her hand over her stomach.

If she told the truth, the worst thing she could imagine was they'd arrest her and return her to England. Would that be so bad? She could pay for the voyage and explain to the Justice of the Peace about her predicament.

The last time she appeared before a court, the magistrate charged her with starting the fire that killed her brother. They'd believed her then, even with her father giving evidence against her, and this time Honesty could speak on her behalf.

If only she'd been able to bring her gold with her, she could have purchased a return journey before the ship had landed. She had more than enough saved for both voyages. She sighed. She only had a few gold coins in her possession, not nearly enough.

Goodwife Wright tucked her brown hair into her coif and chuckled. "Is the sea causing your stomach to churn?"

Elizabella's gut rumbled as if it heard the goodwife. She nodded.

"I have a supply of ginger in my trunk. This is my second voyage to the Americas, and I've found it helps more than any other concoction I've tried. I'll bring some to you."

"Thank ye, Goodwife Wright," Elizabella said.

"May I remind you that since my husband and I are your chaperones and have no titles, you may call us by our Christian names? The New World doesn't hold with the formality of England."

"Constance." Her stomach clenched tighter than a sailor's knot. Now that she had decided to confess her plight, she couldn't manage to get the words out. "Why did you decide to return to Jamestown after sailing back to England?"

The chaperone turned and stared out into the ocean. "My first husband had an estate in England, and I had affairs to handle personally. Otherwise, I never would have made the journey. Jamestown is my home."

"Oh." Elizabella flushed. "I'm sorry to bring up painful memories. I didn't know you were married before."

Constance's chin quivered slightly. "Death touches everyone in Virginia. It was two years since my first husband and I sailed to the New World. He died during his seasoning."

"Seasoning?"

"Everyone goes through a time of seasoning their first year. It is when you acclimate to the climate and diseases of the colony. Some, such as my first husband, succumb to it."

Elizabella had seen enough death in her lifetime. Was this how she'd end up, perishing from some affliction only existing in the New World?

Another wave of nausea swept over her. Her sister would never know what happened. She had to find a way back to her seamstress shop in the heart of London where she'd be safe.

Constance set her hand on Elizabella's arm. "Don't fret so. Many survive the seasoning. I did. And my second husband has been a godsend. He's a good man, and I love him with all my heart. There are many menfolk to choose from there, strong and adventurous fellows with good character forged in the fire of difficulty. You'll find a suitable husband who will provide for you. You might even grow to cherish him as I have mine."

The churning in Elizabella's stomach roiled to the surface. She leaned over the rail and emptied the contents, then wiped her mouth with her sleeve, the sour taste remaining. "At least my queasiness is not as bad as what Widow Ferrier is going through."

Nancy Ferrier, a widow about Elizabella's age, had earlier confided the only reason she embarked on the journey was because her husband had died six months after the wedding and had left her penniless. Within an hour of the ship sailing, she had taken to her bed, bucket in hand, with a severe case of seasickness.

Constance's brow wrinkled. "Poor Widow Ferrier is beyond what ginger can cure."

Elizabella squared her shoulders. "I'm more in need of counsel than of ginger. You said we could come to you with any confidential matter."

Constance touched her arm. "I meant it, Honesty."

Elizabella winced inside at the sound of her sister's name, reminding of the lie she told to board the ship. If she'd confided in First Mate Rogers as soon as she'd arrived, none of this would have happened. The sailors would have protected her from those murderers, and she wouldn't be in this predicament. Why had she lied?

Father's twisted face and accusing voice rose from the waves. *Nobody will ever trust you again. You don't deserve to live.*

"Nay, it was an accident." Elizabella leaned over the rail again and retched.

Constance touched her arm. "What was an accident?"

She wiped her mouth. "I... I've changed my mind about being a bride." She grasped the rail of the ship and gazed out to sea, trying to find an anchor or land or something she could hold on to. Only blue—blue skies, blue water, emptiness. "I want to go home." She swiped the tear running down her cheek.

Constance gazed at her until it became uncomfortable. "We all have moments of nostalgia when embarking on a new adventure."

Elizabella diverted her attention to the sea. If only she could find the courage to explain what happened. "Is there a way out of this? Is it too late?"

Constance took hold of her hand. "Fifteen is so young to make a decision to leave everything you've ever known. I can appreciate your hesitation."

Fifteen? She stopped herself in time to keep from exclaiming she was a woman of twenty-three years, only a year younger than Constance.

"Unless you have gold or some kind of currency with you to pay for your voyage, it's not possible. When you boarded this ship, you limited yourself to two choices, marriage or servitude. 'Tis a difficult lesson to learn at your age, but some choices can't be reversed."

Another wave thudded against the ship. She knew too well about events that couldn't be undone, but she would never marry and be bound to this horrible land. "Is the life of a bondservant difficult?"

Constance chuckled. "You'll have your share of hard labor no matter what you choose. Jamestown doesn't provide an easy life, but it's worth all of it. The climate is temperate, and the land is even more lush and green than England. The trees and flowers and wild animals are like none I've ever seen. Vast open lands never before explored by the British, and a mission to bring God to a new land and be remembered for future generations. We are laying the foundation for a new colony in a new world."

Elizabella wiped her hand over her face. She didn't want to be remembered. She wanted to be safe at home in her rocking chair, sewing ladies' gowns. "I'm not the adventurous sort."

Constance's hazel eyes danced with amusement. "Stepping aboard this ship for a new land is a bold move for a cautious young woman."

Elizabella bit her lip. If only she could bring herself to blurt out the truth. "I don't want to marry. At least not so soon."

"Even if you decide to indenture yourself and find a husband later, all he need do is redeem your contract. Laws are in place to protect bondservants. Your master will be required to care for your needs, and at the end of the service, you'll be compensated with a tract of land and other goods."

A tract of land? As if she would stay one moment longer than necessary. "Could I trade that for a voyage back to England?"

Constance gazed at the ocean as if she saw something Elizabella couldn't. "You might find you love this new land. Even after my first husband died, I couldn't imagine leaving."

The churning in her stomach felt like a wife wringing out her laundry on washday. Nay, she couldn't remain in Jamestown. She had to find a way to return to England, or at least get word to Honesty about what had happened to her. Royalty and titled ladies paid well for their gowns. She had enough gold saved back home to pay for twenty passages.

Time to tell Constance everything. She took a deep breath. "'Twas something else. I--"

"Stop!" someone shouted.

Elizabella and Constance turned and took a few steps toward the ruckus.

"Get him!"

A boy, barely old enough to shave, ran on deck. His eyes darted around wildly.

"Don't let him get away."

He dashed from the sailors chasing him. One man grabbed for him and tripped, plunging to the deck. The lad brushed past Elizabella and dashed to the railing. He climbed up and stared at the water below.

First Mate Rogers drew closer. "Nowhere else to go. It's us or the sharks."

The boy's shoulders drooped, and he made his way off the rails.

Rogers grabbed his arms. He didn't struggle.

The captain, a stern looking older man with a full beard, bolted out of his cabin. "What is this ruckus?"

"This rogue snuck on board and has been masquerading as a part of the crew, Captain." First Mate Rogers twisted the boy's arm to keep him from moving. The boy winced but made no attempt to escape the grip.

"Please, Captain," the boy whimpered. "It's not what you think. I'm here by happenchance."

"You want we should toss him overboard?" the first mate asked, a hint of a grin under his mustache.

Elizabella gasped. Would they do that to her if they found out?

"Throw him in irons and lock him in the bilge," the captain said. "We'll turn him over when we get to Jamestown, and they can hang him there."

"Nay, I beg you." The boy pulled away from Rogers and knelt at the captain's feet. "I'll work for my passage."

"Not on my ship," the captain said. "I have no tolerance for anyone who tries to steal a passage under false pretenses."

"I'll do anything, Captain. Anything."

The captain jerked his head toward the hull, and a couple of sailors dragged the boy below.

Constance shook her head. "Probably some criminal trying to escape the noose by going to America. It happens from time to time."

Elizabella splayed her hand over her chest. "He said it was by mistake."

"A mistake? With an officer at the top of the gangplank guarding the entrance? The only way he got here was through deception. The captain's being more than generous giving him a chance to explain himself at trial. Most would throw him overboard and be done with it."

"He's so young." Her voice thickened. "Surely, they won't hang him."

"Mayhap not, but even if he is not wanted in England, he robbed the captain of the price of a ship's passage. They might be merciful and give him a good whipping before selling him into servitude. They need the laborers, but it's up to the Burgess."

Whipped? Elizabella's throat thickened until she had difficulty catching her breath. She stared into the endless blue ocean. No escape. Mayhap the sharks would have been more compassionate than the captain on this wretched ship.

Constance brushed out the creases of her skirt. "Now good woman, what did you want to discuss?"

"The ginger," Elizabella rasped out. "I'll be by for it later." She teetered her way to the passenger hold, not sure her legs would keep her erect until she got there.

She would never become a Jamestown bride, and she couldn't admit the truth. Unless she could find a way to get word to her sister, she was doomed to enforced servitude for who knew how long.

Chapter Five

Jamestown, Virginia

Miles passed the servants' quarters on the way to his brother's home. They housed five indentured servants, three of whom he'd purchased over a year ago. He would need the extra help this spring. Four others he'd acquired died from the seasoning. With their deaths, there weren't enough men to keep them from working from sunup to sundown once planting season began.

Then there was William, the tall Irishman, who'd served them for six years now. The man had been invaluable as a foreman to the others, but his contract would be over in a year.

He and his brother prided themselves on treating their servants with dignity, even the ones like Henry and George who'd been sent to the Americas for vagrancy, and it had paid off. Every man on the Bonneville plantation worked hard, as if he were farming his own. When the seven years were up, they would be given a tract of land to farm and the tools and resources they needed, regardless of the circumstances that brought them here.

With Mary's death, they would need to hire a couple of women to do the cooking and sewing and to plant a vegetable garden, care for the chickens, and milk the cow. He hated to pull away one of the farmhands to do woman's work. He should have hired the women before now to make Mary's life easier. A maiden could have attended her during labor. Women knew about such things.

A lump formed in the back of his throat. He would have, but the colony didn't have enough females to go around, and almost all of them were married or the daughters of plantation owners.

Either way, he was glad he'd built a small one-room home next to his, sharing the fireplace with his kitchen. He'd planned to house female servants there for Mary, but now, he needed them more than ever.

Hopefully, he could convince a couple of women to become indentured for a time instead of marrying right off. Mayhap if he lessened their servitude to five years instead of seven, they'd be willing to stay on that long.

Of course, if he or his brother were to marry, they'd have plenty of help, but he wasn't ready for that. However, it might be just what Hugh needed to tame his desires.

He entered his brother's house with a sack full of meat and vegetables and set them on the table. Perchance, a hearty meal would make Hugh more amiable.

The fire was cold. Hugh lay in the bed against the wall, under a down blanket, asleep even though the sun was high in the sky. Only a patch of his long, dark hair showed. The stench of rum filled the room, and a jug lay empty on its side.

Miles grabbed a flint and some logs and kindling from the wood bin and built a fire. He considered leaving Hugh to his drunken state or waking him with a bucket of cold water and lecturing him about the evils of drink, but the reason he'd come was too important. Addressing his brother's indiscretions would have to wait.

At least there wasn't a Native woman in his bed as the Burgess members had suspected. What would he have done if he'd found Hugh so occupied? Would he report his own brother as he had his friend?

He shook him.

"Whaaaa rrr you doing here?" Hugh shielded his dark brown eyes.

"I need your help."

Hugh dragged himself from his bed and plopped onto the bench at the wooden table in the middle of the room. "At this time of the morning?"

"It's nearly noon." Miles couldn't help the hint of reproach in his voice.

Leaning back, Hugh wiped his brow with his sleeve. "What could I possibly do to help you?" The hint of scorn in his tone was hard to miss.

"The Burgess wants to arrange a meeting with Chief Opechancanough and the Powhatan council of elders."

"Why?" Hugh swiped his hair out of his eyes. "How is the council of Burgess planning to cheat them this time?"

"They want to meet with the village leaders, see if they can work out their differences." Miles didn't mention some of the men on the council suggested other remedies to take care of the problem. "If we can come to some understanding with the new chief as we had with Chief Powhatan before he died, we might be able to avoid a conflict."

Hugh raised an eyebrow. "If we hadn't treated the Natives with disdain from the beginning, you might already have the good will you desire."

"What do you want from me?" Miles grabbed a kettle and filled it with water. "It's not easy to get the Burgess to unite, but they all pledged to meet with the chief and try to find some way to bring lasting peace." He emptied some turnips, carrots, and rabbit meat out of the sack and set about making some stew.

After a visit to the outhouse, Hugh cleaned himself up in a copper basin, dressed for the day, and sat at the wooden table in the middle of the room. "I'm not sure I can eat. My stomach is wrecked."

"Your constitution will improve once the stew is finished." Miles threw in the last of the vegetables and sat across from his brother.

"Opechancanough won't cooperate," Hugh said. "Even if he pretends to go along, it will most likely be a deception. He blames the white man for his niece's death."

"You know some of the Natives, and you speak their language. Could you arrange a meeting with the chief?"

Hugh tugged on his ear. "Mayhap. It will add a bit of amusement. I grow weary of inactivity now that winter has set in."

Miles picked the jug off the floor and placed it on the table. "It appears you've already found something to occupy your time."

"Not all of us devote our days to Bible studies and pious prayers, Brother. Some of us find merriment in a little diversion now and then."

"Like Father did?" Miles' stomach knotted. He'd planned not to bring up Hugh's immoral behavior. Every time he did, the conversation became a quarrel. "My pardon. I know you're nothing like him."

"Do you?" The muscle in Hugh's jaw twitched. "If I am, would you reject me as you disowned your own father?" He sprung up, knocking over the bench, and turned his back toward Miles.

"I brought you with me to Jamestown, didn't I?" Miles placed his hand on Hugh's shoulder. "You're the only family I have left, but you vex me greatly. You seem... I don't know. Lost."

"Mayhap I am." Hugh pushed Miles' hand away and turned the bench upright. "I won't find my way by you nagging like an old shrew." He sat at the table and wiped a hand over his face. "I'll go to the village first thing in the morning--after I've sobered up."

"Thank you, Brother." Miles sat across from him. An awkward silence filled the space between them. "I'm planning to buy a couple of indentured women when the bride ship arrives in a few months."

"Wise decision," Hugh said. "We need domestic help. My fingers are raw from washing clothes at the creek, and my greatest desire is to not have to endure your cooking another fortnight."

Miles raised an eyebrow, pretending to be insulted. "I never claimed to do well at womanly arts. If you prefer someone else to cook, perchance you should consider taking a wife when the ship arrives."

Hugh stood and stirred the stew. "I have no need for a wife."

"I entreat you to reconsider. It would keep you from..." Miles swallowed hard. "Being tempted to pursue inappropriate relations."

"Inappropriate relations!" Hugh threw the wooden spoon down. "Don't hold your peace, Brother. If you have an accusation against me, speak it."

"Not an accusation. An inquiry mayhap. The men in town have suggested you've been fornicating with some of the Native women."

Hugh gazed at the fire. "What if I have? The women don't protest, and you can't tell me I'm the only one in the colony guilty of, how did you say it? Inappropriate relations. John Cooper has been known to fornicate quite a bit, as well as commit adultery, and he's on the council."

"He paid the penalty for his adulterous behavior."

"After you reported him." Hugh plopped down on the bench at the table. "You turned on your closest friend as you did on Father?"

Miles didn't answer. His brother couldn't possibly understand how hard it was to leave, especially since Mother's illness had prevented her from travelling. She insisted he take his younger siblings to the New World to get them away from Father's influence. Only his oldest sister had remained to care for her.

"All right. If that's what you want, I confess my transgressions," Hugh said. "I have fornicated with a Native woman, and often. So now, you can report me like you did John. I won't deny it or resist. The Burgess can have me flogged in front of everyone at the fort, just as they did him."

Hugh's admission hit Miles as if he'd been punched in the gut.

"You're my brother."

The words sputtered out of him. If it had been anyone else, he would have felt it his duty to report him. Why did Hugh have to be so forthright?

Miles let out a breath and tried to calm his tone. "I would never subject you to that, but if you were to take a wife, you'd have a moral outlet for those desires."

A pinched expression crossed Hugh's mouth as he tapped his fingers on the table. "I will do your bidding when it comes to Chief Opechancanough, and I'll work hard to help create a prosperous plantation, but taking a wife is my decision to make." He grabbed a pitcher of water and took a swig without bothering to pour the contents into the tin cup sitting on the table. He swiped his mouth with his sleeve. "Stay out of my personal affairs."

Miles' shoulders slumped. "How can I? You're my family."

"Should be easy. You were able to sail off and forsake Mother and Father."

"Hugh, please."

"Best you take your leave."

Miles gave a crisp nod before throwing on his cloak. Hugh was as belligerent as always. If only he could find a way to help him.

~~~~~

Hugh entered the Powhatan village. Women sat in front of their longhouses made of birchwood called *yehakins* with large fires to keep them warm. None of the women looked up. During the winter, when it was too cold to farm, they spent their time sewing hide skins, weaving baskets, and making pottery. Today, they were weaving baskets.

There were no men around. Perchance they went hunting, something they often did in the winter months. He'd stay in the village until they returned.

The women of the tribe didn't wear dresses like the Europeans. A few
~~~~~

wore shorter leather skirts, but most, like the men, wore leggings made of deer hide and tied leather aprons around them while they were working. He gazed at each of their features to try to see past the long hair hanging down and the red markings and paint on their faces.

Suleta wasn't among them. He made his way to her longhouse.

He'd been considering his brother's words since the day before. He'd never allow Miles to know, but he had been disgusted by his own behavior of late. He needed to mend his ways. It was time to find a wife, and he could think of none better than the Native squaw he'd become fond of over the last few months.

Suleta sat outside, leaning back against the wall of the house, and sewed a rawhide boot. She looked at him and smiled.

His heart raced faster, and he sat beside her. "I'm glad I found you."

A timid glance down. "So am I."

He kissed her passionately. "Let's go into the longhouse."

She nodded and followed him inside.

Afterwards, they were lying under the blanket, holding each other.

He nuzzled her neck, then worked his way to her lips. "I'm going to speak to Wupun today."

"Why would you desire to speak to my mother?"

He reluctantly pulled away from her embrace, rose, and dressed. "We can't continue this way. I want you to be my wife."

"She won't agree to it." Suleta wrapped the blanket around herself. "I'm pledged to another."

Pain seeped into the cracks of his heart. "But... Who... When did this happen?"

She touched his cheek. "Since I have been widowed, our family doesn't have a man to support us and to bring us fresh meat and hides from the hunt. Mother arranged it."

"I'd support you and your family."

"It's for the best." Suleta took hold of his hand. "I could never leave my family to live as you do. You would take me away from them, away from this village."

"That doesn't mean I wouldn't provide for your family. I'd offer a large dowry if your mother would only agree to this, and you could see them as often as you like."

Suleta let go of his hand and turned away. "She won't allow you to take me away from here."

Hugh swiped his hand through his hair. "Then I'll stay with you. I'll join your tribe."

She shook her head. "Would you really leave your brother and come to live with our people?"

The pain covered his heart like a hand gripping it. He wanted to deny it, but they both knew he could never leave the plantation he and Miles had worked so hard to cultivate.

"She plans to marry me off when planting season is upon us. The warrior I'm betrothed to has gone on a long journey to hunt in the mountains. He won't be back until then."

"How can you marry another when we've been together like this for over a year?"

Suleta touched his cheek. "Hugh, you still do not understand our ways. My future husband shall not object since we have not wed yet. He might even allow us to continue this after we are joined."

"I'm not an adulterer." The pain now squeezed his heart like it was caught in a brawny fist of a wrestler, but there were some indiscretions even he wouldn't commit. The loneliness and guilt overtook him. "We can't be together."

"Why not? He won't be back until spring."

He didn't bother to answer. Instead, he kissed her tenderly on the forehead, a farewell gesture, and left the village as quickly as his legs could carry him.

It would be torturous to stay at the camp, so near to her. He'd meet with them in the spring. The Burgess would understand once he told them the leaders were on a hunt. He headed toward home.

Chapter Six

April 1620

They'd spotted land. Elizabella couldn't stop gawking as the ship edged closer to the seashore.

Her friend, Hannah Walker, stood beside her and pointed at the dense wooded area obscuring the shoreline. An abundance of trees blossomed with yellow, red, and white. "Isn't it beautiful?"

Elizabella gave a nod, but her chest tightened at the sight of them. In England, the trees would still be bare, devoid of any outward show of life this early in the spring. Here, they were so close together, it was difficult to see into the forest. Nothing here familiar or comforting to remind her of home. She might as well be in the jungles of Africa. Once summer came, how would anyone be able to find their way in this foliage?

"Look, the fort." Hannah pointed to it.

It stood near the shore with a forest surrounding it as if it had been dropped accidentally. Only an acre of land with five walls, it wasn't what Elizabella expected. The fortifications made of oak and poplar logs stuck out of the ground. Not nearly as strong as the stone walls around the castles and forts in England.

How could logs hold off an attack of savages?

"I feel safer knowing the men have a strong fort in place," Hannah said. "Any place would be safer than living on the streets of London, but this land is a paradise I couldn't have imagined."

"It doesn't look safe to me." Not any safer than on the ship.

Ten women had died on the voyage to Virginia, including Widow Ferrier. Another woman, Joan, was standing beside her on deck when a jib swung and knocked the poor girl into the ocean. A shark grabbed her before they could attempt a rescue.

Images of Joan flailing her arms flooded Elizabella's mind. The worst part was the screams as the shark swam closer. The monster dove, disappeared, and pulled Joan under. Blood stained the water where she had been.

Elizabella trembled at the memory and wrapped her arms around herself. *Don't dwell on it.* As Hannah had said, they were safe. But was she? According to what she'd heard from Constance, the seasoning would kill off another thirty or forty of them before the year was out. She'd always been hearty, resisting most childhood diseases, but it wouldn't matter here.

The wind had a chill to it, but she had to place her hand over her eyes to block the searing sun. No clouds in sight, the sky as endless as the seas on the journey here. Best not to think about the dangers, or she'd go mad.

The ship drew closer to shore.

A knot formed in Elizabella's stomach. "Isn't it dangerous to get this close to shore? There isn't even a dock to moor the ship."

"No need to fret," Hannah said. "Constance told me the Jamestown River has a deep channel that runs up to the shore. The ship will moor there, and the sailors will tie it down to something to keep it from drifting."

The command was given to drop anchor. A couple of sailors climbed down a rope ladder onto land while others let drop a rope they tied to a tree. The gangplank was shoved out until it reached the sandy beach.

"Look at the flowers." Hannah pointed again, this time to a patch of purple wildflowers. "They don't have flowers that pretty in London."

"I don't know. England is known for her bluebells and honeysuckle." This time of year, Honesty would open the window to allow the aroma of the daffodils in their window box to fill the room no matter how cold it was.

Red and yellow blossoms dotted the red maples surrounding the fort, and the elms were covered in pink buds. Crocuses and irises blanketed the ground around the walls. Elizabella's sister would have loved them.

This new land might have been mistaken for a paradise if it weren't for the high cost it extracted. Instead, it was a colorful graveyard. At least Honesty was safe from its grasp.

Constance clapped her hands. "Ladies, I must have your attention before we leave the ship."

Bridgette, another who had friended Elizabella, scooted beside her and grabbed her arm. The sixteen-year-old girl had latched onto her during the voyage, but she didn't mind. Having Bridgette and Hannah around helped with the emptiness and longing for home. Hannah was the good friend Elizabella had never had, and Bridgette reminded her of Honesty.

Constance placed her hand on her growing stomach. It became obvious since boarding the ship, she was with child and would deliver in a couple of months. "We shall sleep on the ship tonight. On the morrow, when we disembark, families inside the fort will give you lodging until an auction can be arranged within the month. That will give you an opportunity to meet some of the eligible men."

Heat flushed Elizabella's face. If those ruffians hadn't stabbed Honesty, she wouldn't be here, paraded in front of men like a prime goose at market. At least she could be grateful her sister wasn't facing this indignity.

"If you find a suitable husband, he'll bring the bride price of one hundred-twenty pounds of tobacco to pay for your voyage and supplies. Once that is done, a Certificate of Banns will be posted the evening before your wedding, giving anyone who objects to the nuptials an opportunity to speak. This is only a formality since your references were deemed satisfactory before you boarded the ship. Are there any questions?"

Hannah cleared her throat. "A month isn't very long to have a proper courtship."

Constance grinned and placed her hand on her belly. "Many of you will be married off before the week is out."

Bridgette leaned toward Elizabella. "Nobody decent would want me."

Elizabella hushed her. Bridgette was on the homely side with orange hair, blotches of freckles all over her face, a long, thin nose, and a gangly build, but she had more to offer than she realized. Bridgette was strong and hardy, even if she did talk too much.

"If, within a month, you haven't found a suitable mate to pay for your voyage, you'll be auctioned as an indentured servant," Constance said. "That doesn't mean you still can't marry. If a man meets your fancy after that, all he need do is buy out your contract. Your master is required to release you if a suitor meets the price. Within six months, most of you should find the husbands you desire."

"If we decide not to marry," Hannah said, "what guarantees do we have that our masters will treat us fairly?"

Elizabella gave her friend a sympathetic nod as she remembered their conversations. Hannah had boarded the bride ship to better her circumstances, but she was concerned men in such a savage colony might try to take liberties.

Hannah had confided how often she had escaped men who tried to attack her in London. She believed only God's care and a well-positioned kick protected her. Elizabella envied her faith. If only she could trust God's providence in her life.

"The laws forbid mistreatment," Constance said. "If you work hard during the seven-year contract, your master must feed you well and provide you with clothing and a roof over your head."

"What if our masters don't want us to be courted?" Hannah said. "Once we're owned by them, what guarantees shall we have?"

Bridgette's eyes widened. "Does that mean we'll have to wait seven years to marry? I'll be an old maid."

Elizabella couldn't help but chuckle along with the other brides.

Constance glared at them and waited until everyone had quieted. "As long as you finish your daily chores, he must provide opportunities for callers. Of course, you'll have to abide by the courting rules of the household."

Bridgette squeezed Elizabella's hand. "What if I have a master who isn't satisfied with my labor for him? A girl I knew was a servant in a big fancy house, and her mistress once had her whipped."

Elizabella had seen a man whipped in the square once, and it terrified her. The bloody lashes across his back still haunted her nightmares. If the Justice of the Peace had judged against her, that might have been her fate – or worse.

"That won't happen in Virginia." Constance crossed her arms over her belly. "He's not allowed to beat you unless he proves just cause to the Council. He must give evidence you have tried to run away or have shirked your duties. If that happens, you'll have a fair hearing."

"Good to know a council of men will be fair to a servant girl," one of the women in the back yelled out in a sarcastic tone.

Constance held up her palm until the snickers stopped. "In America, you have choices a woman would never dream of in England. You can be a bride to a landowner of your choice, not arranged by your father, or you can decide not to marry and become an independent landowner when your contract is done. Most of you will have paid off your passage to America within seven years. Some can do it in five, depending on your skills and your agreement with your master."

"What if a master makes unwanted advances?" Bridgette twisted the tie on her cap. "We'll be trapped on his farm away from civilization. How can we protect ourselves?"

"It is against the law for a master to take undue advantage of his servant or to commit fornication with any maiden. Anyone who buys your service is responsible for your chasteness. Besides, these are Englishmen."

"That's reassuring," Bridgette said.

The women giggled.

"Living on the streets as I did, I know what Englishmen are capable of." Hannah fanned herself. "If it hadn't been for the vicar who took me in, I would have had my virtue compromised a long time ago."

"Good women," Constance said, "your fears are unfounded. There hasn't been one instance of a woman servant given a beating, and no one has reported unwanted attentions toward a female indentured servant."

"Do you think any woman with any wits about her shall report the master she's enslaved to for seven years?" Bridgette glanced at Elizabella. "She'd be worse off than she was before."

"Bridgette." Constance delivered a glower that would have produced trepidation even in First Officer Rogers. Her patience was clearly at an end. "I assure you, this is not London. If you decide to marry, you have any number of good men to choose from. If you decide not to wed, the full force of the Burgess will protect you from abuse."

Duly chastised, Bridgette gazed at her feet.

Elizabella sighed in relief. Since she had no intention of marrying, at least she would be guaranteed fair treatment. It couldn't have been any worse than her seamstress apprenticeship with Goodwife Johnson had been. The apprenticeship had been difficult, her fingers sometimes raw with excessive needlework, but through hard work, she had learned a valuable skill leading to a prosperous business. This work would have an even greater reward, her freedom and return to England. At least she hoped it would.

Perchance she shouldn't even try to find the right master. If she told Constance the farce that compelled her to this hostile land, with a guarantee of future payment, she might very well be sailing home within a few months when the *London Merchant* headed to England.

Scuffling noises caused her to turn. Two large sailors escorted the boy who had snuck onto the ship down the gangplank. He didn't beg or resist, despite the fate awaiting him. To do so would have been folly. There was no escape for him now.

"I suggest you slumber well," Constance said. "Our arrival on a Saturday is fortuitous. Everyone is required to come to town on Sundays for church meetings, and the women of the fort are preparing a meal for after the service. You can make the acquaintance of eligible men there."

They gathered their ration of food and moved below deck for their last evening meal on the ship. Elizabella, Hannah, and Bridgette had found a spot to eat and sleep near the barrels, away from the others, and had laid claim to it.

As they ate, Bridgette couldn't stop asking questions. "Do you think any of the men will want me as a bride?"

"Of course they will." Elizabella finished the last bite of her potato. "You're young and strong, the perfect wife for a Virginia planter who wants lots of children."

Bridgette bit her lip. "Father said that I was foolish thinking I could get a husband better than the one he'd chosen for me. He said, 'A homely girl has to take what she can get.'"

Elizabella wiped and cleared away her tin plate and cup. Was there a father alive who treated his daughter with kindness? If there was, she'd never met him. "You may have red hair and freckles, but you're only sixteen. In a few years, when other women's faces are distorted with wrinkles, your fair complexion will be the envy of many."

"I doubt that."

"Look at Queen Elizabeth," Hannah said. "She had red hair and freckles, and yet by the time she became queen, she was considered one of the fairest women in the world."

A smirk crossed Bridgette's face. "She never married."

Hannah chuckled. "That was her preference. She had many suitors. No doubt, you shall as well."

"Bridgette," Elizabella said, "why didn't you marry the man your father chose? Even though the law now allows it, I've never heard of a young woman refusing her father's selection before."

Bridgette paused and pinched her lips together. "Thomas and I grew up together and went to the same parish. I always thought I would marry him. Father and Mother arranged it when I was a young girl."

Elizabella spread out her bedding on the floor of the ship's hold beside where her friends slept. "What changed your mind?"

"He had a meanness about him. When he was a boy, I caught him in the woods setting fire to his tomcat's tail. I threatened to tell, but he twisted my arm so hard I thought it would break, and I promised not to."

"Why would you even think about marrying him after that?" Hanna asked.

Bridgette shrugged. "He told me he was sorry he scared me and that I was right. He'd never do something like that again. For the next couple of years, he went out of his way to win me over. He picked flowers for me and sometimes would come over to the farm and help me finish my chores. I thought he'd changed. More likely, he wanted to inherit my father's farm."

"What made you decide that?" Elizabella removed her skirt and bodice.

Bridgette hugged her arms around herself. "One afternoon, he pulled me into the bushes. I tried to pull away, but he kissed me roughly and tore my dress. I screamed for him to stop, and he punched me in the stomach. He told me I was pledged to be his wife, and I needed to do what he said. I was so scared. Somehow, I managed to kick him and wiggle free. I ran home as fast as I could to tell my father."

Hannah shook her head. "How did your parents respond?"

Bridgette played with the edge of her blanket. "I never had the chance. Father took one look at my disheveled condition and told me he would force Thomas to marry me right away since he took liberties with me. I refused and tried to explain what happened, but he called me ungrateful and said I would never find another man who would want me after this. Mother told me if I didn't marry, I would no longer be welcome in their home." She swiped a tear running down her cheek.

Elizabella touched her arm. "You have my deepest sympathy."

"Father gave me one week to do as he bid or leave his home. I was in great distress over it."

"I can well imagine," Hannah said.

"When Father went to London the next day to deliver crops and came home with news from the Virginia Company, he told me if I didn't marry by the end of the week, he was sending me to Jamestown to find a husband." She shrugged. "So here I am. Not sure I'll find anyone who wants me, but if I do, I'll take my time deciding. I want to be a wife, but I won't marry someone like Thomas, no matter how many years I have to work as a servant."

"Well said." Hannah settled into her blanket. "Perchance we should take to our beds. The morrow no doubt shall prove wearisome.

Elizabella rested her head on her pillow. "I bid you a good night."

Her intent had been to fall quickly into slumber, but sleep eluded her. She tossed and turned for hours. She might never see her home, her sister, or her shop again. Being taken against her will to sail to this wilderness where she might perish from disease or an Indian attack had to be a punishment from God for allowing her brother to die under her care.

If it was the Lord's discipline, it was well deserved. She'd do her best to bear it well.

Chapter Seven

Miles wiped the sweat off his brow as he stood by the graves of Mary and James. The four months since their deaths had done little to relieve his grief. Reverend Cochran had implored him to take a wife, and he knew it was wise counsel, but he couldn't imagine wanting to marry again. Nobody could take Mary's place.

Hugh came running up to him. "I thought I might find you here."

"What do you want?" It came out harsher than Miles meant, and he shrugged an apology.

Hugh glanced at the grave and ignored the curt tone. "When I was at the fort to get supplies, the governor bid me to convey to you he's calling a meeting of the Burgess on Monday morn."

"Did he say why?"

"Some matter of a young man gaining passage to Jamestown by deception. They're sentencing him then."

Miles nodded his head. "A simple matter of deciding if he should be whipped and sold or hung. Shouldn't take long."

"There's more. The man in question arrived with the bride ship. They're having a feast after church tomorrow to introduce the maidens."

"It's about time."

"I'm considering taking a bride." Hugh's voice was so soft Miles barely heard him.

Miles took a step back, astonished by his brother's announcement. "You've never shown interest in taking a wife before. Every time I've brought it up, you've become irritated."

Hugh grinned in the infectious way that reminded Miles of his mother. "Maybe one of them will catch my fancy. You never know. A wife might tame my baser instincts and soothe my loneliness from this isolated land."

Miles raised an eyebrow. "I didn't know you wanted to be tamed."

"Don't be crude." Hugh wiped his hand over his mouth, then let out a gusty sigh. "I know I've behaved poorly, but I need a woman's comfort to help me overcome this melancholy that constantly plagues me. We've been here six years, but I still yearn for London, and I grieve for our brothers and sister... and Mother."

A lump formed in Miles' throat. It was the first time Hugh had spoken of their siblings in years. Sarah died on the voyage, and their three middle brothers had died of the seasoning during the first year here. A year ago, they had received word of their mother's death. "I miss them too. I know we've had words, but I would do anything to ease your burden."

Hugh set a hand on his shoulder. "Methinks a suitable wife might help."

Miles didn't bother to ask if there was further fornication with the Natives. Hugh would be truthful, but he had no desire to know. "Mayhap it would."

Hugh snorted. "'Tis not often we agree so completely. Even if I don't find a bride, we still have need of female servants for the household chores."

He wanted to believe Hugh was mending his ways, but was he? Would it be wrong to bring servants girls onto their plantation when he didn't trust his brother to be chaste and honorable toward them? "Perchance we should wait before hiring more servants."

"If I have to do all the women's work, I won't have time to harvest the crops. Mary's death affected more than just you."

Miles' face grew hot. "I'm sorry my wife's death inconvenienced you so much."

"Come now. You know I meant no offense, but we need a couple of women to do the cooking, sewing, and laundering around here and to help with the livestock and vegetable garden. Your wife was a hard worker, but it was too much, even for her."

He resisted an angry retort. Hugh spoke truly. Mary might have survived if she hadn't worked herself to exhaustion. If his brother chose a bride, he wouldn't allow the same to happen to her.

"These women would have never made this journey unless they had matrimony as their goal." Hugh raised his eyebrow. "If we both marry, the quandary we're in would be resolved."

"Nay, I have no desire to do so, but even if you wed, I'm sure we can find a couple of maidens to help with the toil. Not every woman shall desire to marry the first man she sees."

Miles took one last look at the gravestone. What Hugh said made sense. Marriages didn't normally take place because of love but for practical reasons. Still, there wasn't a woman in the civilized world, let alone Jamestown, who could take Mary's place on the farm or in his heart.

~~~~~

Elizabella stood at the rail of the deck. Dawn had not yet begun to light the sky, but she'd been up here for hours, fretting about what was to come. If only there was a way back to London.

Hannah stepped beside her. "You couldn't sleep?"

She shrugged. "My mind is too occupied by the events of the day."

"Aye, mine too."

"May I ask, why did you make this journey?"

Hannah smiled. "God told me to come."

"God?" Elizabella exclaimed. "He spoke to you?"

She gazed at the stars. "Not in words I could hear, but yes."

"How could you possibly know what the Lord wanted?" Elizabella
~~~~~

waited a moment without either of them speaking. "I do want to hear."

"I told you how my parents died of smallpox and how I lived on the streets until a vicar took me in and allowed me to stay in the church."

"Aye, 'tis an amazing story."

"There's more to it. My pastor reads from the Geneva Bible during church meetings. He still reads the Prayer Book, but he said since we had a Holy Bible we can understand, he wanted those of us who can't read to know what God's Word says. He even taught me to read it for myself."

"Not my pastor," Elizabella said. "He says those who are not learned, such as women and peasants, couldn't possibly have the knowledge to understand the Scripture. They must be guided by spiritual authority."

"My pastor says everyone, even women, can learn to read and understand the Scriptures because the Holy Spirit will guide them. The biggest problem is most people have never heard the entirety of Scripture. He has evening meetings devoted only to reading the Holy Bible."

"That is shocking." Elizabella couldn't believe what she was hearing. "A reverend having meetings just to read Scripture? Is he one of those revolutionary heretics the king warns about?"

"Of course not. My pastor is very devout and a student of God's word. That doesn't make him a heretic, even if he has been chastised by some members for being too much like one of those Puritans trying to reform the church."

Elizabella gasped. The Puritans wanted to discard the Prayer Book, icons, and even celebrations of the saints. Some even went so far as to declare the king should not be the head of the church.

"He doesn't advocate leaving the church," Hannah said, "but he does want the members to have a transformation that comes from knowing God."

"I don't understand." An uncomfortable feeling perched upon Elizabella. "I've been a member of the Holy Church of England since I was old enough to take communion. Isn't that enough?"

"At one time, I felt the same way, but it's not sufficient."

"Nonsense. I follow all the rules of my faith, and I never miss a Sunday mass." Elizabella pulled at the neckline of her shift. "I try to do everything God expects of me." She wasn't about to admit she'd never managed to be good enough no matter how hard she tried.

Hannah placed her hand on Elizabella's. "I've found religious duty to be lacking until I learned this truth for myself. One Sunday, my cleric read a verse in Ephesians. 'For by grace are ye saved through faith; and that not of yourselves: it is the gift of God.' It is not what we do for God. It is the sacrifice He provided that makes us pure."

Elizabella had to work hard to please God, especially after the great sin she'd committed. She cleared her throat. "What does that have to do with you coming to Jamestown?"

"I have no father to provide a dowry and little chance of marrying in London. I was praying one evening, and the next morning, my vicar told me about the ship carrying brides to Jamestown. I knew God was in this."

"Do you hope to find a man as devout as you in this wilderness?"

Hannah bit her bottom lip. "I've prayed about this often. I've seen good Christian men attend services every week and pretend to be fine and upstanding, yet the way they treat their wives and children is not good nor Christian. I'll settle for an honest man who vows to treat me with tender affection and leave the rest to the Almighty. God knows the heart. He'll show me the right man to marry.

The sun was beginning to rise. Red, yellow, and orange lit up the sky. Elizabella stared at it as if it held the answer to how Hannah could possibly know what God wanted.

Hannah's voice interrupted her thoughts. "Why did you sail to Jamestown?"

Elizabella let out a gusty sigh. "It's a long story."

"I've been known to be attentive."

Her heart beat faster. As scared as she was, she needed to tell somebody. Hannah had shown herself a true friend. "I have a secret."

"Honesty, whatever it is, I shall keep your confidence."

Even her sister's name taunted her. "I'm on this ship under false pretenses."

Hannah wrinkled her brow. "What do you mean, false pretenses? You had references and papers, or they wouldn't have allowed you on board."

She sighed. "My given name is Elizabella. Honesty is my younger sister." She told Hannah the whole story of how she'd come to be on the ship.

"Why didn't you say something before?"

"You saw how they treated that boy who snuck aboard. I was fearful."

Hannah's intense gaze unnerved her. What if she broke her vow to keep this quiet? Mayhap it was a mistake to tell her.

"It's not too late," Hannah finally said in a voice so quiet Elizabella barely heard her.

"Nay, I can't tell the truth now after being silent for months."

"You can confide in Constance. She'll appreciate your reluctance to speak while aboard this ship. She might even speak to the council on your behalf. Mayhap they'll allow you to return to England and pay for the voyage when you arrive."

If the council would agree to it without her having to subject herself to servitude or marriage proposals, that would be good fortune indeed. It would almost be worth the risk. "What if they don't believe me? I did use deception to board."

"You did what was needed to save your life."

Clatter sounded behind her. The women were making their way up the ladder onto the main deck.

Elizabella pulled back and motioned Hannah to be still. "I'll consider what you've said, but please remain silent on this matter."

Hannah nodded. "I'll keep your confidence until you have the courage to share it."

By then, Constance and her husband drew near. "Come, good women." Constance motioned the brides to gather around. "It's time for your first church service in the New World. You'll find Reverend Cochran an inspiring orator."

"When do we make the acquaintance of suitable bachelors?" Hannah asked.

"After church," Ethan said.

Elizabella's stomach churned. She wouldn't be able to meet with Constance easily after the church meeting. If she didn't confess the truth now, she might not have another opportunity or the courage to do so.

Constance headed toward the gangplank with her husband. "Follow us, and we'll sit together. Reverend Cochran has reserved a space for us on the front bench."

Hannah nudged her with her elbow, then tilted her head toward Constance.

"Wait!" Elizabella's heart raced, but she needed to speak before it was too late. "I have need to discuss an important matter with you first. Alone."

Constance placed her hand on her stomach. "Whatever you have to say can be postponed until after service. We can't keep our Lord or the men of Jamestown waiting. Come along, good women."

Elizabella considered blurting out the truth in front of everyone before her resolve failed, but she couldn't. It would be hard enough to confess the truth in private. There would be an opportunity to meet with Constance after church. There had to be. She followed the others off the ship.

Hurrying down the gangplank, she stepped on dry land for the first time in months. The sensation of the rocking of the ship continued even though the ground beneath her feet was solid. 'Twas not only the ground. Her whole world shook.

They entered through the fort gate, then past the cemetery just inside the walls. Too many wooden crosses for a colony settled only twelve years ago. If she didn't get out of this horrible place soon, she might be buried in that graveyard.

Small wattle and daub buildings similar to the homes and stores in London littered the fort, and one fairly large hall stood near the wall. The church was larger than the other buildings and was made entirely of wood beams. The only brick structure she could see was the armory.

Her home in central London had been built entirely of brick, a purchase she'd been delighted with. Here, she'd never live in a brick house. She'd never have the luxuries she'd worked so hard for. No doubt, she'd end up in a one-room shack with a dirt floor. It would be worse than growing up in Pudding Lane.

A mob of bearded men with tricorn felt hats assembled outside, smoking their pipes. They wore their hair long and mangled or wore wigs in need of a good brushing, and their beards were scruffy and unkempt. Their white cuffs and collar duffs looked dingy gray, their britches were dirty and had patches, and their stockings needed darning.

If the men had dressed as peasants, she wouldn't have given them a second look, but dressed as gentlemen who had fallen into disarray gave them a comical appearance. As she and the other women passed, the men pointed at them and chattered like old women gossiping in a London marketplace.

A tall chap with a narrow, clean-shaven face, clean clothes, and well-groomed long dark hair greeted the women. "Ladies, I'm Governor Yeardley." His burgundy wool long coat, red waist coat, and black britches were more colorful than even the wealthiest commoners wore, and his cuffs, collars, and linen stockings were stark white. He topped the look with a cavalier hat with an ostrich feather. His wife and servants had obviously taken great care in making him presentable, unlike the other men. "On behalf of the Virginia House of Burgess, we would like to welcome you to Jamestown. We look forward to making your acquaintances. We pray you fare well here."

A man with a full scraggly beard, who looked as if he hadn't bathed in months, grabbed Hannah's hand. "I own ten acres, and I had a good crop last year. Marry me, and I'll provide handsomely for you."

Hannah pulled her hand away. "Good man, unhand me. We haven't even been properly introduced."

Other men surrounded them. "I want that one," one man with missing teeth called out.

Another pulled Elizabella away from Bridgette, twirled her around, and secured her in a hug. "You're a pretty lass."

She tried to shove free of the lout, but she couldn't pull away.

"Cease and desist," Ethan Wright called out. He pulled out the flintlock pistol tucked in his trousers and pointed it toward the man who still had hold of Elizabella. "My wife and I are responsible for these virtuous women, and I won't have them accosted."

The man let her go. She brushed off her skirt with trembling hands and staggered to Bridgette and Hannah.

Constance stepped in front of them.

If these were the men Constance had spoken so highly of, it might be time to find some pitchforks to fend them off as she had her sister's attacker in London. A wave of nausea gripped her, and she swallowed to keep from vomiting.

Ethan waved his pistol toward the other men. "You will have time to make your acquaintance with these women in a civil way after they have taken nourishment. But make no mistake about it, the next time one of you tries to waylay one of these brides or make unwanted advances, I will use this firearm posthaste."

Bridgette whispered in Elizabella's ear. "I don't believe I could marry any of these brutes. They're as bad as my former fiancé."

Hannah placed a hand on Bridgette's arm.

Elizabella tried to give them a comforting look even though her skin crawled at the thought of being courted by these louts. She had to find a way to get Constance alone to explain her plight. She would do whatever it took to get back to her sister, her brick home, and her seamstress shop in London, even risk the wrath of the colony.

Chapter Eight

Miles and Hugh arrived at the fort. Outside the church, men surrounded a group of women. Ethan pointed his gun at Richard Lambert and Warren Smithers, a couple of farmers who always seemed to be causing trouble.

The women skirted past them as Goodwife Constance hurried them into the church. The men looked their direction, then turned their gaze on Ethan. Lambert, Smithers, and another man took a step toward him.

Miles rushed to Ethan's side. Whatever the incident at hand, he was confident his friend was in the right. Hugh took his place on the other side of Ethan. Miles gave his brother a crisp nod.

Richard raised his hands in the air in mock surrender. "You got no call to be lording over us. It's not often we lay eyes on all those pretty maidens looking for husbands."

"Service will commence soon," Ethan said as he tucked his gun in the band of his trousers. "You'll have plenty of time to converse with the brides later." He placed his hand on the butt of his gun. "Provided you behave like Englishmen."

Richard shrugged and headed into the church followed by most of the other men. Warren glared at Ethan and Miles a moment longer before meandering through the church doors.

Miles shook his friend's hand. "Good to see you back so soon. Did everything work out to your advantage?"

"Better than I expected." Ethan nodded toward the doors. "I could use your help with the brides. Keeping all these fine, upstanding Englishmen from pouncing on the ladies and scaring them senseless before they even have time to familiarize themselves with colony life is becoming a difficult task."

Hugh chuckled. "You can't blame them. It isn't every day a gathering of beautiful young women comes to the fort." He slapped Ethan on the shoulder. "Even so, you can count on us to stand with you."

Miles gave Hugh a sideways grin. Every time he'd decided his brother was unredeemable, Hugh would step up and do something honorable. It caused hope for his brother's redemption to spring up in him. "How many brides did you bring?"

"We brought a hundred," Ethan said, "but ten died on the way. They plan to send another fifty or so in another a year."

Hugh gazed at the church door with a longing Miles hadn't expected. "When will you allow the men to interact with the brides?"

"Reverend Cochran has arranged a social after church. After a stern warning to the men, I'll introduce each of the maidens before allowing them to congregate, but I'll instruct them not to leave the fort without permission."

"A wise plan."

"By your leave, I'll head into church and watch the fair brides as they worship." Hugh grinned and winked before entering through the heavy wooden door.

"I noticed your wife's condition. Congratulations." A lump lodged in Miles' throat. "How is she faring?"

Ethan glanced toward the church door. "Constance visited a midwife in London who assured us her health is good, and we can expect a healthy newborn this time."

The two babes Ethan's wife delivered before had been stillborn just as James had been, although Constance had survived the birthings. Miles cleared his throat. "That is good news."

"My wife would take me to task if I didn't invite you and Mary to dine with us soon."

"Mary..." Miles' voice caught. "She's no longer with us."

Ethan placed a hand on Miles' shoulder. "What happened?"

"She and the babe... they died in childbirth."

"My condolences. Mary was a good woman."

Miles turned away and grabbed the handle on the church door.

"Before you head back home, we need to talk," Ethan said. "I have tidings of your father."

Miles tensed, hand still resting on the wrought iron handle. The congregation sang a hymn loud enough for them to hear with the doors closed. "What news?"

"Not now," Ethan said. "We'll speak of it in due time."

Miles nodded, pulled the church doors open, and stepped inside. He wasn't sure he cared to hear whatever his father had done now.

~~~~~

Elizabella tried to keep her attention on the sermon, but all she could think about was how to get her chaperone alone to explain her situation. The sooner she left this horrible colony with these brutish men, the better. She sat on the right of Bridgette. Hannah sat on the left of the girl. Without a spoken agreement, they'd both decided to stay close since the incident before church.

Finally, Reverend Cochran said the benediction. Elizabella was about to rise and stride to where Constance was sitting when the reverend cleared his throat. "Married men and women and children are dismissed." A few couples and fewer children made their way to the door and took their leave. Once they were gone, he continued. "Goodman Ethan Wright would like to say a few words."
~~~~~

Ethan stood and strode to the front. "Gentlemen and goodmen of Jamestown, I shall present each of these unmarried women to you as potential brides, but a word of warning. They are to stay in the fort in plain view, and we shall tolerate no liberties taken with them. You may consider this your formal introduction."

"Get on with it," one of the men called out. "Or do we have to wait until they're old maids before we can meet them?"

Many of the men laughed.

"Why don't you forego the introductions altogether?" This time it was the man who accosted Elizabella on the way to church. He snorted. "I can find plenty of ways to get acquainted with one of these fine lasses." More laughs.

"Goodman Smithers!" Ethan placed his hand on his gun and glowered at the man. "I'll remind you again, I'll do everything in my power to guard their virtue." His glare scanned the rest of the men, and the murmurs quieted. When there was no further interruption, he continued. "As I was saying, I shall call each prospective bride forward and introduce her. When I have finished, we will dismiss them. You may speak with them during the feast." He directed his scowl at Goodman Smithers. "If any of you try to lure them away for a stroll outside the fort or a kiss behind the armory, you'll answer to me."

There were grunts of agreement, but they didn't sound convincing.

"Gentlemen and goodmen," Ethan said. "I'd like to introduce Hannah Walker."

Hannah came forward.

"Miss Walker is twenty-two years old. She was born to merchants who left her an orphan. Her cleric took her in as a caretaker and cook for him and his wife. He recommends her as a respectable cook and a hard worker."

Hannah blushed and glanced at her feet.

"She is strong, and healthy, and should bear many children. She would make anyone a fine wife."

The men cheered. Elizabella cringed. It sounded more like an auction of a cow or pig in the marketplace than an introduction of a virtuous maiden.

"Miss Walker, you may sit."

Hannah rushed back to her seat.

"Next we have Bridgette Atwood."

Bridgette bit her lip. All Elizabella could do was offer a nod of encouragement. She stepped forward.

"Miss Atwood is sixteen years old. She is a strong lass from the countryside who worked on her father's farm her whole life. She is young and should be able to survive the seasoning and produce many healthy children."

Bridgette's face turned as red as her hair. She quickly returned to her seat with her head lowered.

One by one, women were called forward and their attributes espoused until Honesty Clark's name was called. At first, Elizabella didn't respond. She still couldn't get used to being called by her sister's name. Embarrassed by her reaction and the indignity of this proceeding, she stood and ambled toward where Ethan was.

This was her chance. She could announce in front of all of them her name was Elizabella, and she had no desire to become a bride or anyone's servant. This had all been a dreadful mistake.

Nobody's ever going to believe you, girl. Not after you started the fire what killed your brother. Remembering her father's words, her knees almost buckled.

She turned and faced the men but couldn't force what she desired to say past her lips.

Chapter Nine

Miles couldn't keep his focus off Miss Clark. Her soft blue eyes narrowed and glazed over. She stared at her feet as if she were afraid to make eye contact. So lost and alone. He wanted to reach out, to somehow reassure her.

Hugh leaned over and whispered in his brother's ear. "I've made my choice."

Miles shushed him.

Ethan continued with the introduction. "Miss Clark is only fifteen years old and should produce many children."

Her face reddened. She was so young, barely old enough to marry. He cleared his throat. Not that he planned on marriage.

"She is a tradeswoman, spinner, weaver, and seamstress. She and her sister owned a shop in London providing gowns for titled ladies. She once helped sew a gown for Queen Anne."

Murmurs rose throughout the room.

That explained her gown. It had a high bodice and was blue satin with pink flowers embedded in the fabric. Her cuffs with black glass buttons and neck ruff were white linen, and her coif was made out of the matching linen. She had a slight heel on her leather shoes, and her hat was made out of felt, not straw. Her finery was not opulent like the ladies of court wore but appealing and testified of wealth. If he had been looking for matrimony, she would have caught his eye.

Miss Clark looked toward Heaven as if she were praying. Nothing more attractive than a woman devoted to God, and she was accomplished for one so young.

Ethan hushed the men. "She's a good cook and accomplished in spinning, weaving, and sewing. She would be a fine addition to any household but especially a larger plantation with servants to manage."

Miss Clark looked back at her feet and opened her mouth as if she wanted to say something, but she kept quiet and folded her hands in front of her.

Miles couldn't help but be intrigued by this humble woman. His farm had grown beyond his ability to effectively manage it. Hugh was right when he said they needed additional household help.

Miss Clark was young, but she apparently had the skill to oversee a household and make sure the servants were fed and clothed. That would be one less thing to worry about. With someone like her in charge, he could devote his attention to the crops.

Perchance, she could be persuaded to consider forgoing matrimony for a time if he offered her generous compensations. If not, mayhap it was time to consider matrimony for practical reasons. It wouldn't hurt to make her acquaintance and learn more of her.

What did Hugh say? Something about making his choice. Heat soared up his back, and he leaned toward his brother. "Are you considering courting Miss Clark?"

"No, not her, but I see you are."

Miles coughed hard.

Hugh pounded him on the back until he stopped. "She is a beauty."

Miles cleared his throat. "Aye, she is." He realized he had said the words out loud and groaned. He gazed at her again. She looked at him, and he quickly glanced away. "I have no interest in her other than our need for servants."

Hugh raised his infuriating eyebrow.

Miles did the only thing he could to stop this maddening accusation. He changed the subject. "Are you really considering settling down with a wife?"

"I am."

"If not Miss Clark, who?"

Hugh grinned. "Miss Hannah Walker is a fascinating woman and fair to look at."

Miles glanced toward Miss Walker, relief flooding over him.

His gaze found its way to Miss Clark again. She bit her lip, fidgeted with her hands, and directed fleeting glances toward her chaperones. Mayhap she was shy. All this attention would be overwhelming to a timid maiden. Still, she seemed more distraught than the situation warranted. A strong wind blew over him, urging him to become her protector.

"So, what say you?" Hugh asked.

"What?" Miles turned his attention to his brother. "What say I about what?"

"Miss Walker." Hugh grinned. "Does she meet your high standards for a sister-in-law?"

A hard worker and good cook who worked in the household of a reverend – that was how Ethan described her. "She's a fine choice providing she agrees to court you." She might be the sort who could calm Hugh's vices. At any rate, she would be a good addition to the plantation.

Hugh stared at the woman. "I'm not much to offer as a husband. She might prefer another."

"Nonsense, your charm affects the fairer sex as flowers attract bees." Miles meant it as a jest, but after seeing the hurt look on Hugh's face, he regretted the words. "Even if you do marry, we'll need household servants."

"It will be a month before any of these women are eligible to become indentured," Hugh said. "They might all be married off by then." He pointed to the scrawny orange-haired girl with freckles. "I'd be willing to wager she'll be available."

Miles glanced at the girl. "She's young and a hard worker. Some planter wanting many strong sons to work his land would be happy with her."

"Then you're willing to take the wager?"

A smirk crossed Miles' face. "It's tempting, but you know I don't game for profit."

"Brother, you need to learn to relax and have some fun."

"And you need to make amends with your God." That hurt look again. Miles shrugged an apology and softened his tone. "We do need a couple of household maidens, but we'll wait to see who's available when the time comes. In the meantime, let's see if we can arrange a meeting with a few of the brides."

Hugh crossed his arms. "I'm only interested in Miss Walker. If she says nay, I'll remain a bachelor."

"There's another bride ship due in a year. If she turns you down, perchance you'll find another who meets your fancy."

"We'll see."

Miles glanced back at Miss Clark. She and Miss Walker seemed to be reassuring the red-haired girl. "I'll talk to Miss Atwood and Miss Clark and see how set they are on matrimony."

Hugh smirked. "You seem smitten by Miss Clark. Are you considering servants or a bride for yourself?"

"Nonsense." Miles' mouth twitched as he tried to suppress a grin. "Even if I did marry, I couldn't possibly consider someone so young. She's only fifteen."

Hugh nudged him. "I believe you protest the notion far too much. There are advantages to a young bride. She would be more likely to survive the seasoning, and she would bear many children."

Miles responded with a smirk. He didn't want to wed, no matter how charming Miss Clark was. Still, marriage might be the only way to entice her to manage his household. He had loved his wife dearly, but love was a poor reason to marry. With his first wife, it had been a pleasant occurrence after the nuptials had taken place.

He would start a conversation with her first. If she were willing to be indentured, excellent, but if she would only come to his household as his wife, he would do what he must to keep his plantation prosperous. Hopefully, it wouldn't come to that. The thought of replacing Mary with another so soon was distasteful to him.

After Ethan dismissed the brides, they headed outside to eat. Miles considered staying and talking to Ethan about his news but rejected the idea. Too many around to hear. There was plenty of time later to hear what mischief his father was up to.

Instead, he followed the brides outside and kept a close eye on Miss Clark and Miss Atwood. They stood with Miss Walker in line at the table overflowing with food. Although the youngest of the three, Miss Clark acted more like an elder sister protecting her brood.

Miss Walker whispered something in her ear. She shook her head.

Wild turkey and pheasant roasted on spits over a large fire. Grilled fish and lobster were displayed on large platters. Nuts, cheeses, corn breads, and stews showed the married women of the fort had worked hard on this feast. The colony had come far since the starving time when food was scarce, and they feared the colony would end in disease and starvation.

The aroma caused Miles' mouth to water, and he entered the line behind Ethan and Constance, but he couldn't manage to divert his attention from Miss Clark.

She and Miss Walker whispered to each other. She shook her head, and Miss Walker crossed her arms. Miss Clark shrugged, and she left the line and approached her chaperones.

"Could we talk – alone?" Miss Clark asked.

"Of course," Constance said.

They started to step away.

Reverend Cochran strode toward them. "Ethan, Constance, there are matters I must discuss with you. Do you have a moment?"

Constance patted Miss Clark's hand. "We'll talk presently."

Miss Clark pressed her lips together and nodded.

Her chaperones followed the reverend to the church.

"Is there something I may do to assist you?" Miles spoke without thinking it through. He had no intention of appearing forward.

Miss Clark startled as if she hadn't known he was there. She shook her head and rushed to join her friends.

Most of the bachelors congregated around the table waiting for an opportunity, but even though they had no difficulty approaching the brides before church, now it appeared none of them wanted to be the first. Perchance, the men required a hearty meal to fortify themselves.

Miss Clark and her companions dished out their food and found a place outside the trading post to sit in the grass and eat.

Miles headed toward them, but Warren Smithers got to the women first.

"I have a farm about a mile from here." Goodman Smithers removed his hat and rubbed his hand through his hair. "It isn't big, but I do all right. I could provide for you, and you wouldn't have to work too hard."

The women stood.

Miss Clark placed herself slightly in front of Miss Atwood and Miss Walker. "We haven't even met. Surely, you're not proposing matrimony at this point, Goodman... We don't even know your name."

Miles grinned slightly but stood a few feet away. Miss Clark might be young, but she wasn't afraid to put the man in his place.

Smithers twisted his hat in his hands. "I'm Goodman Smithers. You came here to marry, didn't you? Well, I need a wife. I'll tell you what. I'll even take the ugly one." He grabbed Miss Atwood by the arm.

Miss Atwood tried to pull away. "Stop, you're hurting me."

Miles strode toward him.

"Unhand her, you brute." Miss Clark slapped Goodman Smithers across the face so hard the sound carried throughout the fort.

Smithers let go of Miss Atwood and placed his hand on his reddened cheek. "You shrew. What crime did I commit deserving such fury?"

Miles stepped in front of Goodman Smithers. "Since these maidens aren't interested, perchance you should look elsewhere."

Smithers scowled at Miss Clark, and Miles was afraid for a moment he wasn't going to give up so easily. "You're right, Master Bonneville. These wenches are too much trouble. I'll find another more pleasant in nature." He wandered toward a cluster of women outside the bakery.

Miles nodded to the women and bowed slightly. "My pardon for the unfortunate occurrence. Goodman Smithers means well, but he does lack manners."

"Perchance, the men are a bit too enthusiastic." Miss Walker turned to the others. "Now that we've had our meal, I'll take my leave. Fare you well, Honesty, Bridgette. I prefer to meet any prospects on my own."

"Are you sure?" Miss Clark asked.

Miss Walker grinned. "I'm sure." She hugged the other two women and strolled toward the center of the fort where groups of men still congregated.

Miss Clark's eyes then locked on Miles. "You're still here? I suppose you want to propose now. Which of us do you plan to drag to the church?"

"Neither... I mean..." He flustered. "I only wished to make your acquaintances, nothing more."

Miss Clark raised an eyebrow. "Why?"

"Why?" Miles couldn't help gaping. This woman had a way of making him feel as unsure as he had been when he first sailed to America. "I only wanted to inquire if you were set on matrimony."

"I am." Miss Atwood wiped her hands on her apron. "I prefer a kind young man with good manners though, not a lout like Goodman Smithers."

"Well, I'm not." Miss Clark crossed her arms and delivered a glower that would make any sensible man step back. "I don't intend to become a broodmare for some ill-mannered colonist. I'll return to England as soon as I earn enough to pay for the voyage."

Miles couldn't help the grin spreading over his face. He couldn't comprehend why she would journey so far only to return to England, but it was his good fortune indeed. "I would like to invite you to work for me."

Miss Clark tilted up her chin. "You're not looking for a bride?"

A gratified sigh escaped his lips. "I have no interest in marrying, but my plantation does have need of household servants to do women's chores."

"My impression was every man here would be looking for a wife," Miss Clark said. "What makes you different? Are you already wed?"

"If you must know this to consider my offer, my wife died four months past. I have no desire to find another this soon."

Miss Clark blushed. "My pardon." She gazed toward the ocean. "What arrangements have you made for the accommodations?"

Miles rubbed his hand across his mouth to hide the smile forming on his lips. Miss Clark would make an excellent household manager. Not only was she capable, she had the moral fortitude he was looking for. "You'll have a room attached to my house by the stone fireplace and chimney. It has a separate entrance. My brother lives in another near the servants' quarters. I have four rooms in the main house. You'll share your room with any other female servants I procure." He cleared his throat. "I'm sure you'll find it comfortable."

"Attached where to the main house? How many other female servants?"

Miles tried to hold back a smile. "The kitchen stands on the right side of the hearth. My bed chamber is on the left side of the house, and I vow I shall never enter your room while you're in my employ. I haven't purchased anyone yet, but I do plan to acquire at least one other female, perchance two."

"Your offer sounds acceptable, but I plan to return to England as soon as possible. Seven years' service and a parcel of land in Virginia doesn't hold much appeal to me."

Miles' forehead furrowed. He couldn't resist the temptation to ask what she was about. His curiosity would not be abated. "Pardon me for being forward, but may I ask why you'd make the journey to Jamestown if you have no desire for a husband or land?"

Miss Clark splayed her hand over her neck as her gaze darted toward the ship outside the fort. "I... I changed my mind is all. I miss London, and I didn't expect Jamestown to be so primitive."

Miles chewed the inside of his cheek. How could someone coming to a new land not expect it to be primitive? It didn't make sense. She didn't seem like the type to make hasty decisions, but sailing to Jamestown and then wanting to turn around and journey back was odd. "I'll make an agreement with you, Miss Clark. If you'll come and work for me and manage my household for five years, instead of the usual compensation, I'll pay for your voyage back to England. Provided you don't take off and marry before the time is up."

A hint of a smile broke through Miss Clark's somber expression. "You'd be more likely to see a bird in last year's nest, but how do I know I can trust you to carry out these intentions?"

"I am a member of the Burgess and a man of my word. I'm not known for making falsehoods." Miles removed his hat. What was it about this girl that made him feel so unsteady? "Even so, I'll sign a paper with the terms of our agreement. That should ease your concerns."

"Aye, that would be satisfactory, provided you have the vicar read it out loud to me. My training includes mostly spinning, weaving, and sewing. Reading is for preachers, aristocrats, and educated men, not for tradeswomen." Miss Clark's gaze darted around. "How do we go about this?"

"I'll work out the details with Ethen. I'm staying at the fort overnight. Tomorrow, I'll come fetch you with the document in hand."

Miss Clark gave a crisp nod.

Miles turned his gaze to Miss Atwood. "What say you? Are you willing to work for me?"

"Mayhap." Miss Atwood's brow furrowed. "I still prefer to marry if I find a kind man who will have me, but I would like time to learn of him ere I make my choice."

If the girl was that set on a husband, it might be wise to wait until the auction. "I have a meeting in town on the morrow. I'll return to my plantation after that, and I'll need your answer before then."

Miss Atwood's mouth twisted. "That won't be enough time to consider my decision, let alone find a groom."

"If you'll agree to remain with me a year," Miles said, "I'll allow any man interested to court you, provided your work is done and you agree to abide by my courting standards. If you decide to marry before the seven years is up, I'll even provide a small dowry."

"Seven years!" Miss Clark placed her hands on her hips. "Why seven years for her and only five years for me?"

"Miss Clark, I am making you a manager of my household. Miss Atwood will work as a general servant."

Miss Clark blushed. "Parden me. I didn't consider that."

"If you do decide to join my household, you'll need to work on that pointed tongue of yours. I tolerate no impertinence on my farm."

Miss Clark's glare was fierce, but she nodded and didn't say any more.

He admired the woman's spirit in protecting her companion, but it didn't make any sense. Why would anyone, even a woman as young as Miss Clark, journey this far only to change her mind? She bewildered him.

Whatever she was about, she captivated him enough to overcome his objections. She would make a fine wife.... He wiped his hand across his neck. Servant. Hugh's jest must have rattled him. Now that she had agreed to become his servant, he had no intention of marrying.

Chapter Ten

Hugh sat on the steps of the bakery and watched Miss Walker. Men flitted around her like bees around a hive. Her smile was pleasant but never promised more than cordial conversation. Even though she was dressed in a plain red linen dress with a simple white linen tartlet around her neck and chest and an undyed waistcoat, the confidence she exuded made her look like a fine lady holding court.

It amazed him how attracted he was to this woman he'd never met. He never thought he'd long for any woman as he had Suleta. Suleta. It had broken his heart to tell her goodbye. He'd been so lonely, a couple of times, he'd started to go to her, but he'd resisted the temptation. Miss Walker's smile gave him hope he could love again.

Each man who came by extolled their virtues and offered courtship or marriage to Miss Walker, but she rejected each one in the same gracious manner he remembered his mother displaying when she received guests.

Master Douglas introduced himself as a member of the Burgess and a prosperous planter. Hugh couldn't help but be amused that a crotchety old man like Douglas would try to court someone as young and pretty as her. He couldn't wait to see how she refused the man's attentions.

"I have a large plantation about three miles from here, over three hundred acres of prime land, with quite a few servants including household maids, so you wouldn't have to toil endlessly if you chose me. May I have the privilege of courting you?"

Miss Walker had tucked her reddish-brown hair into a coif, but one curl escaped onto her cheek. "I'm honored you would even consider me, Master Douglas, but I must refuse your kind offer. Someone in your position and place of honor couldn't possibly accept a penniless girl from Pudding Lane as your wife. I implore you to find another."

He'd never seen Master Douglas at such a loss for words before, but the man accepted her rejection as if she'd bestowed a great honor upon him. Hugh was impressed but a little troubled. If she refused all these men who were worthy of her hand, she would never agree to marry a scoundrel like him.

After waiting until she'd chased away all the other suitors, he ambled toward her. Halfway there, he paused. 'Twas a fool's errand. Even so, none but the brave deserved the fair. He let out the breath he was holding and approached her.

She smiled at him, a dimple indenting her right cheek, and the sun somehow shone brighter. The unruly curl had escaped her bonnet again, but somehow it seemed right for it not to be contained or hidden away. This bride was fair like none other he'd seen. Her rosy, high cheekbones would be the envy of any angel. Suleta could not touch her glow.

"Good day, Miss Walker." He kissed her hand. "I see you've dismissed all your other suitors. I thought I might give it a go."

She gave him a quizzical look. "Your name?"

"I'm Master Hugh Bonneville."

She turned away from him. "I saw you watching me."

"You knew?" Heat spread across his face as he circled her until she was facing him again. "My elder brother and I have a plantation at the Neck of the Woods by the river. I could provide for you."

"Every suitor in Jamestown boasts of fertile land. What else do you have to offer?"

Hugh swallowed hard. Everything she said was true, and there was nothing else he had to vouch for him.

Her green eyes glowed in the sunlight, muddling his thoughts. He was a wretched man. The way he had mistreated Suleta proved that. "I'm told I might not be good husband material, and I deserve the rebuke, but if you agree to marry me, I'll be faithful, and I'll do my best to change my rogue ways. I'll vow to cherish and protect you to the best of my ability. Although others may believe they have a right to be harsh with their wives and rule with an iron fist, I'll be a loving and caring husband all the days of our lives."

That dimple appeared again. "And what transgressions have caused you to describe yourself as a rogue?"

A sinking feeling lodged in the pit of his stomach. He'd done a lot of deplorable things, but he wasn't in the habit of lying. Better to tell the truth and let her decide if she wanted to end the conversation. No matter what his brother suggested, it seemed false to try to charm her with his winsome ways. He cleared his throat. "I have been guilty of fornication with a number of Indian women."

She stared at him as if her green eyes could bore into his soul. "And yet you promise to be faithful? How can you hope to fulfill that vow?"

He lowered his eyes, ashamed to gaze into hers. "I had a romance that ended badly. I vowed not to succumb to fornication again and have kept that vow for many months now. Even if you should reject me, I have determined to live honorably toward the fairer gender."

She touched his arm then drew her hand away. "Any other vices I should know about?"

"I do like my rum. I can't guarantee I'd give that up completely, but if we were to marry, I would do my best to stay sober most of the time."

"I see. If I may offer sound counsel, the only way you can really change your life is to give it to the Lord, the one who created it and knows your heart." Her face showed no repulsion, but it didn't have to.

He let out a heavy sigh. "My only virtue is honesty. If we wed, I would never lie to you or keep secrets from you, but I understand if you prefer to find another."

"Master Bonneville, you have more to offer than you know. Indeed, you are the first man who has given me an honest tally of his faults as well as his virtues, and you're the only one who has pledged to, how did you put it? Cherish and protect me." She placed her hands on her hips. "The others only want a broodmare and kitchen wench, and although they profess to be fine Christian men by their blustering demeanor and false promises, I suspect they're Christian in name only. I'd rather have an honest man."

Hugh flustered. "Does that mean you'll marry me?"

"You don't give a damsel much time, do you, Master Bonneville?"

"You can call me Hugh since we'll soon be man and wife." He grinned in a way he hoped would captivate her. No harm in a little charm to win her hand. "I see no merit in waiting unless you prefer to be a bondservant."

A fake pout made her lips even more desirable. He almost wished he hadn't pledged to be honorable. "Master Bonneville, I insist on a proper proposal before we start calling each other by our Christian names."

He kissed her hand and bowed on one knee. "Miss Walker, would you do me the honor of becoming my wife?"

She placed a finger to her cheek as if she were the queen considering whether to bestow favor or imprison him in the Tower of London. "Yes, Master Bonneville. I believe I shall."

He hugged her and spun her around.

"I have one condition."

A lump lodged in his stomach. He let her go. "What condition?"

"We marry tomorrow. I agree with you on rushing this. I have no desire to go through an extended courtship while indentured to people I don't know."

He let out a laugh. He couldn't help himself. She'd made him so happy. "Tomorrow it is. Let's go to the church now and let Reverend Cochran know he can post the Certificate of Banns tonight."

"What about your elder brother? Won't you desire his blessing?"

Hugh rubbed the back of his neck. Miles wanted him to marry, but sometimes he could be obstinate about propriety. Hopefully, he wouldn't cause any trouble about it taking place so soon.

~~~~~

"You said you had tidings." Miles sat on the front pew of the church with Ethan. "I'm ready to hear them."

Ethan's Adam's apple bulged. "Your father has been arrested by the king's guard, and his title and property have been seized. He's being held in the Tower of London."

The muscle in Miles' jaw twitched. "What did he do this time?"
~~~~~

"Tis nothing to do with his indiscretions." Ethan stroked his beard. "You know of his many enemies in King James' court since that incident with the wine."

A familiar knot lodged in Miles' gut as he remembered the disdain the lords and ladies of London showed toward his family. Ten years ago, they'd finally decided his father had gone beyond the pale by entertaining women while unclothed on his balcony. If that wasn't shameful enough, he desecrated the wine and had the gall to toast the king with it.

Father had shown himself a reprobate long before that with his many mistresses and drunken parties, but until his incident with the wine, the royal court never seemed to care. Afterwards, they heaped their disgust on every member of his family. They couldn't show their faces in public without being shunned or receiving a tongue lashing by gentlemen and ladies who, before that, were clamoring to be invited to his father's parties.

After the king banned Father from his presence, Mother had taken to her bed and refused to allow herself to be seen in public. She had forgiven him so many times before, but the public humiliation was too much for her.

Miles, the oldest sibling though barely a man at age twenty, had decided to take his mother, brothers, and sisters to the New World to depart from the disgrace his father had brought on the family, but Lady Bonneville was too weak to travel. He desired to stay in London to take care of her, but she insisted he take his siblings and sail to unknown lands. His older sister by two years would stay with her, and they would come later when she'd recovered.

Mother never did recover. A year ago, she'd died of her ailment, and his sister married a vicar soon after and moved to Scotland.

"What are the charges?"

"He's been accused of treason."

"Treason!" Miles rubbed a hand over his mouth. "Father is a reprobate and a sinner, but he's always been loyal to the king."

"Apparently, the Duke of Bedford has brought evidence against him."

Miles grabbed hold of the edge of the pew. Duchess Bedford was one of his father's favorite mistresses and the duke had sworn revenge on his father. "He's giving false testimony, Ethan. He has to be."

Ethan gazed at the floor. "It's possible. The ship returns in a few months. You could travel to London to sort this out. Hugh can see to the land while you're away."

"Nay." Miles stood. "I shall not set eyes on him again in this lifetime."

"He's your father, man. What about the fifth commandment?"

"He doesn't deserve my honor." If it hadn't been for his father's scandals, mayhap his mother would still be alive. "I've worked hard to secure a good name and a profitable farm. I shan't toss it aside for him."

Ethan placed a hand on Miles' shoulder. "Heed my words. If you don't attempt to make peace with him, you might not get another chance."

"They wouldn't execute him." A sour taste assaulted Miles' mouth. As much as he wanted not to distress over this, the thought of his father being put to death for a crime he didn't commit troubled him.

"Prepare yourself. The king is still undecided, but he won't wait forever before hanging your father's head in the Tower of London.

"What do they think he did?"

"He's accused of being involved with the gunpowder plot."

"Impossible. That was fifteen years long past, and the conspirators have already been hung. He's not even Catholic."

"Nevertheless, he's been charged with supplying the traitors with information as to the king's whereabouts."

"How could he possibly have any knowledge of the plot?" Miles slunk into the pew and rested his elbows on his knees. "I need to consider this. Hugh will be troubled by this report. For better or worse, he still idolizes Father. He was barely a lad of fourteen when we left England, and he still doesn't understand why we had to depart."

The door burst open. Hugh entered with one of the prettier brides and grinning ear to ear. "Meet Miss Walker. Only on the morrow, she'll change her name to Mistress Hannah Bonneville."

Miles stood and stepped back, reeling from tidings of his father's possible execution and now the news of his brother's hasty wedding. "On the morrow! You just met."

Hugh shrugged. "You told me to find a wife." He took hold of Miss Walker's hand. "I could find none finer."

"But so soon?" Miles stuffed the shock inside and forced a smile. This was what he wanted for his brother, but the timing was startling. He shook Hugh's hand. "Congratulations."

Ethan slapped Hugh on the back. "Does Reverend Cochran know?"

"Not yet," Hugh said. "We preferred to tell Miles the good tidings first and secure the tobacco payment for her journey. We'll let him know as soon as we leave here."

Miles nodded, took Hannah's hand, and kissed it. "Welcome to the family."

Hannah blushed. "Thank ye, Master Bonneville."

"If you plan to become my brother's wife, we must be on a first name basis. I'm Miles."

"Sir Miles." Hannah curtsied slightly.

A half-grin reached the corner of his mouth. Hugh had not only chosen a beautiful woman, but one with grace and decorum. "Just Miles will do. We tend to be informal here in the colony. I also have some tidings to share."

Ethan's shoulders stiffened, but he had no need to fret. Miles would never ruin this day for his brother. News about their father could wait. "I have secured payment for a female bondservant. Another is considering my offer. Your new bride will have plenty of household help."

"I'm grateful, brother," Hugh said. "I know we sometimes quarrel, but it means everything to me to have your blessing."

"You have that and more." Miles forced a grin. He would wait to tell Hugh about Father until after the nuptials.

Chapter Eleven

Elizabella spent the next hour shooing away would-be suitors. The sooner she got through this day, the better. At least, she wouldn't have to risk explaining to Constance who she really was. All she needed to do was keep the deception up for five years, and she would be able to sail back to London... to her sister.

Five years. An eternity. If only she could find a way to get word to Honesty sooner. Mayhap her sister would send the necessary funds to buy her way out of this and pay for her journey home.

Another man approached them. This one had pimples, fair skin, and a lisp, and looked like he hadn't eaten a decent meal in months.

"Nay, we have no desire to wed you," she blurted.

The man stumbled over her feet, and apologized, then scurried away. Bridgette let out a gusty sigh.

"Mayhap we should take some time to explore the fort before Master Bonneville comes for us," Elizabella said.

Bridgette rubbed her temples. "You go ahead. I wish to stay."

"Haven't you had enough to eat?"

"It's not my belly I wish to fill. I want to meet some eligible men. There might be a few decent among them, but you shoo them away before I can even say good day."

Elizabella flushed. "Of course." She could have kicked herself for being so dull. "I have no more brain than a stone. You came to Jamestown to marry."

Bridgette crossed her arms. "Aye, that's why I'm here. I can't fathom why you would make such a long voyage if you don't want a husband."

Elizabella pressed her lips together. The way Bridgette liked to chatter, she wasn't about to tell her the reason. It would be all over the fort by nightfall.

"Greetings." A handsome man in his mid-twenties with sandy brown hair and a winsome smile approached. "My name is John Cooper. I'm one of the Burgess. I hope you're enjoying yourselves."

"Very much so." Bridgette delivered a glare, warning her not to interfere.

Elizabella's jaw clenched. "If you'll excuse me, I have matters to attend to." She headed toward the church. Mayhap, she could find refuge from marriage proposals there. The doors had been left open, showing the church was empty, so she entered and sat on a bench.

"What am I to do?" She said the words out loud in prayer, even though she didn't expect the Lord to answer her requests. "Is there no way to get word to Honesty? She must be so vexed about me."

If she was even alive. For all she knew, infection could have set in and killed her. *Don't even think of that.* If her sister died, it would be her fault. She couldn't bear another sibling on her conscience. Her brother's death was already too great a burden.

She wiped a stray tear running down her cheek. How did this happen? Why? She had never wanted anything more than opening a small seamstress shop where she could get her sister away from Pudding Lane and support them both.

When the time came, she would have found Honesty a suitable husband, but she assumed they would both live in central London and visit each other often.

Things started unraveling when her sister met Sir Robert Weathersby while she was delivering a gown to his mother. Elizabella tried to convince her it would end badly, but she wouldn't listen. She knew her sister was nursing a broken heart, but she was delighted she would still have her by her side a little longer. After all, Honesty was only fifteen.

Every event since her sister announced she would sail to Jamestown had led to Elizabella being thrust into this venture she didn't want. She had to find a way to get her life back.

An idea started to form. Although First Mate Rogers was an unpleasant man, he'd been helpful on the journey. Once, a couple of sailors had cornered her, making rude suggestions. Not only did Rogers stop them, he whipped them severely and told the other sailors they could expect worse if he caught them around any of the brides.

He could be trusted to take a message to her sister. She dug around in her purse and found two pounds and one-half pound coins. A half-pound should do it, but if he wanted more, she would pay it.

Ethan and Constance exhorted them to stay in the fort within view, but the ship was moored just outside the gate. Surely, they wouldn't oppose this, but she would do her best to avoid being seen. She didn't want to answer any questions about why she was on the ship.

Walking outside, she looked around. Although crowds had been around here all day, she had good fortune. The area around the church was deserted, and nobody looked her way. She darted behind the chapel and outside the fort gate.

She glanced back. Nobody noticed, so she strode to the ship, coins in hand.

Even if this message didn't get to her sister in a timely manner, she could work for Master Bonneville five years and return to England. Her sojourn in Jamestown wouldn't be that long if the message was delivered. Her sister could get the money to a ship's captain. Elizabella might be sailing home within the year, provided she didn't die from disease or a savage

Indian attack. Even if misfortune did besiege her, at least Honesty would know what had happened.

She climbed aboard the gangplank and searched for First Mate Rogers. It didn't take long to find him towering over a couple of sailors swabbing the deck.

He bellowed out insults. "Put some muscle in it. You're not at a ladies' tea party."

She walked toward him. "First Mate, I need to speak with you about an urgent matter."

Rogers glared at her with narrowed eyes and furrowed brow, his normal annoyed expression. "Aren't you supposed to be in the fort finding a husband?"

Elizabella shrugged and ignored his irritation and his question.

Rogers let out a gusty sigh. "I suppose I can give you a moment. What are you about?"

"When you return to London, I have need for a message to be delivered to the Clark Seamstress Shop. It's west of the Royal Exchange, about two rods. Do you know the area?"

"Aye, but I'm not an errand boy. Find another to deliver your missive."

Elizabella showed him the coin in her hand. "Do you really believe these sailors are trustworthy enough to do my bidding? Nay, I know you shall carry out your word. I'll pay you a half-pound, and when the message is delivered, tell the woman you find to give you another pound."

The officer's scowl slipped. "Make it a pound."

Elizabella dug in her purse and pulled out a one-pound coin. Well worth it if she made it back to London. "As you wish."

He took the pound and tucked it in the pocket inside his trousers. "What do you want me to say?"

Elizabella's heart beat faster. She hadn't thought far enough ahead to consider how she could word the message without giving herself away. "There's a woman at the dress shop named Miss Clark."

"Same name as yours, huh?"

"She's my sister." He nodded, and her heart slowed to normal. "Do you write?"

"Aye?"

"Perchance you'll wish to write it down, so you'll remember."

Rogers glared at her. "I run this ship, don't I? I'm not addled. I can remember a simple message."

Her stomach churned. He had to get it correct. "For a pound, I have the right to insist you write it down."

Another gusty sigh. "A moment while I get parchment and quill." He headed toward the captain's berth.

Elizabella gazed toward the shore. Nobody had seen her yet, but if she didn't return to the fort soon, it would only be a matter of time. Why didn't he hurry?

He marched back to her, quill pen, inkwell, and parchment in hand. He sat on the deck and dipped the pen in ink. "Well? I haven't got all day, have I?"

"Write 'Elizabella is in Jamestown. Send funds to redeem her from service and pay for her voyage back to London.' You remember where to deliver it?"

He wrote the words and folded the paper. "I remember. Clark's Seamstress shop, two rods west of the Royal Exchange, but who's this Elizabella? I don't remember her aboard the bride ship."

Elizabella bit her lip and tried to come up with a convincing lie. "She was here before we arrived. She's an associate of mine from London and –"

"I've no time for your life's story."

"One more thing," Elizabella said. "This must be kept in confidence. Nobody else need know I came to you."

"I'll get the message delivered." He dismissed her with a wave of his hand and strode toward the captain's berth.

"There you are." Master Bonneville's voice startled her. He stood on shore by the gangplank with his arms crossed. "What are you about here?"

Heat rose to her face. How much had he heard? "I had an errand. I have need to make arrangements to have my trunk delivered to my new home."

"No need. My land is on the James River. I'll have a couple of my servants take a raft to the fort to fetch your belongings." Master Bonneville's brow furrowed. "I thought you were charged not to leave the fort."

Her mind scurried for an explanation. "Tis but a short walk from the gates. I knew Constance wouldn't mind."

"Could we talk? Mayhap somewhere off the ship?"

Elizabella's stomach tightened. If he'd heard her conversation with the first mate, he might withdraw his offer. Or worse. "Aye."

She approached him down the gangplank. He offered his hand, and she took it and stepped onto dry land. Depending on how much he heard, he might report her to the Burgess. Who knew what punishment they would mete out for her deception?

He led her to a nearby grove of trees close to the ship. "My brother is getting married on the morrow."

She tilted her head to the side and tried to keep the relief from showing on her face. He hadn't overheard. "One of the brides?"

Master Bonneville grinned slightly as a dimple appeared on his rugged left cheek. "Aye, Miss Hannah Walker."

"These matters move swiftly in Jamestown. I'm happy for them." More surprised than happy. Hannah seemed too level-headed to marry a man she'd just met so soon, but she did confide how much she longed for a truthful and caring man who would shield her from the cruelties of life after what she'd been through in London, as if there was such a man. "She's a wonderful person."

Master Bonneville leaned against a tree. "So far, I know of four couples who will wed in the morn."

"Four? Amazing. One wedding surely does bring another."

A family of deer wandered nearby, and she took a step toward them. Such beauty in this untamed wilderness. One day, she would tell Honesty all about it. Hopefully soon.

"You haven't changed your mind about our arrangement, have you?" He stepped beside her.

Ducks quacked as they made their way out of the James River. "I have no intention of marrying, if that's what concerns you."

"Tell me about your life in England." He picked up a stone and skipped it along the water. "It must have been quite an accomplishment for a woman to run a seamstress shop frequented by gentleladies of noble birth."

"There's not much to tell." She grabbed a rock at her feet and tried to throw it toward the river. Instead of skipping along the surface, it sank.

"Here, let me show you." He handed another stone to her. "It's all in how you toss it. Stand sideways, like this." He stood behind her, took her arms, and led her through the movement.

She could feel his breath on the back of her neck, and a twinge of excitement went through her. She knew she should move away, but she didn't.

He placed his hand over hers and moved it from side to side. "Toss the rock across the water instead of throwing it." His rough hand was warm against hers. He cleared his throat and stepped back. "Now you try."

She tossed the rock. It skipped a couple of times before sinking. She clapped her hands together. "I did it."

He chuckled, making his brown eyes squint. "Another fine accomplishment."

Her ears grew hot. She was acting like a young girl still hanging on to her mother's apron. What he must think of her.

He seemed not to notice her discomfort. "Keep practicing, and you'll become as much of an expert at rock skipping as you are at sewing." They walked a little farther. "You never answered my question. How did you manage to acquire your own shop?"

Her thoughts jumbled. "In my youth, I apprenticed with a reputable seamstress in London."

"In your youth?" The corners of his mouth turned up a little. "You're only fifteen."

Heat rushed up her back. "I was only eight when I started my apprenticeship." She'd known a few girls starting that early. It sounded plausible. "My older sister, Elizabella, worked there and helped secure a position."

"That was young." His eyes twinkled in a way that made her wonder if he believed her fable.

"After my father died, my sister and I used the small inheritance he left us to open a shop near the Royal Market. Soon, word of our work reached nobility. After we made a gown for Duchess Marjory of Worthington, she shared our work with Queen Anne, who commissioned us to sew a gown for King James' royal party."

The muscle in his jaw twitched. "You… You knew my mother?"

"I don't understand. Who is your mother?"

His voice caught. "Duchess Marjory Bonneville of Worthington."

She touched his hand. "I am so sorry for your loss. She was a lovely woman."

His Adam's apple bulged. "Yes, she was." The intensity in his gaze made her knees shaky. "Then you've heard of my father, no doubt."

She paused for a moment. It had been the talk of London for years. Of course, she'd heard.

"I don't listen to idle chatter."

"Thank you for that." He held out his arm. "Would you like to see more of the countryside?"

She grinned slightly as she looped her arm in his. "I would enjoy that, if you're sure Ethan won't shoot you."

He let out a laugh. "Nay, I believe I'm safe if we don't tarry long. He's a good friend and a good neighbor."

"Neighbor?"

"Aye, their farm borders mine."

Elizabella nodded. It would be good to have Constance close by. They walked a little further.

A tree by the riverside was filled with bluish white buds. "What kind of tree is that?"

"It's called a juniper." Master Bonneville picked a bud off the tree. "There are many among the Virginia forests."

"I've never seen such dense woodland. I've heard about the jungles of Africa, and I imagined them looking thus. When I was young, Mother and Father took me to the country outside of London." She swallowed hard. That was one of her favorite memories before the drink took hold of her father. "It was a wonderful adventure, but I don't remember this much foliage even then."

"England has its grassy knolls and rolling hills, even some forests, but for raw, untamed wilderness, nothing compares to Virginia." He stopped and gazed at the western sky. "There's room to expand here, to breathe. London is getting more crowded every day."

She had to admit the truth of that. She enjoyed all the conveniences of living in the most civilized city on Earth, but sometimes it was stifling.

"The sun is beginning to set. We should go back." The corners of his mouth twitched. "I wouldn't want to be shot by your chaperone."

Elizabella chuckled. "I, for one, am relieved he takes his responsibility so seriously."

"Ethan is a godly man of impeccable character."

She strolled with Master Bonneville back to the fort. He seemed like a decent sort, and it didn't feel right to deceive him. If she'd met him in London, she might even consider him a likely prospect, but not here.

Before they left for his plantation, she would tell him everything about how she came to be in Jamestown. Something about his manner convinced her she could trust him.

Chapter Twelve

On their way back to the fort, Miles walked beside Miss Clark along the shore. Gentle waves washed over the sand. The sun on the western horizon lit up the sky with red and yellow. He loved this time of day, right before dusk. He used to walk this shore with Mary when they visited the fort.

As they came near the entrance to the gate, John Cooper and Miss Atwood approached them. Miles' jaw tightened. John knew better than to take a stroll with one of the brides outside the fort.

His hypocrisy made heat rise up the back of his neck. He was strolling with a beautiful woman outside the fort also, wasn't he? That was different. He had the reputation to prove he wouldn't take liberties with her.

John waved to him. "Miles, may I have a word with you?"

Miles glanced toward Miss Clark. "Say your piece."

"I plan to marry Miss Atwood, but she has informed me that she believes in a long courtship, which she'll require before she even considers a proposal."

If John set his cap toward Miss Atwood, Miles would need to look elsewhere for a servant. He wouldn't allow John to seduce a woman in his charge. "What has that to do with me?"

Miss Atwood smoothed her hand across her skirt. "I haven't given my consent yet. I wish to become more acquainted with Mr. Cooper first. I desire to become your servant until such time as I choose to marry."

Miles raised an eyebrow. "And how long do you believe that will be?"

"I don't know." Miss Atwood glanced toward John. "A year should suffice."

"Aye, well..." John's lips clutched together. "However long it takes, I want to make the courting arrangements. I know you pride yourself on being an upright, religious man. I wouldn't want to take advantage of our association in this."

If that were true, it would be the first time John had such considerations.

Miles swiped at the back of his neck. He still needed the girl. Her farm experience would be valuable, but John courting her complicated things. "If I wish to purchase her as a servant, that is."

Miss Atwood stared at her feet.

Miles turned his back on John. Even if the women didn't fathom what was happening, he would deliver fair warning to his former friend before allowing this courtship to take place on his land. He waited a moment longer before facing John. "I know how persuasive you can be. If you can guarantee a year without fornication or pregnancies, I'll take her."

Miss Atwood's face turned red. "You question my virtue?"

"Otherwise," Miles said, "I'll wait for auction."

Miss Clark stepped between them and gave Miles the same glower Mary used to deliver when he'd angered her. "Aren't you bargaining with the wrong person, Master Bonneville? Bridgette is trustworthy. You have no cause to imply otherwise. If she says she'll wait a year to marry, she'll wait. And she'll remain virtuous until that day."

"Don't interfere in my affairs, Miss Clark. This doesn't concern you."

Her blue gaze intensified.

Miles tugged at his shirt collar. "Miss Atwood, what say you? Do I at least have a year's service from you without immoral behavior?"

The girl's blush traveled to her ears. She glanced toward Miss Clark, then to John. "I... I give my word."

"Without improper relations?"

Miss Atwood turned even redder and nodded.

John grabbed the girl around the waist and twirled her around.

Every muscle in Miles' body tensed. The man was already taking liberties. "There will be none of that." He caught hold of John's arm and pulled him away. "If Miss Atwood is to become a member of my plantation, you will treat her with the utmost piety."

John backed up a step and raised his hands in a mock surrender. "I meant no harm."

Miles turned to the women. He needed to talk to John without them overhearing. "I'm sure your chaperones will expect you to arrive in their care soon. I wouldn't want them unduly concerned. If you'll excuse us, Master Cooper and I shall make the arrangements. My brother's wedding will take place in the morn, then I have a meeting to attend. I'll fetch you both after that."

John winked at Miss Atwood.

Miss Clark opened the gate to the fort and ushered Miss Atwood inside.

Miles strode off without another word, with John following, and waited until they were out of earshot. "We need to talk."

"Of course," John said with his deceptively innocent smirk.

"Not here. You don't want anyone to overhear this conversation."

John nodded, and they walked along the shore until dusk was upon them.

Miles motioned to stop. "This isn't like you. Why Bridgette Atwood?"

"I don't know what you mean." The vein in John's neck pulsed. "I desire a wife. I've chosen her."

"I gathered that." Miles wiped his hand over his face. "Miss Atwood doesn't have the appearance you'd normally require."

"I find her appearance acceptable. She's young, and I like red hair and freckles."

"Mm huh." Miles crossed his arms. "Her hair is orange, not red. Her freckles cover her face to the point where it's difficult to find a part of her without freckles. Her nose is long and pointed, and she has the figure of a boy."

John shrugged his shoulders. "She may not be a great beauty, but she makes up for it with her spunky personality. She brings merriment to my lips. And she's strong. Who knows?" His voice cracked. "She might even survive the seasoning, and if we marry, she might endure childbirth." He turned away and stared at the ocean.

Heat rushed to Miles' face. "My pardon." He placed his hand on John's shoulder. "I didn't consider you've already lost two wives."

John cleared his throat. "It might be profitable to wait a year. Not what I want, but at least I'll know if she makes it through the seasoning."

Miles nodded. "I have some reservations about you courting a servant on my farm, but if you'll agree to my terms, I'll allow it."

John let out a gusty sigh. "What terms?"

"You may see her once a week on my land, but she'll only be permitted to leave the plantation on Sundays for church. You may sit with her during the meeting and eat with her inside the fort walls afterward. When you visit the plantation, you may take a short stroll after dinner, but that's the only time I'll permit you to be with her without a chaperone present."

"A fair proposal."

"One more thing." Miles paused while he decided how to word the next part. Bundling did not stop John from fornicating during his previous courtships. Both of his wives were compromised during their betrothals, causing the wedding days to be hastened. Miles would not allow this on his land or with any servant under his protection. "I won't permit you to stay overnight."

John snorted. "Surely, you don't intend for me to make that long walk back to my farm every time I come to court? By the time I arrived, I would have to start on the journey home."

Miles' jaw clenched. "Do I need to remind you of your past transgressions?"

Color rushed to John's cheeks. "You're being unreasonable. I assure you I've changed my ways. I have only the purest intentions, and I shall prove it to you."

The muscle in Miles' cheek twitched. He'd been the one who'd caught John in the act of adultery with his indentured servant, Katherine. He was married to his second wife at the time. Miles had felt it his duty to report John to the governor, even if it did cause a wedge in their friendship.

After John was fined and publicly whipped, his wife was so distraught, it brought on early labor and death. Katherine became ill shortly afterward and succumbed to the seasoning, but Miles suspected the cause of her demise was shame for the sinful act she'd committed.

John had acted differently since then, broken somehow. He'd sought Miles' forgiveness and had worked hard to regain his reputation in the church and the community. He'd even been elected to the Burgess. Miles said he'd accepted the apology, but he hadn't forgiven him. A leopard couldn't change his spots easily.

The thought of John taking advantage of one of his own servants shortly after marrying a woman he'd impregnated made Miles' blood boil. "I won't have my servant subjected to undue temptation."

"Do you really think I would seduce someone as homely as Bridgette?"

Miles grabbed John's shirt, then let go and took a steady breath to keep from giving the man the thrashing he deserved.

John held up his hands. "I know I've sinned greatly in the past, but I've paid a high price for my transgressions. I've worked hard to put those days behind me and become an honorable man. I want a woman who I can spend my life with, not one who only has beauty to offer. You have my word I won't seduce Miss Atwood or take her into my bed."

"Not if I can help it."

John gazed out at the ocean. "You may live only an hour's walk from Jamestown, but my farm is a five-hour stroll away. What am I to do?"

Miles let out a heavy sigh. "No bundling. You can stay in the servants' quarters when you visit."

"I find that acceptable."

"Mark my words. There'll be no late-night visits to the women's home or any secret rendezvous after the women have retired for the evening."

"Done and done," John said.

Even though the man had agreed to his terms, it didn't ease his anxiety. Miles couldn't shake the suspicion he was risking Miss Atwood's virtue with this compromise.

Chapter Thirteen

Hannah looked so happy on her wedding day. Elizabella couldn't help but wonder if that would change with the burdens that came with living in Jamestown. At least, it wasn't her sister standing there.

Marriage was a dangerous prospect for any woman, even one who didn't face the difficulties of taming a new land. Her own mother had died giving birth in a civilized land while attended by a midwife. How could a woman survive childbirth in this land?

The last wedding was completed, and everyone moved to the common area outside the church while the Burgess had their meeting. Even though two women Elizabella knew well would live on the farm with her, she still felt completely abandoned in a desolate land. Would there ever come a time where she could accept her fate? No matter. Once she told Master Bonneville how she came to be here, he would find a way for her to go back to London where she belonged. Even if he didn't and insisted she fulfill her contract, at least she wouldn't be living a lie.

Hannah giggled as Hugh whispered in her ear, and they headed toward the shore.

Lord, please let her joy last.

"Weren't the weddings beautiful?" Bridgette said.

Elizabella nodded. "Why did you decide to wait to wed Goodman Cooper? A year is a long time, even in London."

"He seems kindly." Bridgette bit her lower lip. "I want to make sure he won't be cruel or violent toward me. A year will give me time to know for sure."

Elizabella shrugged. "A wise course of action."

Bridgette wandered off to take some nourishment. Elizabella was glad of it. She leaned against the church wall, waiting for the meeting to end. She didn't want anyone to hear when she confessed all to Master Bonneville.

The sun rose high in the sky, and she sat on the church steps. What was taking them so long? The master said the meeting would be brief, and she wasn't sure she could maintain her courage if it lasted much longer.

A murmur of noise came from the church. The men on the council burst through the door, and Elizabella stood and darted out of the way just in time to keep from being trampled underfoot. The Burgess dragged a young man to the walls of the fort. It was the boy who'd deceived his way onto the ship on their voyage to America.

Elizabella stared in horror as the men tied ropes around the boy's wrist and secured him to logs. The lad didn't resist.

Master Bonneville walked over to her. "We'll leave as soon as this business is attended to."

"What business?" Panic rose in her throat. "What are you going to do to that boy? You're not going to hang him, are you?"

"Nay, nay, the Burgess has decided to be merciful. Master Douglas has paid for his voyage. He'll receive twenty lashes and serve ten years of indenture."

"Whipped?" Bile rose in Elizabella's mouth.

One of the men took a horsewhip, and another tore off the boy's shirt. This couldn't be happening.

"He should consider himself fortunate," Master Bonneville said in an expressionless tone he might use to describe the weather.

The whip came down with a swish, and the boy screamed.

Tears formed in Elizabella's eyes, and she looked away, but when the whip swished and the boy screamed again, she couldn't block out the sounds. Nor those of the next eighteen lashes. What she heard next caused her stomach to churn. The people in the fort cheered.

She ran through the gates and retched. Was this what would happen to her if she admitted she was here under false pretenses? Would she be whipped while people cheered?

It's what you deserve.

Her father's words attacked her mind. What made her think she could escape? Wasn't that why God sent her to Jamestown, to punish her?

Master Bonneville found her outside the fort. His brow furrowed. "I'm sorry you found this so disturbing." He placed his hand on her shoulder and spoke tenderly. "If I'd known you'd be so affected, we would have left before the sentence was carried out."

"You're a member of the Burgess. Were you a part of this?" She couldn't help the accusation in her tone.

He looked at the ground. "I did vote for him to be whipped and indentured and convinced the others to agree, but I did him a kindness."

"A kindness? You call that a kindness?"

He grabbed her hands and gazed intently into her eyes. "If I hadn't done so, he would have been hung. He's just a boy. I couldn't allow that."

Elizabella let out the breath she was holding. She could never admit to the truth now, even to Master Bonneville. They might do even worse to her. She had to get out of this horrible place as soon as she could manage it.

~~~~~

Miles strode home, deep in thought, with Hugh and Hannah a few yards in front of him. Sometimes they would whisper to each other, sometimes exchange glances and smiles. They reminded him of the way he was with Mary on their wedding day. He couldn't ruin it by telling his brother about their father's predicament. He would at least give him this one day.
~~~~~

Miss Clark and Miss Atwood walked a few steps behind him. They hadn't said a word since leaving the fort. They were too quiet.

It was obvious Miss Clark was disturbed about the public whipping, but Miles couldn't understand why. Surely, she'd seen her share of public whippings and hangings in London. Perchance she was one of those women who cared too deeply for the oppressed.

Mary had that trait. Although Hugh believed Mary to be the one causing Miles' antagonism with him, Mary had spoken on his brother's behalf. She always admonished him to show mercy, even to John. She almost stopped him from reporting John's adultery and was angry when he went through with it.

"He's your friend," she'd said. "You know what will happen to him. 'Tis for God to judge."

It was the memory of her mercy that caused him to speak on behalf of whipping the young man today. If only Miss Clark had known how set the council was on a hanging.

Why did he care what she thought? Hugh had accused him of considering her for a bride, but it wouldn't work. She was a servant girl who wanted to return to London in five years. A husband was not something she desired.

He shook his head. Of course, he missed having a woman to care for him, to talk with him, and to partner with him. The loneliness since Mary's death had been overwhelming, but that was no reason to marry, even if Miss Clark was a suitable replacement.

He sighed. Nobody could replace his wife.

A thud and stifled sound of surprise roused him from his thoughts. He turned to find Miss Clark on the ground, looking just as astonished as he felt. He ran to her. She brushed off her skirt and tried to stand. He reached out and offered his hand. She took it and was soon on her feet.

"I stepped in a hole," she said.

Hugh and Hannah were so intent on each other, they didn't notice. They continued to stroll ahead of the others.

"Are you well?" Miles asked.

She nodded.

"Perchance, you and Miss Atwood should take my arms. The path through the forest is uneven, and at times, treacherous."

Miss Clark bit her lower lip. "I suppose it would be acceptable."

Miles held out his arms. She took one, and Miss Atwood took the other. It amazed him how right it felt for Miss Clark to stroll beside him, holding on to his arm. Too right.

Chapter Fourteen

Elizabella and Bridgette took inventory of the kitchen supplies and foodstuffs in Master Bonneville's kitchen. When they'd arrived the day before, all they'd had a chance to do was prepare a hasty meal for everyone.

Hannah had offered to help with breakfast, but Elizabella insisted she take the morning off. After all, she was a new bride, even if it was in this wilderness.

Bridgette stood and peered over the edge of the top shelf. "There's a twenty-pound bag of flour up here and a bag of oats. Neither one's been touched."

"Good." Elizabella reached down and pulled a large iron pot off one of the lower shelves. "We'll make oat porridge and biscuits for breakfast."

Bridgette grunted as she pulled the bags of flour and oats off the shelf. They landed with a thud. She grabbed a dipper and scooped some of each into some copper bowls. "With all the vegetables in the cellar, I could make some stew with fresh bread for supper."

"An excellent idea." Elizabella poured some milk and cracked an egg into the flour. "We should take time to reorganize things. Heavy bags have no place on the top shelf. If you make the stew, I'll consider the plantation and its resources and decide what needs to be done. I'll meet with the master after breakfast and discuss his expectations."

A knock sounded on the door, and Elizabella answered. Two men stood outside. One was taller than any man she'd ever seen. The other was young, even younger than Honesty.

"Good day." She didn't offer to invite them in because she wasn't sure if Master Bonneville allowed his field hands in the house.

"Good day," the tall one said in an Irish broque. "We have your trunks. Do you want dem in your room, or should we place dem outside your door?"

"Inside is fine. Thank ye."

The men nodded, and she closed the door behind them.

Bridgette poured oats into the kettle of boiling water Elizabella had started earlier while she had churned the butter. She poured some flour and water in a bowl and started mixing the dough for biscuits. "I've never seen such a big house for one man."

Elizabella had to admit, this affluence was not what she expected. Master Bonneville had four large rooms, including this spacious kitchen, and a wooden floor. A stone fireplace twice the size of her own in London, with a solid crane large enough for any kettle, covered the back wall.

Two wooden rockers sat in front of the hearth. She had purchased rockers for her and Honesty to sit in while they sewed, but she didn't expect this luxury in the middle of Virginia. A sturdy pine table in the center of the room with benches enough for ten people wasn't a surprise, but it amazed her there was still enough room to walk around.

Even the women's room was large enough to not only have a bed, but a small table and a few stools to sit on as well. She had expected a dirt floor with a couple of tick mattresses in the corner.

"My sister and I own a shop in London, and we don't have this much space." She dropped the biscuits into the large skillet. "Not to mention the servants' houses and a separate home for Master Bonneville's brother and Hannah."

"Don't forget the cow and five chickens," Bridgette said.

"We might have more work than we can handle. He's well stocked for a bachelor in the middle of the wilderness." Elizabella grabbed a large copper kettle with a wooden handle. "I'll get some more water from the well." She carried it outside.

The rooster crowed as the sun peeked over the horizon, painting the sky with orange and yellow. A melody of birds sang their morning song. The light scent of morning dew on the wet grass and honeysuckle encouraged her to take in a big whiff of the fresh smells.

In Central London, the air was stale. The horses clopping down the city streets would stir up dust, deposit manure everywhere, and trample any grass daring to peek out from the ground. Instead of the pleasantness of the dew, the stench of wastewater being poured out in front of every home would assault her nose every morning.

Here, even with the acres of land cleared for farming, oak and poplar trees crowded in on it as if the wilderness wasn't content to be tamed.

It was majestic, but Elizabella couldn't allow herself to enjoy it. A pang of emptiness sprang from her innermost being. Honesty must have stopped looking for her by now. Had her sister considered she might be on the ship?

Of course not. Why would she ever leave her home without a word after chiding Honesty for going to Jamestown?

She strode toward the well at the edge of the clearing. The overturned dirt was different than the sludge in the city. She never thought of dirt as clean before, but the rich bronze color covered the fields like a freshly washed blanket. An eagle, larger than she'd ever seen, with white feathers on its head, glided across the sky. Such a beautiful land to start a new life.

Nay, this would never be her home. How would her sister handle all of the shop work on her own?

A doe darted out of the trees, startling her. Its fawn followed close behind. It gazed at her with big brown eyes, then took off after its mother to the far end of the farmland where several wooden crosses stood.

A heaviness lodged in her stomach. The master's wife was no doubt buried there. Even with all this beauty, the price of colonizing this wilderness was too high.

A flock of geese flew by.

She didn't want to be here, no matter how beautiful it was. She wanted to go home. Wiping her face with her apron, she tamped down her despair. For now, there was nothing she could do to change her situation. Somehow, she had to find a way to cope.

Lord, please help me to survive this first year.

The anxiety eased. Enough of feeling sorry for herself. She needed to make haste before everyone came to the table expecting breakfast.

The other servants wouldn't eat with them, but they were still required to provide the men with two meals a day. Because the servants would be working in the fields until late every day, the women would have to carry the meals to them. Between cooking, laundry, sewing, weaving, and planting a garden, there was more work to do than three women could handle. Her days would be kept busier than when she was apprenticed, mayhap busy enough to help her stop thinking about her sister and her sewing shop.

She hurried to the stone well and found a bucket attached to a heavy rope. The rope was tied to a wooden beam above the well. Elizabella lowered the bucket.

A voice came from behind her. "Have you found everything you need?"

Her heart jumped, and she dropped the rope. A splash confirmed the bucket had reached the water.

"My pardon." Master Bonneville gave a reticent smile, and again she noticed deep dimples in his cheeks. Until now, he always looked somber.

"I didn't see you there." She took hold of the rough twine.

"Let me help." Master Bonneville placed his hands next to hers and pulled on the rope.

A twinge unsettled her stomach. She let go and placed the kettle on the side of the well.

He pulled on the rope, his muscular arms bulging tight against the threadbare sleeves of his shirt.

Heat flushed her face, and she looked away. "The porridge and biscuits will be ready shortly." After she established a routine, she would need to make him some new work clothes.

He pulled up the bucket and poured the water into the kettle. "I'm happy to hear that. My hunger knows no bounds." A slight grin betrayed his melancholy.

She reached for the handle, but he grabbed it before she could. Water sloshed over the sides as he carried it toward the house. She tried to catch up with his long strides. "You needn't do my chores. I can fetch the water."

He halted sharply and stood in place. "Forgive me." He set the kettle down. "Every morn, my wife and I..." There was a catch in his voice. "We'd draw the water together."

"I beg your pardon, Master Bonneville. I sometimes speak ere I think."

His crooked smile couldn't hide the pain in his eyes. "How could you have known?"

A breath caught in her throat. She didn't know what to say to cut through the awkwardness. After a crisp nod, she turned from him and carried the kettle into the house. She glanced back before closing the door. He hadn't moved a step, his expression blank. She knew that forlorn look well. It had been her constant companion every day since her brother died.

~~~~~

Miles took a moment to gather his erupting emotions. When he'd spotted Miss Clark fetching the water, he fell so easily into his old routine with his wife – only this girl wasn't Mary. He'd acted shamefully. Carrying water for a female servant wasn't decent. He could see by her blush how much he'd embarrassed her.

He drew some water from the well and splashed it on his face. As soon as breakfast was over, he would deliver an apology and assure her he had no intentions other than those stated.

Did he? If he did decide to marry again, as the preacher said he should, he could think of no finer woman to court.

Nay, it was wrong of him to have romantic notions about a servant in his household. Besides, courtship and marriage were about finding a female partner to bear his children and run his household, not about romance. But with Mary, there was romance and tender affections.

Mary, I loved you so much. How could I ever marry another?

Hugh strode toward him with his new wife on his arm. "Greetings, brother."

Miles nodded.

"I'm hungry. Is breakfast ready?" His brother's grin almost reached his ears, showing marriage agreed with him.

A heaviness rested in Miles' stomach. He hated to ruin Hugh's marital bliss so soon, but it was better to deliver the news to his brother posthaste. Hugh wouldn't forgive him if he waited any longer. "I must speak with you. Alone."

Hugh's brow furrowed. "Can't this wait until after we break our fast? I hate lectures on an empty stomach."

"I should see if the women need my help." Hannah kissed Hugh on the cheek and went into the house.

"What's so important you must talk to me before I fortify myself with a hearty meal? What fault will you chide me for now?"

"You did nothing." Miles wiped his hand through his hair. "Ethan brought some news from London."

A gasp escaped Hugh's lips. "Father? Does he fare well?"
~~~~~

Miles swallowed. "In body, aye."

"I've never known you to be evasive." Hugh rubbed his hand across his face. "Tell me plain. What's the trouble with Father?"

"He's been arrested for treason."

"Treason! Nay, I don't believe it."

"The charges are false, of course, perpetrated by the Duke of Bedford."

Hugh faced the trees, took a few steps, then turned toward Miles. "We have to sail. The *London Merchant* is leaving within a few months. We can book passage."

Miles strode to his side. He hadn't seen Hugh this distraught since their brothers died from the seasoning their first year in Jamestown. That first year had been the hardest.

Then he'd met Mary, the daughter of one of the original colonists, and his life found new purpose.

He squeezed Hugh's shoulder. "It must wait. When the ship is ready to depart, we'll be in the middle of harvesting."

Hugh pulled away. "Tis an excuse. You never had any consideration for Father."

Miles' jaw clenched. "I don't wish to see harm come to him any more than you do." He bit back his caustic tone. This was no time for a quarrel. "What can we do?"

The lie stuck in his throat. He would never leave his farm unattended to help a man who cared so little for his family. "The news was three months getting here. The *London Merchant* won't leave until at least September or October, and the journey back would be at least another couple of months, mayhap more. Whatever fate befalls Father, it doubtless has already happened."

Hugh paced a few steps away and back, then shook his head. "We must try. I have to try."

Miles studied his feet, considering all the reasons Hugh should stay. The task of running the farm on his own for at least a year was daunting, and what if his brother decided not to return? "What about your wife? She just arrived."

Hugh's jaw set. "If she's the woman I believe her to be, she'll insist we go."

Miles let out a heavy sigh. "I'll make the arrangements."

"You don't object then?"

Of course, Miles objected, but what good would it do? If Father was executed, and he didn't allow his brother to go, Hugh would never forgive him. "This is something you must do. I'll manage the farm without you somehow."

Hugh set his hand on Miles' shoulder. "Thank ye."

Miles cleared his throat. "We may have our quarrels, but he's my father too. I don't wish to see him executed for a crime he didn't commit with no family there to speak on his behalf." That part, at least, was true.

"I'll let Hannah know. Do you wish me to convey a message for you?"

"No message." The muscle in Miles' cheek twitched. "Hugh, you'll come back?"

His brother paused a second too long. "Jamestown is my home."

An ache rested in Miles' throat. No matter what Hugh said, that longing in his eyes spoke even louder. Once the ship sailed for London, he would never see his brother again. He'd be alone.

Chapter Fifteen

Hannah walked into the kitchen. "What shall I do to assist?"

Elizabella wiped her hands on her apron. "Perchance you might set the table and pour the drinks. I also have some freshly churned butter. If you could wash it for me, I would be grateful."

Hannah nodded. "Might we talk?" She tilted her head toward Bridgette.

Elizabella understood her meaning. "Bridgette, please tell the master breakfast will be served not too long hence."

Bridgette crossed her arms. "If you wish to converse alone, you needn't send me on a useless errand. Only request, and I shall depart and leave you to your secrets."

Hannah smiled. "May I converse with Elizabella alone?"

Bridgette nodded and left.

Elizabella removed coals from the belly of the oven made of red clay and sand sitting on the raised stones in the fireplace hearth. She placed the bread inside the clay oven for it to bake. "Are you enjoying married life?" Even without looking, she could tell Hannah was gazing at her.

Hannah took a dipper and reached into the churn for the butter. "Have you told your master the truth about who you are yet?"

"About that..." Elizabella cracked eggs over a skillet. "After what had happened at the fort with that boy, I've decided not to tell him. I've arranged to have my sister send funds to release me and pay for my journey home."

Hannah pressed the butter. "How do you plan to do that?"

"First Mate Rogers is delivering word to her."

"You'll trust a sailor with this?" She placed the butter on a plate and started setting the table. "What if he doesn't survive the journey back? What if he doesn't find her?"

Elizabella set the skillet down, a sick feeling rising in her stomach. He would find her, he had to, unless she had succumbed to infection and died.

Hannah grabbed the pitcher, then set it down and placed a hand on Elizabella's arm. "Confess to Miles. Once you tell him why you deceived everyone, he'll understand."

Her father's contorted face filled her mind. *Nobody's ever going to believe you, girl.*

Hannah shook her. "What's wrong? You appear as if you've seen a ghost."

Elizabella snorted. "Nay, not a ghost."

"What then?"

"'Tis nothing." She wished it were only a ghost. "Memories from the past sometimes haunt me." She took a wooden spoon and knelt to stir the porridge. "No need to fret."

"Then you'll tell your master everything?"

"Nay. If word from my sister doesn't arrive with the next ship, I'll confess it then."

"There's another matter to consider." Hannah poured the drinks into the cups. "Before I wed, my husband and I vowed to not keep secrets from each other. I'll give you time, but I shall not hold it from Hugh for long."

Heat rose up Elizabella's back. She stood and stepped away from the hearth. "You'd break my confidence? I thought better of you."

"Marriage vows are stronger than those of friendship. I'll implore my husband to keep your secret, but if you haven't declared the truth within a month, I'll have to tell him."

Elizabella stepped back to the hearth. A lot could transpire in a month. She let up a silent prayer asking the Lord to help her. Did God answer such petitions to keep deceptions hidden? Whether He did or not, she couldn't help calling out to Him. "I'll let you know my decision."

~~~~~

The dishes had been washed, and Bridgette and Hannah went to clean up the plot next to the house for planting a vegetable garden.

Elizabella now sat next to the master in a rocker by the fireplace. "I'll have a list of supplies we need when you go to the fort."

The master brooded, staring at the fireplace, as if he hadn't heard a word she said. She cleared her throat.

He glanced up as if he suddenly realized she was in the rocker next to him. "My pardon. What were you saying?"

Elizabella's mouth turned up. "Which part?"

He shrugged. "My mind is elsewhere. Mayhap we should revisit this discussion later."

"Of course, if that's what you wish." She straightened her skirt and started to stand. She dropped back into the chair. "Later won't do. Bridgette and Hannah will be back soon. They're cooking stew for the evening meal so I can spend the day taking inventory and scheduling tasks that need to be done."

Dimples deepened in Master Bonneville's face. "Is that so? I wouldn't want to delay you in your work."

Elizabella grunted. "You're the one who made me manager over your household."

"Aye, I did." His attention went back to the fireplace. The brooding returned.

"Is there anything I can do to assist?"

"What? Assist with what?"
~~~~~

"Obviously, something's amiss. If I could aid with whatever is distracting you, I might gain as much of your attention as that fireplace."

Miles glared at her. "You're an outspoken woman."

"I've been told that before. What's troubling you?"

He stared at her a moment longer, then clasped his hands in his lap and focused on the fire. "My brother is traveling to England with his new bride to handle family business there."

Excitement stirred inside. "When?" If Hannah was traveling to London, she could contact Honesty personally and let her know of her plight.

"The ship sails in five or six months."

A reprieve. Mayhap God had answered her prayers.

"I don't look forward to harvesting a crop without my brother here."

"You'll miss him?"

Miles wiped his hand over his mouth. "Aye."

"I have a sister in England. I miss her very much."

"Is this the older sister who helped you get an apprenticeship?"

She bit her lip. "Aye, Elizabella. May I have your permission to send word to her through Hannah?"

"I'm sure Hannah won't mind. You may ask her."

A weight lifted from her. If Hannah would agree to wait to tell her husband until they departed and would deliver word to Honesty, her worries were over. All she had to do was survive the next year.

~~~~~

Hugh's stomach churned. He hadn't eaten much, but he wasn't hungry. He couldn't stop thinking about his father. And about returning to London. He hadn't had a chance to talk to Hannah after breakfast. After assigning work to the men, he chopped wood while Hannah helped with the women's chores.

Now evening had come, and they sat at the wooden table in front of their fireplace. The one-room wattle and daub home with a dirt floor wasn't much, but with Hannah there beside him, it finally seemed like home.

He took her hand. "I have need to talk with you."

She glanced over to him. "I could see your thoughts are troubled. What is it?"

Squeezing her hand, he told her about his father. "We must return to England as soon as possible. The ship is planning to sail within a few months."

Hannah stared at the fire and bit her lip. "Of course. We must go."

Hugh noticed the subtle change in her demeanor. "You have reservations?"

"Nay, it's nothing."

Hugh took both of her hands in his. "We agreed we would keep no secrets from each other."
~~~~~

She nodded. "I hated London. I was an orphan there with no means of support. I wandered Pudding Lane every day looking for food and lived in fear every moment until a kindly vicar hired me as the family servant. I was so delighted to escape that life." She glanced down, wet her lips. "I don't want to go back, but I shall for your sake."

He stood and pulled her into his arms. "It'll be different this time. You'll have me to protect you. I have rich and powerful friends who would never let harm come to my wife. You'll see. You might even grow to love the city."

Hannah lay her head on his shoulder. "My place is with you." She kissed him tenderly. "We'll do what we can for your father, then we can sail home."

"The journey there'll take months, but we'll only be in London a month, mayhap two." After he showed her the London he remembered, she might grow to love it as he did. "Unless you decide you prefer it to this uncivilized wilderness." He longed so much to stay in England, but he would allow her to decide.

Chapter Sixteen

Elizabella and Bridgette had finished the last of their evening chores and were putting away the dishes. Overall, Elizabella felt better than she had since the journey to Jamestown had begun. Hope had begun to spring up in her. A year at most, and Honesty would send the funds for her to travel home. Even if the first mate didn't find her sister, Hannah would not stop looking.

She reminded herself it was too early for hope to take root. There were many dangers ahead. The seasoning could overtake her with disease, or she could be attacked by Indians or bears. The master could find out she'd gained passage to the colony under false pretenses and turn her over to the Burgess.

Even so, hope would not be contained. She began to whistle her favorite hymn.

Master Bonneville entered.

Elizabella flushed and stopped whistling.

"Don't stop." Master Bonneville sat in one of the rocking chairs. "*A Mighty Fortress is Our God* is one of my favorites."

Elizabella dried her hands. "Mine as well."

He stared at her for a moment as if he wanted to say something. "I won't need you for the rest of the evening, but you are both welcome to sit with me at the fireplace. I read Scripture nightly before retiring, and I could read it aloud if you desire."

"Nay," Bridgette said. "I prefer to find comfort in my bed." She bowed slightly and departed.

Elizabella didn't want to retire yet. A nervous energy had overtaken her, and she desired to stay. "Scripture reading would be nice, but should we sit here unchaperoned?"

His brow furrowed. "'Tis only for an hour. I believe it to be proper, but if you prefer not to..."

"A short time of Bible reading would be acceptable." She sat in the rocker beside him. "I've never had the Bible read to me before, except a few verses in the Prayer Book at church."

A smile caused his dimples to deepen. "I believe every Christian should read or hear the Word of God for themselves."

"That's what Hannah said aboard the ship. Her vicar read the Geneva Bible in meetings throughout the week."

He grabbed his Bible from the mantle. "I read from the version King James authorized a few years ago. I brought it with me to Jamestown." He read from the Gospel of Matthew, chapter eleven. Most of the chapter was about judgement, as she expected. Then he read the last three verses. "Come unto me, all ye that labour and are heavy laden, and I will give you rest. Take my yoke upon you, and learn of me; for I am meek and lowly in heart: and ye shall find rest unto your souls. For my yoke is easy, and my burden is light."

She tilted her head and pursed her lips. Rest unto your souls? It sounded so comforting, so hopeful, but what did that mean? "Would you read the last three verses again?"

"Of course." He read them again.

"What does 'rest unto your souls' mean?"

His dimple indented slightly. "When you trust in God and give Him your burdens of life, He will heal your soul."

"Master Bonneville, have you ever experienced that?"

"Aye, many times." He wiped his hand across his mouth. "Most recently, I have been coming to the Lord with my grief over my wife's death."

She gazed into his dark eyes full of sorrow and saw something, maybe hope. "Pardon me for bringing up such a painful memory."

"Not at all. In truth, I long to have someone to discuss her with. Everyone avoids speaking of her, perchance afraid they will, as you say, bring up a painful memory, but I can't help remembering her. I'm not sure I want to forget."

"Does it bring comfort, giving it to God, I mean?"

He sat for a moment staring at the fire. "The Bible says we don't grieve as the world does. I know someday I'll see her again, but as far as helping me get over my sorrow..." His jaw twitched. "He hasn't taken it away, but He has eased my burden by walking through it with me."

"I don't know how to give my grief to God."

Master Bonneville regarded her with compassion so strong it surprised her.

She turned from his gaze and stared at the fire. "My mother died a few years back and then my brother."

"My sympathies." His tone was so kind, and his brow knit together in a way that showed her he meant it.

"May I inquire more about the Scripture you read?"

"Please do."

She didn't know how to say the rest, but she turned toward him and blurted it out. "The first part of the chapter talks about judgement. Doesn't the Lord want to punish us? If we come to Him, won't He show us why we are so wretched?"

Master Bonneville leaned forward in his chair. "Jesus was declaring judgement on the people who rejected Him. When we come to Him with our burdens and with our sins, He provides mercy and grace."

She'd been too wicked for God to pardon her. "If we do enough good acts of service and are not wicked in our actions toward others, God shall provide mercy. Otherwise, we can only expect judgement for our wickedness. That's what my vicar taught." Her throat thickened. She knew what the answer would be. "How can I expect mercy or rest when I've sinned against Him?"

"Miss Clark, everyone alive has sinned against Him. If we were good enough, we wouldn't need mercy."

She felt disoriented, like the room was spinning. Surely, this couldn't be true for her. "Nay, I've transgressed too greatly to be forgiven."

He took hold of her hand. "What could you have possibly done that is so evil?"

"I killed my brother." She clasped her hand over her mouth. She hadn't meant to say it out loud.

~~~~

Stunned by Miss Clark's confession, Miles withdrew his hand. Surely, there was more to the story. "Tell me what happened."

"His name was Benjamin." Miss Clark's chin quivered. "My mother made me promise to look after him when she died. No doubt, she knew Father would more likely be at the saloon than home caring for an infant son."

A lump formed in the pit of Miles' stomach. "Aye, my father would have done the same, but how did you kill your brother?"

"I went to check on him in the middle of the night." Her hands twisted together in her lap. "He'd had a nightmare and begged me to leave the lantern lit. I did so, planning to return later to put it out."

Miles worked his chin as understanding dawned about what happened. "There was a fire."

"Aye." Tears welled up in her eyes. "I couldn't save him. He died."

He handed her his handkerchief. "Surely, the fault isn't yours. ''Twas a tragic misfortune only."

"That's what the court said at my trial." She wiped her eyes and blew her nose. "Pardon me. I didn't mean to burden you with my troubles." A stray tear fell down her cheek.

"We all have things we regret." He wanted to wipe the tear away, let her know he didn't blame her, but he wouldn't make such an inappropriate gesture. He clasped his hands in front of him, holding them down as if they might stray to her face of their own accord.

"I can't imagine you would have any regrets." She said it in such a sad way, it made his heart ache for her.

He did have regrets, lots of them, but he couldn't imagine the burden she bore of believing she killed her younger brother. As much as Hugh vexed him at times, he couldn't bear for something to happen to him. "Aye, I left my mother in England with my father when we sailed to Jamestown.
~~~~

I should have insisted she come with us. She died a year ago."

"My sympathies," Miss Clark said. "Your mother was a gentle and kind woman with a heart of compassion, so unlike the other ladies of the royal court."

Miles rubbed his hands on his pants and clasped them together again. "Aye, she was kind." His face warmed. "I shouldn't have left her after the disgrace Father had brought to our family's reputation, but she insisted."

"It appears we have that in common. We both have reprobate fathers who've caused us great harm, but aren't we responsible only for our own actions, not the actions of our family?

He pondered that for a moment. There was wisdom in that simple statement. If true, he wasn't responsible for his father or Hugh's actions. "What you say rings true." As much as he enjoyed this conversation, it was becoming too intimate for a master and servant. "Perchance I should bid you a good night. It's getting late."

She blushed and stood. "I have stayed far too long. I shall retire to my bed." Her face turned almost as red as Miss Atwood's hair.

A lump lodged in his throat. He hadn't meant to embarrass her, only to protect her honor. "I only meant that an hour has passed, and the time has come to part." He paused for a moment. "I enjoyed our Bible reading. Farewell."

"Farewell." She rushed out the door.

Chapter Seventeen

Sleep escaped Elizabella most of the night. It wasn't because of the noise. Since she'd come to Jamestown, her sleep had been restful despite her worries. The chirping of crickets, the song of night birds, and the croak of an occasional bullfrog helped lull her into slumber.

Not at all like London. Her home city had been called the city that never sleeps, and it was true. Carriages and horses tromped up her street at all hours of the night delivering milk and bread and picking up trash. Then there were the drunks that would loudly find their way home at all hours of the early morning. She had been used to the clatter, but the noise here was soothing in comparison.

The verses the master had read kept milling around in her mind and heart. Could she find rest in the Lord? Could even the tragedies she'd faced in the past be healed through the Lord's grace? And how could she find mercy after what she'd done? All she knew was that she wanted to hear more.

At some point, she did doze, but the rooster crowed far too soon. Groggily, she dragged herself out of bed and dressed quickly with barely a nod toward Bridgette. She would want to know about what transpired after she retired, but Elizabella didn't want to talk about it, at least not with her.

She went to the kitchen to fetch a pot and headed to the well. The air was crisp, and frost covered the ground. Mayhap the weather here wasn't that different than England after all. She dipped the bucket into the water and started pulling it out when Master Bonneville came walking toward her after feeding the livestock.

"Good morn." He crossed his arms and gave her a faint smile, large enough for one dimple to show through.

"It is a crisp one today." She pulled the bucket out and poured the water into the pot, hoping he wouldn't notice her blush.

"Aye, we shall have a few more frosts, I dare say, before 'tis time to plant the crops."

She grabbed the handle of the pot, and at the same time, he reached for it. Their fingers touched. She pulled her hand away.

"Pardon me," Master Bonneville said. "I know it may seem improper for me to carry the water, but your work has been exceptional, and you have so much to do. Please let me do this small favor."

Elizabella bit her lip and nodded. "As you wish." She followed him into the house. Fortunately, Bridgette wasn't there to remark on her letting the master carry the water.

"I enjoyed our Bible reading last night, but I fear I might have embarrassed you by bringing up personal matters."

"Nay," Elizabella said. "I'm not sure I should have been so forthright. The fault was mine."

"I consider forthrightness an admirable trait." The dimple deepened again. "Would you be willing to meet with me again tonight for Bible reading? As long as we end at dusk, I feel it would be proper."

Proper, but mayhap not wise. As much as Elizabella wanted to agree, she wasn't sure she should. She had revealed things about herself without meaning to. He had a way of making her feel at ease in doing so. "Could I have time to consider it?"

His dimple disappeared, and his forehead creased. "Of course. If you'd rather have a chaperone during that time, I could order Miss Atwood to stay, or perchance my brother and his new wife would join us."

She pressed her lips together then nodded. "As you say, 'tis only until dusk."

"Then shall we press forward?"

She nodded. As much as she was sure it would lead to trouble to spend too much time with him, the night before had felt like a healing balm pouring into the cracks of her soul. She wanted nothing more than to hear him read God's Word again as she listened.

He carried the water inside and set it on the table. "I'll leave you to your cooking." He went back outside into the cold morning air.

What had she done? Hannah or the first mate would find her sister in London, and she could be back home within a year, two at the most. As much as it called to her, she couldn't allow herself to become attached to this life.

Bridgette returned and immediately started setting bowls out for the porridge, so Elizabella hurried to pour some oats and water into a kettle. She'd already wasted too much time daydreaming. The master and his brother would be hungry.

"So, how was it?" Bridgette asked as she filled the cups with drink. "Did you get your fill of the master reading the Holy Bible to you?"

Elizabella kept her face to the fire as she stirred the porridge. "I enjoyed it."

Bridgette snorted. "I can't think why. It's bad enough we have to attend church services every week, and if we doze during the sermon, we'll end up in the stocks. I can't imagine having to sit through Bible reading every night." She set the pitcher on the table and placed a hand on Elizabella's shoulder. "Unless 'tis the man reading it that interests you and not the words being read."

Heat shot up Elizabella's back, and she turned to the girl, wooden spoon in hand. "I have no intention to become a wife, and it wouldn't hurt you to listen to Scripture occasionally either."

Bridgette turned pale. "I don't need it read to me. I got my belly full when my father used it to show me what a wicked girl I was every time he wasn't pleased with me."

"Forgive me." Elizabella set the spoon down. "I spoke too sharply."

"I was only jesting."

"My pardon. I overreacted."

Bridgette nodded, but she didn't say any more while they made breakfast. The change from the way she usually chattered on showed Elizabella she had hurt the girl's feelings, but she hadn't meant to any more than she'd meant to hurt her sister by not going with her to the ship. How could she expect mercy from God when she continually was cruel to those around her?

~~~~~

Over the next few weeks, Elizabella fell into a pattern. In the morning, Master Bonneville would help her carry water. Bridgette had helped her organize the supplies and had taken over laundry and sweeping, and Hannah helped with the cooking. The land for the garden had been prepared, and planting would begin in a couple of weeks.

Elizabella had even been able to get in some time for weaving. She desired to make the master and his brother new stockings and shirts, so no colored thread was required. Honesty had packed a myriad of threads, yarn, needles, and cloth in her chest. The master's late wife had a loom and a spinning wheel, so she had everything she needed.

Every evening, after the dishes had been washed and put away, Bridgette would retire to her room, and Elizabella would sit in front of the fireplace and listen to Master Bonneville read from God's Word. She heard about how Jesus had rebuked the religious leaders for not wanting Him to heal on the Sabbath, the parable of the sower, and how Jesus fed the multitude, healed the sick, and walked on water, as well as how He died and rose again.

None of these stories sounded like the angry Lord her vicar had portrayed. Christ only seemed to be angry at the religious leaders who rejected Him. Perchance He would forgive her if she asked Him to.

She sat there now, in her rocker in front of the fire, listening. The loneliness of being in this strange land still overcame her at times, but as she did her chores during the day and listened to Master Bonneville as he read God's Word, a peace had settled over her. She would leave Jamestown soon enough, but for now, she was content.

The master had finished reading the Gospel passage and had begun reading in Psalms. Tonight, as they sat by the fireplace, he turned to Psalm six, verse one. "O Lord, do not rebuke me in Your anger, Nor chasten me in Your hot displeasure."

Heat rushed to Elizabella's face. How had she forgotten so easily that the Lord sent her to Jamestown to punish her?
~~~~~

Master Bonneville read on until verses eight and nine. "Depart from me, all you workers of iniquity; For the Lord has heard the voice of my weeping. The Lord has heard my supplication; The Lord will receive my prayer."

She gasped. "How can that be true?"

The master stopped reading. "How can what be true?"

"In the Psalm, the Lord was angry with David. He was punishing him. How could he say the Lord had heard his prayer?"

Master Bonneville set the Bible aside and turned to her, compassion shining in his gaze. "Don't you see, Miss Clark? Remember the passage I read about the Lord taking away our burdens? He is merciful and quick to forgive when we turn to Him and ask for His pardon."

Tears welled up in Elizabella's eyes. She wanted so much to believe that. "All I have to do is pray and ask Him for mercy?"

"Aye." He took hold of her hands. "We can do it together, right here if you like."

She nodded and poured out her heart to God. What happened then astounded her. It was as if a heavy burden had been taken from her.

Chapter Eighteen

After church, Hugh and Hannah strolled on the beach. Miles had a council meeting, and the women stayed to find supplies they needed at the shops. Hugh enjoyed spending time just being with Hannah. It amazed him how quickly his deep affection for his wife had grown.

Hugh suggested they take a respite and walk along the shore together. It was well into May, and the warmth of the sun was abated by a cool breeze from the river. As much as he wanted to sail to his homeland, he'd miss days like this.

As they were returning, Miles and the council gathered outside the gate near the ship. Governor Yeardley waved and shouted. "Greetings."

They turned and headed toward him. Miles followed after them at a slower pace, his brow furrowed. Whatever the Burgess had decided, he wasn't happy about it.

Governor Yeardley shook his hand. "Hugh, we have an urgent mission for you. Go to Chief Opechancanough and ask him for that meeting. We can afford no more delay."

Hugh shook his head, trying to find a reason not to go. He didn't want to run into Suleta or her mother. "I agreed to go to the village after planting season. Why such haste?"

Captain Lawnes stepped forward. "This meeting is of utmost importance. One of our men has been attacked by some braves while hunting. They stole his musket and the buck he'd shot."

"Why don't you go since there's such an urgency?"

"You've been to the village often. You know their ways better than we do."

Hugh's jaw twitched. 'Twas true only because they chose to regard the Natives with disdain. They only visited the village to do trade. "If I go, you'll honor the agreement we make with them? Vow this, or I won't do it."

Governor Yeardley looked toward the other men. They all nodded.

"Perchance this could wait until we plant our crops." Miles rubbed the back of his neck, something he often did when he was anxious.

Hugh let out a heavy sigh. "We have at least a couple of weeks before the planting." There was nothing for it but to carry it out and hope he didn't see Suleta. This was too important to the colony to refuse. "I'll journey to the tribe two days hence."

"Well then, I have matters to attend to." Miles turned abruptly and climbed onto the gangplank of the ship.

Hugh doubted his brother really had business there. They had paid for his and Hannah's journey a week earlier. More likely Miles was concerned he'd go back to his old ways. The other men said their goodbyes and dispersed.

The village did offer temptations Hugh had succumbed to in past visits, but that was before Suleta had decided to marry another, and before he'd taken Hannah for his wife. He would never betray her. He grabbed hold of his wife's hand.

He'd confessed to Hannah about liaisons with Native women but not much about Suleta. He glanced toward her, hoping she'd forgive him. "I need to tell you something."

"Let's move away from the fort where nobody can hear us." She glanced toward the ship where Miles stood watching them.

Hugh nodded, wondering how she knew they needed privacy. He walked with her down the beach.

"You can tell me anything." She gazed at him, her green eyes boring into his soul. "What is it?"

He let out a noisy sigh. "A little over a year ago, I met a Native named Suleta."

Hannah's mouth formed into an O. "Is she beautiful?"

Hugh wished he hadn't vowed to always be truthful. "Very."

"More beautiful than me?" Her brow furrowed as if she were afraid to hear the answer.

He grasped her hands in his. "That's not possible, my dear, but she is beautiful."

She turned away.

His throat tightened, but he forged on. "I met her when I was on a trading mission. She was friendly and kind, and I was so lonely..." His voice trailed off as he remembered that first day.

"Go on," Hannah said.

"The Powhatan have different customs than we Europeans do." He cleared his throat. "At least different from what we espouse to have. They don't believe amorous relations should be confined to the bonds of matrimony."

She didn't say anything or look away, and he wouldn't no matter how much he wanted to. He needed her to see the truth in his eyes.

"There were others before, but since the first time I met her, I only was with her. Every time I visited the village hence, we were together. I did ask to marry her."

Tears filled her eyes. "She refused?"

"Aye, her mother had promised her to another."

Hannah turned and strolled further down the beach, putting a few feet between them. "Did her mother know about the... relations? Surely, she would have allowed the marriage if she'd known."

He followed Hannah but kept the distance she'd created. "She knew, but she didn't care." He stopped, letting Hannah get further away. The guilt caused his stomach to harden.

Hannah paused and stared at the ocean. "So, she's married to another. That's why you wed me, to help you forget."

"I didn't love Suleta. I realize that now. What I felt for her was desire only." He hurried to catch up with his wife. "I never planned to visit the village again, but since I am required to do so, I shan't keep this from you." He touched her cheek, wiping a tear off with his thumb. "I love only you. Do you believe me?"

"Aye, I do." She embraced him.

He reached down to devour her lips, drinking in her grace and love. How did he deserve someone as wonderful as her when he'd been such a reprobate? He nuzzled her neck. "Thank ye for believing in me. I'll never hide anything from you again."

She pulled away.

"What's wrong?"

She bit her lower lip. "I've been keeping something from you as well."

"Whatever you're hiding couldn't be worse than what I just confessed. Out with it."

"The fault is not mine. I'm keeping the confidence for a friend."

Hugh pulled her back into his arms. "Surely, you know you can trust me to stay silent."

"It's not that simple." Hannah allowed him to kiss her again. "I told her..." Another kiss... "I'd give her a month..." And another... "before I tell you." She pulled back.

"Well then. A month is not that long. If it is a confidence between you, you needn't tell me even then."

"The month has passed, and I must speak." Hannah nuzzled her head against his shoulder. "It concerns your brother and Elizabella."

"Who?"

She let out a sigh and moved away from his embrace. "Honesty Clark is going by a false identity. Her true name is Elizabella. Honesty is her younger sister."

"Why would she deceive us about her name?" He dragged his fingers through his hair, trying to understand. "Did she travel here to escape the law? Has she committed a crime?"

Hannah told Hugh how Honesty had planned to become a Jamestown bride, but Elizabella saw a murder. Honesty had been stabbed, and to escape the murderers, Elizabella boarded the ship and pretended to be her sister.

"An amazing tale. I can't fathom why she doesn't confess her deception. I can't believe anybody would think less of her for protecting herself from murderous thugs."

"I told her that, but she insists it's too late. She thinks because she didn't tell Constance or Miles who she was earlier, they won't believe her. She desires me to deliver word to her sister when we reach London."

Hugh rubbed his hand against his chin. "Miles does have a standard of virtue nobody can live up to, but he values honesty. The longer she waits, the worse it will be."

"I know. Will you keep her confidence?"

"He is my brother. I don't know." How could he keep such a deception? Miles would never forgive him. It was plain Miles had a fondness for Honesty – or Elizabella – or whoever she was. He had to know the truth before he developed a relationship with her. "Tell your friend to confess soon, or I'll have no choice."

~~~~~

The next day, Elizabella stood at the wooden table kneading bread for supper. Since Bridgette and Hannah weren't there to help, she'd chopped some vegetables and turkey into a large pot and was making soup for the evening meal.

She rolled the bread in a ball and pounded it. At home, she and her sister would have cooked supper together after a day of sewing in front of the fireplace. A twinge of sadness tightened her stomach.

That was foolishness. She would be in London within a year or two. Hannah would find her sister and send the necessary funds. Then she would be back where she belonged. She blew out her frustration.

How many times had she wished things were different? Nay, it was not to be. She would remain here, stuck in this uncivilized land, living a deception with no way back to London... to home.

At least now, in this isolated place, she knew God loved her. If only Hannah would wait a bit longer to tell Hugh the truth about who she was. She knew God wanted her to tell the master herself, but she needed more time to shore up her courage.

She sensed Miles' presence and turned around. His face had the sheen of sweat on it, and dirt stains soiled his untucked shirt. His dark brown hair had fallen in his eyes, and mud crusted the soles of his brown boots. He grabbed a pitcher off the table and poured himself a mug of water.

"Where is Bridgette? Did she leave you to prepare the evening meal alone?"

"She's doing laundry by the creek, and Hannah is working in the garden." Elizabella placed a cloth over the bread and wiped her hands on her apron. "We're having a simple meal, turkey and vegetable soup. I'm almost done with the preparations."

Miles nodded. "Would you sit and talk with me then?"

She sat across from him at the table and folded her hands in front of her. A knot formed in her stomach. Hannah surely wouldn't have betrayed her confidence without warning her first. "Is there a problem with the way I'm carrying out my duties?"
~~~~~

"Nay." He delivered his crooked smile. "I would say the household runs better now than it ever did." He patted his stomach. "I've never eaten so well."

Her stomach unwound, and she let out an easy breath. "I'm sure your wife made you very good meals indeed."

He rubbed his hand across his mouth. "Mary was a fine cook, but I fear she worked too hard without female servants to assist her. One of my many regrets."

She touched his hand without realizing it. Her face flushed, and she pulled it back. "What did you wish to enquire about?"

"My brother and his wife will be leaving in a few months to sail back to England on family business."

"This troubles you?"

"Aye. I fear he may not return." Master Bonneville cleared his throat. "That will leave you without Hannah's assistance."

"I'll manage."

That crooked grin again. "I'm sure you'll do whatever you set your mind to. I'm often amazed one so young is so industrious and organized."

"One does what one must."

"Mayhap, but I don't desire to work you to the point of exhaustion. Would you like me to inquire about purchasing another servant?"

"I thought Bridgette and I were the only ones still unmarried. Are there any brides left to purchase?"

"There aren't, but another bride ship should arrive sometime within the next year. Perchance, I could find another woman who would wait for matrimony."

A warmth traveled through Elizabella. She'd never seen a man who would consider a woman's feelings about such matters, especially not a servant girl. "I'm used to hard labor and long hours. I'll fare well. No need to trouble yourself."

Now Miles touched her hand. "If it becomes too burdensome, you'll let me know?"

She resisted the urge to pull back her arm and gave a crisp nod. He was so different than other men she'd been aquatinted with, different from her father. Perchance it was because of his strong faith in God.

Her stomach fluttered with such ferocity she could swear she'd swallowed a flock of pigeons. He used his other hand to swipe his unruly hair out of his brown eyes, but he didn't divert his gaze.

Perchance, he could be trusted with the truth now. Her face grew warm. She had to return to London to care for her sister, but there were times she wondered what it would be like to stay here with him. Finally, he released her hand, but the warmth lingered.

If he knew how she'd gotten to Jamestown, he would put away any foolish romantic notions – if there were any. She'd had little experience with matters of the heart. Mayhap the affection was only on her part. "There is something I have need to discuss with you."

His crooked smile lit up his eyes. "I await your every word."

She giggled, and immediately clamped her hand over her mouth. She couldn't remember the last time she laughed. What must he think of her frivolity?

"So, what did you wish to tell me?"

"I..." The image of that boy being whipped while everyone at the fort cheered came into her thoughts. Would that be her fate? *Lord, give me the courage I lack.* "The boy who was whipped in the courtyard..."

His face turned grim, and he patted her hand. "An unfortunate business, but that was a month ago and nothing you need concern yourself with. From what I hear, he is doing well in his new life."

"Please, I need to ask you about it."

Miles nodded. "Go on then."

"Of course, the boy needed to be reprimanded for sneaking aboard the ship, but wasn't ten years indentured service enough? It more than paid for his journey."

"Young women don't appreciate these things." He shrugged. "My wife was the same way. She desired me to be merciful in matters like this."

Elizabella bit her lip. "Would you help me to understand?" If she knew why it was so important to punish the boy, mayhap there would be hope that if she confessed, she would escape the same fate.

"When he lied to get aboard the ship, that was theft." Miles leaned back in his rocker and stared at the fire. "In London, theft would have required a noose."

Elizabella gasped. Was that what they would consider her actions? Would they brand her a thief?

Master Bonneville raised an eyebrow. "There were some on the Burgess who felt that was a just reward, but he was young. I convinced them being whipped in the public square was enough to pay for his crime."

"So, if someone else was caught in such a lie to gain passage on the ship, even though that person had good reason, would they also be whipped?"

Miles nodded. "I suppose so, but why are you so disturbed by this? Surely, you've seen criminals punished in London."

Elizabella's words caught in her throat. She should confess everything and be done with it. The last time she was hauled before officials, everything turned out all right, but could she really trust any man, even Master Bonneville, to show mercy? She couldn't risk it.

The master's brother burst through the door. "I'm leaving for the village tomorrow." He glared at Elizabella for a moment longer than needed.

There was no mistaking that look. He knew. Her heart thumped loudly in her chest. Hannah must have told him.

"I'll see that your wife has everything she needs in your absence," Miles said.

She had to find a way to talk to Hannah.

"Thank ye," Hugh said.

She had to find out what Hugh knew and what he intended to do. "I'll leave you alone to converse."

The men said their farewells, and she hurried out the door and ran as fast as she could to where Hannah was planting the garden.

Hannah looked up, stood, and wiped the dirt off her apron. "I was planning to come and see you. Sit here with me awhile." She motioned to a felled tree.

Elizabella sat, her jaw clenched. "Did you tell your husband my confidence?"

"When Hugh and I married, we promised we wouldn't keep secrets from each other. I had to tell him."

"Could you at least have waited the time you promised to me?"

Hannah took her hand. "I gave you the month I promised."

Elizabella swallowed the lump in her throat. "I'm astonished Hugh hasn't already told his brother, unless that's what he's doing as we speak."

"Nay, he has agreed to keep it quiet for a time, but he shan't allow you to keep this deception for long."

"You must convince him to hold his tongue. Let me tell Miles in my own time."

"You're fretting too much about this. When you tell him what happened, he'll understand. Why should he care about your name when you've worked hard for him?"

"He cares." The thickness in her throat grew until she could barely speak. "The boy who was whipped is proof of that."

"It's different with you. You didn't intentionally steal a ship's voyage to Jamestown. Unless you wait and let him find out from my husband, he'll forgive you."

Elizabella let out a sigh. How could she explain to Hannah how terrified she was of telling the truth? When her father wouldn't believe the fire that killed her brother was an accident, how could she trust strangers to accept her word, especially when she'd already deceived them? "Hannah, he said the boy deserved to be whipped."

Hannah gazed at her with an expression so deep and thoughtful, it shook Elizabella to the core. "I'll talk to Hugh when he returns."

Relief flooded through her. "Thank ye."

"I doubt it will sway him. My husband is an honest man. Ask the Lord to give you the courage you need."

Elizabella's stomach roiled. "I need to take a walk to consider what I am to do." She rushed into the woods, memories of the past flooding her.

Chapter Nineteen

Nine years earlier

Elizabella had shaken her sister, sweat pouring off her. It had been so hot, and she'd barely seen through the smoke filling the room.

Six-year-old Honesty rubbed her eyes and coughed.

Elizabella spoke softly, trying not to alarm her. "Come with me." She grabbed her blanket, wrapped it around them both, picked her sister up into her arms, and pushed through the door.

She turned toward the room where her brother and father slept. Flames skirted from down the narrow hallway between her and the room.

Setting Honesty down, she said, "Stay here!"

Her sister sobbed but obeyed. She ran to her brother's room. Too hot. She couldn't get through. A burning beam fell, and she jumped back to keep it from hitting her. A heaviness overwhelmed her. She couldn't leave him there.

Father slept in the same room as Benjamin. If he got out, he would have brought the boy with him. The wall of fire was too intense to get through. Besides, she couldn't carry them both. She had to get Honesty out of here first. If her father and brother hadn't made it, she'd climb the staircase at the back of the house to rescue them.

She ran to Honesty, wrapped the blanket around them again, then hurried to the staircase. The flames hadn't reached it yet. Adjusting her sister in her arms, she made her way down the first flight of stairs, one step at a time.

The oppressive heat scorched her, and she looked back. The fire roared across the staircase and up the walls. *Lord, please help me.* She dashed down the second flight.

Coughing violently, she pushed her way out the door and ran across the narrow lane. She set her sister down and began to look for Benjamin.

Men, women, and children, all in their nightclothes, stared at the burning building. The fire consumed it now and had spread to the houses on either side of it. Families poured out of them and joined the others.

The smell of burning wood nearly choked her. How could it have spread so quickly? Benjamin had to have made it out. She peered through the faces of the crowd trying to find him.

A little girl, younger than Honesty, cried for her mama. A woman ran up to the child and swept her up into her arms.

Elizabella grabbed Honesty's hand and pushed her way through the people. "Benjamin!" Panic rose from her gut.

Her father lay on the ground a few feet away -- alone. "Father." Was he drunk or overcome by smoke?

A sour taste assaulted the back of her throat as she ran toward him. Benjamin wasn't there. She half dragged Honesty to him. "Where is he? Did you get him?"

"Who?" Her father's speech was slurred.

"Benji." Honesty sobbed.

"Hush, honey." She patted her sister's arm and glowered at her father. "Where is Benjamin!"

Father squinted his eyes. "Benjamin?"

She grabbed his shirt and shook him. "Where's my brother?"

He pointed to the three-story apartment building.

Every muscle in her body quaked. She pelted toward the building. Voices called to her from a distance, but she ignored them. As she grew closer, heat scorched her face. Flames shot up around the doorframe. Holding her breath, she pushed past them through the door.

Hands grabbed her, pulled her back. She struggled to free herself, but they had a firm hold. She collapsed to the ground sobbing, heat coursing through her arms and face. "Benjamin!" She tried to get up, but men held her down. An older woman wrapped her in a blanket, and a younger woman poured a bucket of water on her.

Father staggered over to her, his stance unsteady.

She stood and screamed, "Why didn't you try to get him out! Why did you leave him there!" Something inside broke, and she couldn't stop the wails.

Her father slapped her across the face. She drew her hand to her cheek and gulped back the cries.

"Getting high and mighty, aren't you, missy? You started the fire so you wouldn't have to be a nursemaid to him." His face and voice were distorted, and she tried to make sense of what he was saying. "You murdered your own brother."

"Nay, I didn't." Pain shot through her arms, and she struggled to grasp his words. "What are you talking about?"

"The lantern in his room. You're the one who takes care of him at night. You left it lit on purpose."

The people surrounding her stepped back, their faces changing from concern to horror.

"Nay, I just..." She'd gone into his room in the middle of the night. Father wasn't home yet, and her brother was scared. She tried to comfort him, to assure him, but he'd had a bad dream. She had turned the lantern down and kept it lit to ease his fears.

That wouldn't have started the fire. It couldn't have.

~~~~~
~~~~~

Elizabella fell to the ground and sobbed as she'd done that night. It had been nine years ago, but it still haunted her, still made her afraid. She deserved what was happening to her.

Nay, hadn't God forgiven her? Hadn't Master Bonneville believed her when she told him what happened? *Lord, take this fear away? Give me the courage to tell the truth?*

A calm came over her, and she felt the presence of the Lord. Squaring her shoulders, she headed back to the master's house. With God's help, she would somehow find the mettle to confess all of it after the Bible reading tonight.

~~~~~

After they had cooked the evening meal, Elizabella set the turkey soup on the table while Bridgette set the plates out and Hannah poured the drink.

"When will the master arrive?" Bridgette asked. "The food is getting cold."

"He and my husband had business to discuss," Hannah said.

Elizabella looked out the window. "Here they are now." Her heart thumped a little faster at the sight of Miles.

A few minutes later, Miles and Hugh arrived. They sat down and said grace.

"Thank you, Miss Clark," Miles said a short time later. "As usual, the dinner is delicious."

Elizabella's face grew warm. She wasn't used to accolades, but the master provided them often. He was a good man, so different than others she'd known. When she told the truth, it would be all right. A tightness gripped her chest. *Courage, Lord.*

They said no more as they nourished themselves. She finished the last bite of venison and was eating her corn cake.

The door banged open, and Ethan stood in the opening. "Miles, I need help." His breath was ragged, as if he'd run all the way from his farm. "Constance is in labor. I was hoping..." he glanced toward Hannah, "one of your women had attended a birthing before."

After attending Benjamin's birth and watching her mother die, Elizabella had no desire to attend another one. Hopefully Bridgette or Hannah had experience in such matters.

Master Bonneville turned and looked at each one of them. "Well?"

"Nay," Bridgette said. "I was the last of my mother's brood, and she never allowed me to go with her when she attended to neighbors."

"Hannah?" the master said.

"I never have, but I'll go to her and do what I can," Hannah responded.

"What about you, Miss Clark?"

All gazes darted to Elizabella. Her ears burned. If there was anyone else, she would have declined, but Constance had been good to her, to all the brides. What choice did she have? "Aye, I attended with a midwife
~~~~~

when my sister and baby brother were born. The last time, my mother didn't survive."

Miles forehead furrowed. "I thought you had an older sister."

"Aye, and a younger one." A lump formed in her throat. Another lie to be forgiven for, but now was not the time to explain.

Miles nodded and touched her arm. "With you gone, the others are needed here. I can only spare one of you."

Elizabella followed Ethan out the door. It was only an hour's journey to his house. On the way, she tried to remember everything the midwife did when Benjamin was born. The woman gave her mother a potion, then used a long-hooked needle to try to pull the babe out.

The blood. The screams.

Elizabella shuddered. How could she ever do something like that even if she did have the tools the midwife used? The midwife was there to help, but did she make things worse? Mayhap her mother would have lived if she'd been allowed to deliver in her own time, in God's time.

She hurried her pace to keep up with Ethan's long strides. Why didn't she say she'd never seen a babe delivered? Hannah would have gone in her place.

Nay, even before all this happened, it wasn't her custom to lie. The lump rose in her throat again. She had lied lately and often. *Lord, forgive me, and give me the courage to tell the truth when I return.*

They came upon the wattle and daub house, almost as large as Miles' home. Screams came from inside, and Elizabella's heart pounded so hard, she was sure it would burst out of her chest. Ethan ran into the house.

Lord, please help me to know what to do.

She rushed in after him.

Chapter Twenty

Hugh ambled into the Powhatan camp with a bit of trepidation. He needed to find the chief and get out of here as fast as he could. If Suleta crossed his path, what could he say to her?

He looked around. Most of the women were tending the crops, but he didn't see any men around. A young squaw passed by, and he stopped her. "Where are the men?" he asked in the Powhatan language.

She pointed to a trail toward the west. "They are not here. They will return before the sun goes down."

Hugh looked up. The sun was still high in the sky. He let out a heavy sigh. It would be foolish to travel home. By the time he got there, he would need to travel back again. In the past, when he was waiting for the men to return, he would spend time with Suleta. Before that, it would be with another willing squaw.

The young woman before him gazed at him with a seductive look. "You can wait in my longhouse." She rested her hand on his chest. "I'll stay with you until they return." Her meaning was clear. She was beautiful, desirable. His face grew hot.

Nay. He removed her hand. "Tell the men I shall return at nightfall." He rushed out of the village and down the path.

He'd gone at least a couple of miles before he dared stop. He leaned over with his hands on his knees and breathed heavily. It startled him the temptation had been that great. He loved his wife with a greater intensity than he'd ever believed he could. Marrying Hannah had been the best thing he'd ever done. How could he still desire another when she was in his heart and his bed?

He walked on until he found a nearby clearing and placed his heavy musket on the ground. Better to wait for the chief here. He gulped a swig of rum he'd brought with him and sat beside where he'd laid his musket. After a few more swigs, the warmth of the drink went through him. His eyes grew heavy, and he lay on the hard ground.

~~~~~

Hugh woke with a start in darkness. The sun had already gone down. How long had he been here? He didn't know. He stood and brushed the dirt from his trousers. The moon was almost full, but when he looked down the path to the village, the heavy brush obscured it. Perchance, it would be better to wait until first light before traversing it.

Nay, he didn't know how long that would be or if the chief would go hunting again at first light. 'Twas better to finish his business here and
~~~~~

journey back to his plantation at dawn.

Hopefully Opechancanough hadn't already retired to his bed.

He stepped onto the path and trod a few steps, but he couldn't see where he was going. He waited a few moments to let his vision adjust to the darkness and walked further down the path.

A distant growl caused his heart to race. Black bears were often spotted in this forest. He stopped to load his musket. Better not to be caught unaware. He strode to the Indian village a bit faster than before even though the darkness remained thick.

A tree branch brushed against his cheek. He reached up and felt the scratch then continued on. A light glimmered ahead, and he rushed toward it.

When he arrived at the village, the warriors were sitting around the great fire in the clearing at the center of the village. He approached them and called out a greeting in their language.

"Hugh Bonneville," Chief Opechancanough said as he stood and faced him. Although an older man, mayhap in his sixties, he stood taller than most of the warriors in the tribe. A headband full of feathers covered his long gray hair, and he wore a heavy thick necklace made of animal teeth. Normally the chief would greet him with a smile, but today, a scowl crossed his features. "We were speaking of you, and here you are. How fortunate."

Hugh's chest tightened. Something was wrong. The chief had always been cordial to him, but he was a dangerous man, prone to outbursts of anger. Wupun, Suleta's mother, stood behind the chief. Surely, whatever the chief wanted had nothing to do with their relationship.

"Aye," Hugh said, dread settling in his stomach. "Is there a problem?"

The chief took a couple of steps toward him. "Wupun has brought a grievance against you that must be settled."

"What grievance?" His words barely rasped out.

"Her daughter, Suleta, died bearing your child."

A heaviness covered Hugh as if a tree had fallen on him. His mind reeled. The timing was right, but the last he talked with the Native woman, she gave no indication she was with child.

If it was true, what could he say? His mistress and child dead. If he had known before he met Hannah, he would have married her. He would have done the right thing. "I hadn't seen her in many moons. I thought she'd married another."

Wupun stepped from behind the chief. "Her betrothed rejected her after seeing her belly swollen with your child."

Heat flushed Hugh's face. "Mayhap it was her betrothed's babe."

The chief crossed his arms. "You talk with a lying tongue. The warrior had been gone from the camp for six moons with a hunting party when she told him she was having your child. Do you refuse to claim the babe?"

"Nay, 'twas mine." Hugh's knees weakened, and he fell on his knees in front of the chief. A sign of weakness, but he didn't care. "What would you have me do?" At least twenty warriors formed a circle around him leaving no doubt he was on trial before them, and he'd just admitted his guilt.

"Wupun doesn't have a warrior to care for her." Opechancanough said. "Her husband is dead, and now Suleta has gone to the grave and cannot marry." The chief placed his hand on Hugh's shoulder and glared at him. The gesture was not friendly. "You owe her compensation."

He struggled to get to his feet. He wanted to say he would do whatever it took, but he knew these people enough to know he might not be able to agree to what they had in mind. "What compensation?"

The chief's grip on his shoulder became uncomfortable, but he said nothing.

"I have wronged her," Hugh said. "What can I do to work this out between us?"

The chief squeezed so hard he had to press his tongue against his teeth to keep from showing the pain on his face. "You white men, all the same. You think you have a right to take our women and our land."

Opechancanough continued to squeeze until it was all Hugh could do to keep from crying out, but he dared not try to move away. The chief let go.

Hugh grabbed hold of his shoulder and tried to rub out the ache.

The chief pointed to Hugh's musket. "That would be a fine weapon in my hands. With a firearm like that and twenty more, I would agree to care for Wupun and her family."

Hugh grasped the musket so hard his nails dug into his palms. He shook his head. "Nay, I shan't part with it." He would never betray the colony by allowing Opechancanough to have so many firearms. "I'll give her one hundred pounds of tobacco."

"One hundred pounds of tobacco. 'Tis a white man's crop. Is that all you believe Suleta is worth? How does tobacco feed and clothe Wupun's family now?"

The fire was too hot. Sweat formed on Hugh's brow. "It's all I have."

"You offended Wupun greatly, and now you offer only one hundred pounds of a worthless crop." The chief slapped him hard against the cheek.

Pain shot through his face, but he made no move to avoid it. "I could come up with other items more valuable to you, copper bowls and pots and woven sheets of cloth." It would mean going to Miles for it and telling him why, but what else could he do?

"It'll take much to make up for the offence. Wupun, what say you?"

Wupun glared at Hugh. The rage over Suletta's death was evident in that glower. "I do desire woven cloth and cooking pans. At least twenty sheets of the cloth and five copper pans to start, but that still doesn't provide meat for my tent."

"Then he will also provide meat for you at least twice a year, a stag or a few turkeys until your younger daughter, Kimi, is old enough to marry a brave. Would that suffice?"

"It is enough," Wupun said.

"You heard her," the chief said. "The cloth and copper she demands and meat for her table before the next moon."

Hugh's stomach hardened. "Tis not enough time. T'would take three to four months to have that many pieces of cloth woven. And the copper pans will take time to acquire."

"I shall be merciful." The chief's glare showed mercy was not what he intended. "In one moon, you'll deliver the meat. I'll wait only three moons for the cooper and the cloth."

Hugh nodded. It wasn't much time, and he could only think of one way to get that much cloth or copper. He would have to go to the council and confess everything. He wiped the sweat off his brow. "I'll pay whatever she requires, but I can't provide after that. I'm leaving the colony in a few months to return to England."

The chief's voice lowered. "You're going to England? To the land where Pocahontas died and where they are keeping her son even now?"

Lady Rolfe had died of an unknown illness after she sailed to London with her husband. It wasn't the white man's fault, but the chief wouldn't have believed that. All Hugh could do was stay silent.

"Pocahontas is the chief's daughter. Her son should be with our tribe, not in this distant white man's land."

Hugh swallowed hard. So, this wasn't about Suleta. It was about the chief's niece and her son, the grandson of Chief Powhatan, his predecessor.

Opechancanough motioned to the other warriors, and they all took a couple of steps closer, closing in. Hugh tried to remember to breathe.

"Know this, Hugh Bonneville. You and your people need to learn you can't have our squaws without restitution. If you leave this land to sail across the great sea, there will be war."

The air escaped Hugh's lungs.

The chief stepped closer still until Hugh could smell his odor from hunting all day. He resisted the urge to gag.

Grasping his shoulder roughly again, the chief said in a low, menacing voice, "We shall have your women and children this time. We'll kill your men and take your children to become servants and give your wives to our braves."

Hugh kept his gaze focused. As much as he wanted to look away, the guilt of Suleta's death haunting him, he didn't dare. Suleta and his baby dead and now a risk of war. How much more would his sin cost?

Opechancanough swept with his hand as if Hugh was dismissed.

Hugh warily glanced around the tribe, afraid to speak but knowing he must. "I have another reason for coming."

The chief crossed his arms. "What reason?"

"Chief Opechancanough, I am here to ask you to consider meeting with the white man's council."

Opechancanough raised an eyebrow. "Why?"

"They wish a treaty of peace with you."

"I shan't meet with them until you settle with Wupun. We'll talk of an assembly then, but remember, I won't permit you to leave this land without the white man's blood staining the ground of your village."

The chief and his brave turned their backs toward Hugh. He strode to the path in the woods leading home. When he confessed to his brother that he was the reason for all of this, Miles would never forgive him. Even worse, he might lose Hannah's love.

Chapter Twenty-One

Constance lay in a bed by the fireplace, sweat beading her forehead. She had her eyes closed and didn't seem to be in distress. The pain must have subsided for the moment.

Elizabella wasn't sure how much assistance she could be, but she wasn't going to let Constance go through this alone. "Ethan, did she prepare any caudle?" Caudle was thin porridge made with eggs, milk and alcohol the midwife had given to her mother. She didn't know how to make it, but she'd often heard it helped with the pain during labor.

"Aye, it's in a bowl warming on the hearth."

Elizabella held Constance's hand to let her know she was there. "Please, get it for me. I'll also need a basin of water and a cloth."

Ethan set the bowl and a spoon beside Elizabella. Then he poured some water into a basin next to the bowl. "There are some swaddling clothes and blankets in the trunk." He pointed to the wooden box beside the cradle in the corner of the room. "Take care of her. And the babe."

"Pray I have the wisdom I need," Elizabella said.

Ethan nodded. "I'll be close by. Call when it's done." He kissed his wife on the forehead, squeezed her hand, and left the house.

Elizabella spoke soothingly to Constance as she held a spoonful of caudle to her lips. "Drink a little of this. It'll help."

Constance opened her eyes and took a spoonful. "Thank you for coming. Men know nothing about birthing babies, and I was afraid to deliver alone."

"Nay, we can't have that. I'll do what I can, but I've only attended a couple of births."

Constance blew out a heavy groan. Another pain was upon her.

Elizabella didn't know what to do, so she held her hand. When the pain passed, she held up another spoonful of porridge.

"There's nothing you need to do except hold my hand, pray I am found worthy, and slap the babe on the rump once it's born."

If anyone was worthy, it would be Constance, but Elizabella's mother was also worthy. Another pain overtook Constance, and Elizabella placed a wet cloth on her forehead and squeezed her hand.

She no longer believed pain and death in childbirth was God's punishment on all women. How could it be when the Lord took her godly mother? Many women who died were more than worthy in the Lord's eyes. Her mother couldn't have possibly displeased Him. Her death was not from His wrath. It couldn't have been.

If it were true that God wasn't punishing women by having them die in childbirth, then it was also possible that her being forced to come to Jamestown was not a sign of God's displeasure. Hard to fathom such a thing since she had been fearing God's punishment since Benjamin died, but now she knew about God's mercy.

Another pain caused Constance to cry out, then it subsided. This went on for hours as the birthing pangs grew closer together. The sun began to set, leaving the blaze from the fireplace as their only light. Elizabella lit a couple of candles.

Constance closed her eyes after a grueling couple of moments. "Mayhap, it shall happen soon."

Elizabella wet a cloth and placed it on her forehead. "A midwife attended when my brother was born. She used a large hook called a croquet to hasten the birth."

Constance's eyes opened wide. "Nay, I shan't allow that thing near me. Our Lord shall allow this child to be born in his own time."

"I wouldn't ever use that horrible hook," Elizabella said thickly. "I believe it was the torture device that caused my mother's death."

Constance squeezed her hand, but this time, it wasn't out of pain. "Surgeons in the king's court have spoken against the practice. They say it causes more harm than good. I'm sorry about your mother."

Elizabella's eyes watered, and she blinked back the tears. "Thank you." She gave Constance a spoonful of porridge. "What can I do to help?"

"You're doing it." Constance tensed and groaned. "You could pray for the Lord's grace. Mayhap quote a Scripture or two?"

Elizabella tried to remember Scriptures Master Bonneville had read. The vicar had preached on an appropriate passage two days past.

"Please, a Scripture now." Constance cried out.

"I will lift up mine eyes unto the hills, from whence cometh my help. My help cometh from the Lord, which made heaven and earth."

Constance nodded, then screamed. The pain didn't seem to lesson now. "Perchance you should lift my shift."

Elizabella did so. A patch of the baby's head had appeared. "Lord, please give Constance the grace to deliver this baby. Protect both their lives."

Constance groaned again. "Another scripture."

She remembered the Scripture from when the disciples were in the storm. "Peace, be still." The Lord would surely give Constance peace after this turmoil was done.

Another groan. "Again."

She quoted the passage Master Bonneville had read that first day and many days hence. "Come unto me, all ye that labour and are heavy laden, and I will give you rest. Take my yoke upon you, and learn of me; for I am meek and lowly in heart: and ye shall find rest unto your souls. For my yoke is easy, and my burden is light." She couldn't fathom it when she first heard it, but now she relied on it. It had become her favorite.

Constance strained and pushed. The head came out, full of dark hair. Another push, and a hand slipped through.

Elizabella held the babe as it slipped out of Constance's body. "A girl."

"Slap her," Constance said. "She has to cry to get enough air."

She slapped the babe's rump. Nothing happened.

"Harder."

She hit the babe again. Nothing. The babe began to have a bluish tint. She hit harder and harder. Tears rolled onto her cheeks. "Please, Lord, please." At the next slap, the child let out a loud wail. She took the baby in her arms and laughed. "What do I do now?"

"Tie a knot in the cord, take a sharp knife, and cut the cord close to the navel."

Elizabella did so.

"Now wash her in the basin, wrap her in a blanket, and set her in the cradle. I still need your assistance."

She did as Constance said and helped her deliver the afterbirth. When she was done, she handed the infant to her mother. Constance calmed her cries by nursing her.

Elizabella ran to the window. "Ethan! Ethan, it's done."

Ethan dashed from a grove of nearby trees, and she met him outside. "Well?"

"Mother and daughter are both doing well."

"Thank ye, Lord." He stepped inside.

She stayed outside a little longer and gazed at the stars. The memory of her mother dying assaulted her, and she wiped her face. "Lord, I don't know why You didn't save my mother, but please heal this memory of her perishing. I know she's in Your arms."

A peace came over her. She walked back into the house to take care of the new babe.

Chapter Twenty-Two

On the long path home, Hugh had done a lot of pondering on what his sin would cost. When he had married Hannah, he vowed to be a better man, for her sake and for his own. He couldn't help but remember Hannah's words to him that day. *The only way you can really change your life is to give it to the Lord, the one who created it.*

He'd thought it an odd statement at the time. Of course, he believed in God. Didn't everyone? But to surrender his life seemed extreme. He didn't want to become like Miles, judgmental and unforgiving.

Now, he would never be able to leave this colony. His father would die in the king's court with nobody to speak for him, all because of the death of Suleta and his babe. Guilt lodged in his gut.

His wickedness had not only caused her death but could be responsible for the deaths of many more in the colony. He couldn't fix this on his own. He dropped to his knees onto the dirt.

"Lord, please forgive me. I give my life to You. Help me to somehow make this right."

He didn't know how long he stayed there, kneeling on the ground, but it was a while. The damp ground had soaked through the knees of his trousers, causing a shiver. He wiped his face and stood, not sure if his prayer did any good. Then, peace flooded through him, reassuring him of God's grace. He prayed that peace would stay with him and guide him through all of this.

As he walked the path, he tried to rehearse how he would tell all of this to his brother, Hannah, and the Burgess. A couple of hours later, he still knew not what he would say. As the sun was beginning to rise, he reached the fields where Miles and the men were working and let out a heavy sigh.

Making things right meant confessing everything and facing whatever consequences came his way. And there would be consequences. His brother had sheltered him once, but he wouldn't this time.

Hugh wasn't sure he wanted to escape the punishment anyway, no matter how severe. He'd already received more grace from the Lord than he ever expected. What wounded him most was the truth that Miles would never forgive him. Not this time.

Would Hannah when she knew what his sin had caused? He'd already told her about the whole sordid affair before he left. *Thank Ye, Lord, for that.* It would make confessing about the babe a little easier.

When he drew closer, Miles waved and strode to him. "How did you fare?"

"We must talk."

"What happened?"

"Not here. Come to my house, and I'll tell you everything."

Miles nodded and followed him to his home. When they entered, Hannah was sitting in a rocker in front of the fireplace plucking feathers from a chicken.

She wiped her hands on her apron and stood. "Welcome home, husband."

He took her into his arms and held onto her tight. He wanted to hold her forever, but he couldn't delay this for long. He cleared his throat and pulled away. "Please sit, both of you."

They took their places at the roughhewn table.

"Normally, I wouldn't include my wife in such matters, but..." His voice cracked.

"What's wrong?" Miles asked, concern in his voice. "Did the Powhatan refuse to meet?"

Hugh snorted. "Nay, but they have conditions."

Hannah placed her hand on Hugh's. The warmth of her touch strengthened his resolve.

Without lifting his head, Hugh gazed at Miles. He wasn't about to look away no matter how difficult this task. "They are considering war, and 'tis my fault."

"What?" Miles swiped at the back of his neck. "War? Why? What have you done?"

"I've already told Hannah part of this, but I need to make a full confession to both of you and..." Hugh paused, "perchance the Burgess. I don't know."

An angry scowl crossed Miles' features. He stood, took a couple of steps toward the fireplace, and leaned against the stone. "Well."

"I admitted to you a few months back that I committed fornication with Indian women." Hugh glanced toward his wife. She motioned for him to go on. "Over the past year and a half, I had an illicit liaison with only one Native, Suleta. I told her I wanted to wed her, but she refused. She was betrothed to another."

Miles sat at the table again, his eyebrows lowered and pinched so closely together, they seemed to be one. "So, did you continue in this... fornication? Are you an adulterer also?"

"Nay, I have sinned greatly, but I could not continue knowing she was marrying another. I determined to stop visiting the village and to find myself a good wife."

Hugh waited for a moment. When his brother didn't say anything, he continued. "When I was at the village, I learned she had been with child. Both her and the babe, my babe, died in childbirth."

Hannah gasped.

He wanted nothing more than to take her in his arms and comfort her, but he had to tell the rest first. "When I met with the chief, Suleta's mother, Wupun, was there to accuse me. The warrior, Suleta's fiancé, had returned from an extended hunting trip and found her with a large belly. He refused to marry her. Wupun demanded compensation for the wrongs I'd caused."

"What does this have to do with the Powhatan wanting war?" Miles asked. "The Natives are heathens. Adultery is a way of life with them."

Hannah reached over and squeezed Hugh's hand. He was grateful for the support even though it came as a surprise.

"When I met with Chief Opechancanough last night, he was angry. He said I had an obligation to provide for Suleta's family and demanded fifty muskets in payment, but I couldn't do that." Hugh's shoulders slumped. "Whatever else I am, I'm not a traitor."

Miles let out a hard laugh. "Not a traitor? If you don't satisfy the chief and he declares war, you might as well be."

"'Tis true." Hugh couldn't help the crack in his voice. "I offered a hundred pounds of tobacco to recompense her."

Miles rubbed his hand across his mouth. "After paying for your bride and two women servants, not to mention a journey to England for you and Hannah, we have little left between us until harvest time four months hence."

"Doesn't matter. He refused. I must bring him a stag and some turkeys within a month, and twenty sheets of woven cloth, five copper pots, and another stag within three months."

"We only have two copper pots, and the women need those for cooking." The muscle in Miles' jaw twitched. "And how are the women going to weave that much cloth in time, let alone spin enough yarn?"

Hannah cleared her throat. "Miss Clark is an expert weaver, and she has a trunk full of threads and yarn, even a few coverlets. If anyone could weave it in time, she could."

"That still leaves the pots we need. Copper is dear, and we don't have any tobacco to purchase it. Even if we had enough, it's unlikely we could find enough to meet his demands." The vein in Miles' neck pulsed. "How many times have I warned you to mend your ways? How many times have I told you your sin would lead you to ruin? That's apparently not enough for you. You want to destroy our farm and perchance the colony as well."

"You were right about everything." Hugh wanted to remain stoic, but he couldn't stop his chin from quivering. "The chief is angry at the white man for taking away their squaws. He mentioned Pocahontas."

"So, this is really about Lady Rolfe and her child? Your indiscretion was a way for him to exact his revenge."

Hugh didn't bother to say anymore. He had no defense to give.

Miles paced a few steps back and forth, then stopped and bellowed. "Even if we could get Miss Clark to weave enough cloth in time, it would cost at least two hundred pounds of tobacco to buy enough copper. We could never come up with that amount, at least not until autumn harvest."

No matter how disturbing, Hugh needed to tell the rest. "I can't go to London." He swallowed back a sob. "He says I must stay in the colony and bring Wupun meat twice a year until her youngest daughter is old enough to marry, or he will slaughter every man, woman, and child in the colony."

Miles' face turned white. "You can't stay. We need to get you on that ship as soon as possible, and we need to warn Lord Rolfe to do the same. He won't just want war with the colony, he'll take his revenge out on you both."

Hugh shook his head. "I won't let the colony suffer for my actions."

"You have to," Hannah said, tears forming in her eyes. "You can't stay and be slaughtered by these men."

Miles waved a hand toward Hannah. "We'll figure out something."

"There's nothing you can do. I've made my decision." Hugh strode toward the door. "I'll tell the Burgess what I've done. Perchance the town shall provide what's needed. We'll repay after the crop comes in."

"You can't." Hannah threw her arms around him. "They'll have you whipped."

Hugh wrapped his arms around his wife. He was surprised how calm he felt considering what was facing him. He held her tight, grateful for her embrace. "I'm so sorry. On the way home, I gave my life to the Lord and asked for His forgiveness. Now I'm asking for yours."

A tear fell down her cheek. "You have it."

He pulled back. "The council needs to know the truth no matter what they do to me. I must go to them."

Miles' brow furrowed. "No need to involve them yet."

Hugh gazed at his brother, not believing what he was hearing. "Haven't you always said they that dance must pay the fiddler?"

"If Miss Clark works only on weaving for the next few months, and we are able to get the price for the voyage back and we sell one of the servants, we should have enough for the copper," Miles said. "You won't be able to leave, but Chief Opechancanough should be satisfied for now."

Hugh rubbed his chin. "Nay, the Burgess shall want news about my meeting. I must tell them the truth. Besides, even if we get the voyage price back, we can't afford to lose any of the servants."

Miles began to pace. After a few times back and forth, he paused and folded his arms. "You can't stay. Payment is no guarantee Opechancanough's anger would be appeased."

Hugh shook his head. Whatever else he was, he wasn't a coward. "I shan't leave."

Hannah kissed his cheek. "Do as your brother commands."

Hugh disentangled himself from his wife's loving arms. "Nay, I won't." He turned to Miles and extended his hand. "Forgive me."

Miles gave him a stony look but didn't reach for his hand. "I can't condone what you've done, and I don't believe this convenient transformation to get yourself out of trouble. You've proven to be just like Father." He turned and strode out of the house.

Hugh sank to the bench at the table. No matter what else befell them, he had to make amends to his brother.

Chapter Twenty-Three

Miles hadn't talked to his brother since his revelation the day before. What was there to say? Hugh had sinned against God, placed the colony in danger, and might have left their plantation in financial ruin, all because he couldn't keep his lust from overtaking him.

He might have told the truth, but he didn't have a choice after what happened at the Powhatan village. That excused nothing, even if he had received God's salvation.

A kettle of stew hung over the fireplace, and the smell made him hungry. Miss Atwood had prepared it that morning since Miss Clark was still helping Constance. He missed her. He wished he could talk to her about what was happening with his brother.

If the babe was born alive, she would probably be there at least another day or two. Many babes didn't survive childbirth, let alone their first two years of life. James didn't. Neither did Mary.

He rubbed his hand across his face and let up a prayer for God's grace upon Ethan and Constance. He missed talking to Miss Clark. She always seemed to give him wise counsel when he needed it. Most of the time, that counsel involved mercy, but how could he possibly forgive his brother?

The sun was sitting low in the sky. John should be returning from his walk with Miss Atwood soon. So far, John had honored his agreement to behave decently, but who knew how long that would last?

He strode toward the path they took. Up ahead, the corner of a skirt showed behind a wide oak tree. He ran toward it and found John holding Miss Atwood in his arms.

Heat rose up his back, and he pulled John away. "How dare you take liberties with my servant!"

Miss Atwood blushed and turned away.

John held up his hands. "We did nothing sordid. It was an embrace, nothing more."

"It would have led to more if I hadn't spotted you when I did." His hands rolled into fists. "Am I the only man in this colony with morals?"

"Please, sir," Miss Atwood said. "We did nothing wrong, nor would we. We were ready to head back to the house. It was a fare-thee-well only."

"Best you be on your way to the house, Miss Atwood. 'Tis between me and John."

She broke into sobs, dashed around them, and ran to the house.

"You have no reason to accuse us," John said. "Let alone cause her to cry."

"You should have considered that before you held her in such a manner."

"Come now," John said. "Are you trying to tell me you never embraced your wife when you were betrothed?"

"Nay, never. I protected her virtue until our wedding day."

"You expect too much. You only courted her a week. Try a year and see if a hug is not acceptable."

"I should have known to expect no honor from you, given your past dealings with women."

"How dare you? I paid for that crime dearly, thanks to you."

Mile felt the muscles cord in his neck. Heat overtook him. He tugged on John's shirt and drew back his fist. They were all alike. His father, his brother... John. His fist connected with John's jaw before he even become aware of throwing the punch.

He let go, and John landed with a thud on the ground. Shock, then betrayal, flashed in his friend's eyes. Miles' rage lifted, and his head cleared. He gasped at the way he had reacted. There was no impropriety. He could see that now.

Miles offered him a hand. "I'm sorry."

John swiped it away and rubbed his jaw. It was red, and there would be an ugly bruise, but it didn't appear swollen or broken.

"How can I make this up to you?"

"You can't," John said thickly. "You, of all people, know how hard I worked to rebuild my reputation. I've taken the utmost care to treat Bridgette with respect. I thought we had restored our friendship."

Miles' shoulders slumped. He gazed at the ground and wished he could hide in it. It wasn't John he had been angry with. "Pardon my bad humor. 'Twas wrong. To prove it, I won't require you to wait a year. I'll let you buy Miss Atwood's contract now if you like, so you can marry."

John glanced toward the path Miss Atwood had taken. "I'd like that, but she desired to wait. I'll respect her wishes no matter what she decides."

Miles nodded. "Let us go to the house and ask her now. I'm sorry about my behavior."

John shrugged off the apology, but he did shake Miles' hand. They strode toward the house. If this worked, Miles would have more than enough tobacco on hand to buy the copper he needed. Mayhap he could get Hugh on that ship after all. He could provide the meat the chief required.

With Hugh and Hannah in England and Miss Atwood married off, Miss Clark would be required to run the household and work as hard as Mary had. He cared for Miss Clark more each day, more than he wanted to admit. He'd do anything to save her from the same fate as his wife or help her survive the seasoning, but Hugh was his brother. What was he to do?

Forgive.

The word roared so loud in his spirit, he almost looked around to see if anyone had spoken it, but nobody had. This was the voice of God compelling him to forgive his brother, but not only him. He had lived in this offense since his father had ruined their reputations and caused his mother so much grief.

He might be able to forgive his brother, but his father? Nay. That would require traveling to London, seeing him in person once again.

Lord, forgive me, but I shan't do it.

~~~~~

Elizabella sat by the fireplace, rocking the newborn. The babe had been up half the night, and she'd told Constance to take a nap while she cared for the infant.

The glow from the fireplace shone on the little one's face. She was so precious, a blessing from God. She'd prayed, and God had heard her prayers. This babe proved God loved her.

Since the birth, she'd felt His presence beside her. For the first time, she remembered her mother without pain. Oh, there was still sorrow. She missed her so much. But she could remember the good times now, like how Mother would sing while she was making breakfast or sewing by the light of the hearth.

Mother possessed such joy even after Father started drinking, and she spread that joy to her children. She would often quote the verse, "The joy of the Lord is my strength."

If the Lord had seen fit to let Constance live through the birthing and create such a perfect little one, then Elizabella could depend upon Him to heal the other hurts in her life and to confess the truth to Master Bonneville. Mayhap she could even come to a place where she could feel joy again.

Could she possibly experience happiness here in Jamestown? Would God see her safely back to London? That would be a joyful thing indeed.

She kissed the babe's forehead. "I'm going to miss you when I go back to the Bonneville Plantation tomorrow."

"We're going to miss you too," Constance said.

She laid the sleeping babe in the crib.

Constance stood and went to the pitcher of water, wet a cloth, and wiped it over her face. "You've been a godsend to us, but you're only one farm away, and we'll see each other at church."

"Aye, 'tis true." She pressed her lips together. It might be easier to confess to someone else first to practice getting it out in the light. "May I gain your counsel?"

"Of course. How may I help?"

"I've tried to tell you so many times, but something always stopped it." Elizabella glanced at the babe's cradle. "I could always manage a justification to delay it."

Constance's brow furrowed. "Go on."

She told her the whole story then waited for the reaction.
~~~~~

Constance gave her a wide-eyed stare, followed by her hand touching her chest, and the lifting of a single eyebrow. Then, she hugged Elizabella and patted her back as her mother might have done if she'd been there. It was comforting and wonderful and gave her hope Miles might react the same way.

"This explains so much," Constance said. "You poor thing, barely escaping from murderous thugs, having your sister stabbed in front of you, then having to sneak on board and sail to Jamestown to escape. Why didn't you tell me this earlier? I might have been able to arrange something before you became indentured."

Elizabella folded her hands together. "I was about to, but I was afraid."

"Why would you be?" Constance's mouth gaped open into an O. "The boy. You were about to tell me when they discovered the boy who snuck aboard and then again before we left the ship."

"I'm going to tell my master everything."

Constance poured a cup of water and gulped it down. "Do you think that wise? Miles Bonneville can be difficult when he believes he's been lied to or betrayed. Perchance, we can find another way."

A nudging of worry trickled down Elizabella's spine. "His brother already knows and is sure to tell him if I don't. Besides, I can't go on living this lie for five years. The truth shall come out. 'Tis best if he finds out from me."

"Of course," Constance said. "I pray thee well then." The sound of her voice wasn't convincing.

Lord, be with me. Don't let my courage falter.

~~~~~

Miles strode through the door after John. Miss Atwood turned from the basin where she was washing dishes. Her eyes were red. She'd been crying.

He swiped his hand across the back of his neck. He had lost his temper and embarrassed the girl when nothing sordid had happened. Hopefully, this would make amends.

"Master Bonneville, I vow on my mother's life, nothing sordid happened between John and me. You had no call to accuse him."

John took her hand. "I explained everything, and I have good news."

Miss Atwood bit her lip.

"Miles has released you from your promise to wait a year. We can marry right away. Isn't that wonderful?"

Miss Atwood glanced at Miles then at John. She didn't look as pleased as he had expected. "Master Bonneville, have you already sold me to him?"

"Nay," Miles said. What was wrong with the lass? She acted as if she didn't wish to marry John. "It's your decision to make."

Miss Atwood crossed her arms. "John, I must speak to you... alone."

"I'll be outside," Miles muttered and strode through the door. This
~~~~~

wasn't working at all the way he had hoped, and he needed the funds to buy the copper.

When he stepped outside, Hugh walked toward him.

Heat warmed his face. He was doing his best to help his brother through this, but he wasn't ready to talk to him about it.

"I must let you know my decision." Hugh looked at his feet. "On the morrow, I'll hunt game and take it to the village, then when the Burgess meet in a few weeks, I'll go to them and confess everything. Surely, they'll provide the copper I need. We can repay them after the harvest."

"No need." Miles wiped his hand across his mouth. "John is proposing to Miss Atwood. I told him he could pay off her indenture early. If we also sell one of the field hands, we should have enough for the copper. Miss Clark can make the cloth. We won't even need to redeem the cost of your journey. You can sail to England, and I'll provide the meat the chief requires."

"Miles, nay." The muscle in Hugh's jaw twitched. "I won't let you do this. We need every servant we have."

"I'll do what I must." Miles glanced toward the house. "It's already decided. John is proposing now."

"Even if John marries Miss Atwood, how will we manage? We need every fieldhand we have."

Just then, John walked out of the door, shoulders slumped and head down.

Miles' heart dropped to his stomach. "She refused?"

"Nay, she'll marry me, but she desires to wait a month or two. She doesn't want to leave Hugh's wife and your servant in a quandary. She begs me wait a bit longer."

Hugh placed a hand on John's shoulder. "Are you willing to do that?"

John gave a crooked smile. "I know you've both wondered what I see in her. She's no great beauty, but she's kind and thoughtful, and so vulnerable. Since the moment I met her, I had a strong urging to be her protector. I love her."

"It's done then. You'll pay the required price within a month?"

"Nay, I'll give you what you need by the end of the week. I desire to give Bridgette the time she needs, but I want to make sure all is in order."

Miles shook his hand, and John departed.

"We still have another servant to sell," Miles said. "I'll check with the men at the fort to see who's interested."

"Do you plan to sell Miss Clark instead?" Hugh asked.

"Nay, she is too great a blessing."

"I thought not. You care for her, admit it."

Miles nodded. He could no longer deny the truth. "She is godly, virtuous, caring, and hard-working. I never thought I'd wish for another, especially a woman so young, but somehow, she has wormed her way into my heart."

"Everyone has faults. Don't place her on a pedestal so high that she can never live up to it. I could never live up to your expectations." Hugh shrugged. "Mayhap, that's why I never tried."

Miles swallowed back the lump in his throat. "Is that what you thought, that you could never measure up?"

Hugh's gaze fell to the ground, but he didn't speak. Finally, he looked Miles in the eyes. "The fault is mine, not yours. If I had... If I had given my life in service to the Lord instead of trying to spite you, this never would have happened." His voice thickened. "Will you forgive me?"

Miles' throat threatened to close, and tears welled up behind his eyelids. He had always thought of himself as an honorable man, but now he knew the truth. He was judgmental and unforgiving, wretched in the sight of God. "How can I not? I'm the one who drove you away." He stepped toward Hugh. "I also need forgiveness."

"You have it," Hugh said.

Miles embraced his brother.

Hugh returned the embrace, then stepped back. "The Burgess are meeting in a month, are they not?"

Miles nodded. "Please don't go to them. I'll still redeem the cost of your journey if the captain agrees, and I can still sell a fieldhand. I don't wish to see you beaten with the people in the fort cheering."

"I'll do what I must. We can't spare another servant, and even if you were able to convince the captain, the Burgess needs to know the danger the colony is in because of me. In a few days, I'll leave to hunt game and take it to the Powhatan. When the council meets next, I'll be there to confess everything."

"Then I shall stand by your side and plead for their mercy."

Chapter Twenty-Four

It had been five days since Elizabella helped Constance deliver her daughter. Ethan had offered to walk her home, but she insisted there was no need. It was only a short stroll along a well-established path.

She had a lot to think about, and the solitude would give her the time she needed. She still couldn't help but feel amazed and grateful. She had prayed, really prayed, and God heard her prayers and saved Constance and her babe.

They hadn't named the child yet. Constance had explained that it was the custom of the colony to wait two years, just in case.

No more needed to be said. *Just in case* meant the babe might not survive the first two years. Apparently, the seasoning didn't only apply to newcomers but newborns as well.

A morbid thought, but somehow it didn't terrify her as it once did. God had brought her so much comfort in this new land. If the Lord really was listening to her and answering her prayers, mayhap, He would allow Honesty to receive word and rescue her.

First, she needed to tell Master Bonneville the truth. Constance had advised her not to, but she didn't need to fear him. In every way, he had shown himself a good man, a decent man. He could help her get back to London where she belonged.

Nobody will believe you. You killed your own brother.

Elizabella dropped to the ground on her knees. Her father's ugly accusations tore her apart inside as they did the first time he said them. "Lord, can You help me with this? Can You heal those horrible things my father spoke?"

Even as she said the prayer, peace swept over her. Was it that easy? Was the God of the universe really willing to help her with memories that had haunted her for years? It seemed so, but there were so many nightmares from the past to torment her. All she could do was give each one to the Lord as they assailed her. It would take time, perchance years, but she now knew what to do.

"Thank You, Lord." She wiped her face and stood. If God could help her with these memories, He could give her the courage to tell Miles the truth. She headed for the farm.

The heat had become oppressive even though it was still only May. She hated to think how sweltering it would be when July came around. Another reason to return to London.

A sigh escaped her. Truthfully, the land was beautiful despite the heat.

The trees were beginning to leaf and losing their white, yellow, and red buds. The animals she'd seen amazed her. Wild turkey, eagles with white feathers on their heads, and an abundance of deer.

She'd recently become in the habit of reminding herself why she didn't want to stay in this paradise, but she didn't need to bother. Even though she grew to love it here, as long as her sister was alive, she had vowed to protect her. To do that, she had to return to London.

A growl sounded from the woods. She glanced around nervously and wiped the sweat off her brow. A crunch ahead. She peered through the trees, trying to see what was making the sound. Three deer darted past, racing away from something. Or maybe they were just running.

Anxiousness caused her stomach to rumble. She'd been here almost two months now, and she didn't recall one dangerous animal, not even a racoon, but one of the wives at the fort had said there were bears in the forest.

'Twas foolishness. She let out a chuckle. Nothing to fear. Honesty would have found merriment at her imagining all sorts of creatures, but that was one of the difficulties in living in a savage land. Dangerous animals could lurk in the foliage.

Another growl. This time, it sounded almost like a roar. So loud. "If you are a bear, no need to come closer. I'm leaving."

She glanced back and walked a little faster. Another growl, this time low and menacing. She ran. Her stomach wrenched, but she dared not stop.

Up ahead, she saw it. The bear was running straight toward her. She backed away from the large brown creature, broad with a long muzzle and dangerous claws sharp enough to rip someone apart. She turned and ran, tripped, and fell to the ground. She screamed and looked up, expecting to see the bear coming closer, but instead, it ran into the forest.

Master Bonneville and his brother stood at the edge of the forest. Mayhap, that was what scared the bear. The master ran toward her.

"A bear. There's a big bear in the trees."

Master Bonneville raised an eyebrow, and both he and his brother quickly loaded their muskets and moved past her toward where she pointed. Two shots sounded. They loaded again and ran into the trees.

Elizabella couldn't bring herself to move or to take her gaze off them. The lump in her throat threatened to choke her.

Soon they strode back to her. Master Bonneville reached out his hand and helped her to her feet.

Shaky, she leaned against him to steady herself. "Did you get it?"

The master wrapped his arms around her and placed his hand on her head. "It's all right. We didn't get him, but he ran off."

She felt safe in his arms, but after a moment, she was embarrassed and pulled away. "What if it comes back?"

"It was a grizzly, not a black bear like the others," Hugh said. "We need to hunt him down. I'll get the hunting supplies." He ran toward his cabin.

The master rubbed his chin. "We're safe for now, but it could come back." He turned to her, his gaze intense. "Miss Clark, do you think you can find your way back to the house?"

She looked through the woods and could see the house up ahead, only a short walk from here. "I think so."

"You are a brave lass." He took her hand. "Let Hannah and Miss Atwood know all that transpired, and command them to stay close to the house."

Elizabella nodded. "I'll tell them."

Hugh returned with a couple of the men carrying sacks. "The other servants are staying to protect the women."

Elizabella glanced at the path the bear took. "When shall you return?"

He squeezed her hand. "Don't fret. We'll kill it before it has a chance to hurt anyone, and if you need help, Caleb and the others will be there." He let go, paused a moment, then they headed into the woods with great haste.

Elizabella placed her hand on her cheek, still feeling the pressure of his touch. *Lord, keep them safe.*

~~~~~

Miles and the other men followed Hugh along the path. They'd found bear tracks and were now following them to their farm. They had their share of visits from black bear and gave them a wide berth, but a grizzly this close to the plantation? They had to find it and kill it before it hurt someone. The sun had almost set. If they didn't find the animal soon, they'd have to give up until the morrow.

A low growl came from the grove. All four men loaded their muskets and stood ready.

"Bear," Miles shouted. "Come out and be done with this."

The growl came again, only louder, then the bear sprang out of the trees and brush at such speed it startled him for a moment. The blasts from four muskets rang in his ears.

The bear stumbled back.

They took only a moment to reload their guns, but Miles and Hugh didn't manage it in time. The angry bear was coming for them. George, the youngest of their servants, shot again, but it only slowed the bear down. William aimed for the head. This time, the animal fell with a thud. Dust stirred around it. By then, Miles and Hugh had reloaded. They approached it cautiously. It appeared dead, but they had to be sure. A wounded bear could be just as dangerous.

Hugh kicked its leg, but it didn't move. Only then did Miles dare lay his hand on the bear's stomach. No rising and falling with breath. It was dead. He nodded to his brother. The men cheered.

"George, bring the game bags," Hugh said.
~~~~~

The young boy with a slight shadow of fuzz on his chin brought the bags. They pulled out their knives and started dressing the carcass.

William cut through the bear's middle with the skill of a trained hunter. Hugh let out a heavy sigh as he pushed against the animal to get it on its side. The sun was setting quickly, and they would never finish in time to return home.

Miles glanced at the sky. "We're going to have to make camp here. William, George, finish skinning and salting the bear while Hugh and I find some firewood and water and make camp."

As Miles and Hugh walked further into the woods, he heard William giving George instructions. The Irishman had been on the farm six years now. He would hate to lose him in another year. There were few who worked as hard or knew farming as well as him.

Once they were far enough from the men, Miles turned to his brother. "I implore you not to go to the council."

"It's already decided. They have to know everything so they can make preparations should the Natives attack. I thought you would be pleased I'm owning up to my sins."

"It pleases me your character has changed, but I'd prefer not to have you whipped with onlookers cheering. Besides, it'll subject our family to more ridicule."

"So, this is about Father."

Miles didn't answer, but his throat tightened with shame. Was that the only reason he objected to Hugh telling the truth? He emptied the bear's guts onto the ground.

Hugh picked up some kindling for the fire and gazed at Miles. "My pardon for bringing this on you. You were the oldest and the one who took the brunt of our disgrace. I was so young, I never considered how much Father's actions affected you."

"Please travel to London." Miles grabbed a small tree branch lying on the ground. "Father will have nobody to stand by his side."

Hugh didn't look up from his work. "You must sail in my place."

Miles jutted his chin. "Nay." Even as he refused, he knew the Lord bid him go.

"Do you not trust me to take care of the farm while you're away? I've worked as hard as you have to make it prosperous, and we've never had five better servants than we do now."

Heat burned Miles' cheeks even though the air was growing cool. "I know. I could think of none better to take my place."

"At least pray about it."

"I shall." That, Miles would agree to. He had been doing nothing else since Hugh had returned from the village after delivering a large buck to begin his payments.

Neither of them said any more.

That night, Miles lay staring up at the sky. *Please, Lord, I don't want to return there, but I shall if You make it obvious I must.*

~~~~~

When Elizabella had returned to the plantation, she immediately went to Hannah and told her what had happened, not just about the bear, but about her revelation of the Lord and how He had given her peace. When Miles returned, she would tell him everything.

Hannah hadn't responded the way Elizabella thought she would. She had agreed to stay with her and Bridgette until the men hunting the bear returned, but she hadn't said two words since then, and she seemed unable to sit for more than a few moments. Something troubled her.

It was now evening, but they heard no word. Surely, they'd found the bear and killed it by now. Elizabella sat with Bridgette in front of the fireplace in the women's room.

Elizabella set aside the shirt she was sewing and rubbed her temples. Her head had throbbed since she'd arrived home, and she ached all over. Possibly because the events of the last few days had tired her. She longed for sleep.

Bridgette rambled on. Something about marrying John as soon as she was sure Elizabella and Hannah could manage without her.

Hannah stood and rubbed sweat off her forehead. "The fire is too strong. I'll return to my cabin."

"Nay!"

The volume of Bridgette's protest made Elizabella's head pound.

"You heard what Honesty said." Bridgette stepped in front of the door. "We are to stay near until the men return."

"Egad, tis only a short walk from here, and there are other servants around," Hannah said. "I must have some air."

"Bridgette is right," Elizabella patted an empty stool beside her. "Come and sit. Tell us what troubles you."

"'Tis nothing." Hannah's face turned red, and she eased herself onto the stool. "My husband has some business at the fort in a few weeks. It has me preoccupied."

Bridgette stood, paced a little, and sat down again. "John says they're trying to make a peace treaty with the Natives. I'm not sure they can be trusted, though. Their ways are so... savage."

Hannah stood, sweat beading on her brow. "I'll not be trapped in this hothouse for another moment." She took two steps toward the door, drew her hand to her head, and collapsed.

They ran to her. Elizabella felt her forehead. "She's burning with fever. Quick, fetch some water from the well."

"Nay, I'm not going out there," Bridgette said. "What if the bear's nearby?"

"Oh, for Heaven's sake. I'll go." Elizabella fetched the pitcher.
~~~~~

"Please don't." Bridgette's eyes teared up.

"What's wrong? I've never seen you so fearful."

Bridgette grabbed hold of Elizabella's hands. "Bears are dangerous. If the master and his brother hadn't shown up, you could have been killed."

Elizabella hugged Bridgette. "You have nothing to fear. I'm sure the creature won't come near the house."

"The bear you saw wasn't very far from it."

Elizabella paused considering that. She shook her head. Bridgette was being foolish, and Hannah needed the water. She walked outside and checked in every direction. No bear, not even a growl. Now who was being foolish?

She started to head to the well. Her arms and legs felt wobbly, and every footstep seemed sluggish, as if she were walking through molasses. She reached the well and lowered the bucket. Her arms ached.

Was this the seasoning? Hannah was obviously overcome by something. This could be why she seemed so restless all day, but they'd only been here a couple of months. How could it have struck so soon?

She struggled to crank the rope to lift the full bucket. The muscles in her arms burned with every turn. When the pail finally reached the place where she could grab it, she filled the pitcher, then sank to the ground. Her head pounded. When she struggled to stand, she felt so weak she couldn't manage it. Shivers went through her.

"Miss, can I assist you?" It was one of the servants, a scrawny young man named Henry.

"Thank ye." She allowed Henry to help her up. "Get the water pitcher."

Henry complied. She held his arm and took one step at a time toward the door of their room. When she reached for the handle, she heard a growl. Terror caused the hair on the nape of her neck to rise. Not daring to look back, she opened the door and stepped inside. Henry stepped in long enough to set the pitcher on the table, then nodded to the women, and closed the door behind him.

Elizabella ran to the door and bolted it. "The bear is out there. I heard it."

Bridgette drew the back of her hand to her mouth. "Do you think it can get to us?"

Elizabella knelt on the floor beside Hannah and poured the water into a basin. "Nay, this house is well built, and the door is securely bolted. Besides the servants are keeping watch." She felt Hannah's head. So hot. "Get me a cloth.

Bridgette did so, and she wet it and placed it on Hannah's forehead. Elizabella rested with her back against the wall and shivered. So cold. Mayhap, she should send one of the servants to fetch Constance. She'd know how to treat the seasoning. *Lord, guide their steps to find that bear.*

Chapter Twenty-Five

As the cabin came into view, Hugh couldn't help the excitement stirring within. Hunting game had always been a pleasant diversion, especially so with big game like bear, but that was not what coursed through him now. He so wanted to drop the game bags he'd been carrying for over a mile and take Hannah into his arms.

There were difficult tasks ahead of him. After he acknowledged everything to the Burgess, there would be severe consequences. Then he would need to make preparations to return to the village with Wupun's demanded supplies. None of these things caused the trepidation he expected. With the Lord and Hannah by his side, he could face anything.

He turned to his brother. "I'll depart from you now. I desire to see my wife."

Miles nodded. "I look forward to seeing Miss Clark. I missed her while she was away helping Constance."

Hugh grinned. "Why don't you marry that girl? It's obvious you're enamored with her."

Miles gave him a rueful smile, then gazed toward the big house. "I've considered it, but she has made it evident she doesn't want to stay here. Her desire is to return to London."

Hugh set a hand on his brother's shoulder. "None but the brave deserved the fair. Ask her. Mayhap she'll decide being with you has greater attractions."

"Mayhap."

"If not, you could take her to London with you when you visit Father."

Miles delivered a glare that caused Hugh to hasten to find his wife. He opened the door to their home with a grin on his face. "Hannah."

She wasn't there. Only an empty room. Perchance she stayed in the women's room off the main house while he was gone. He hurried to find her.

Before he reached the main house, Miles came from the women's room, face pale.

Hugh's stomach roiled, and he hastened his pace. "What's wrong?"

"The seasoning."

It was all Miles said, but it was enough. Their brothers and a number of their servants had died from the mysterious ailment in the past. Miles and he had suffered from it as well, but somehow, they'd survived. Bile rose from the back of his throat, and he rushed inside.

Hannah lay by the fireplace, moaning and holding her stomach. Miss

Clark lay nearby. He touched Hannah's forehead. So hot.

Miss Atwood placed a cool cloth on hers and then on Miss Clark's forehead. "Master, what would you have me do?"

Miles' Adam's apple bulged. "I don't... I..."

"Go to the Wright farm." Hugh's voice came out raspy. He cleared his throat and tried to remember to breathe. "Get Constance. She'll know what to do."

"But what about the bear?"

"The bear is dead," Miles said, his decisiveness returning. "Go! Now!"

Miss Atwood did what he said. Hugh heard the door close but didn't look up. He couldn't look away from Hannah. How could he ever live without her?

Her eyes opened a little. "Hugh." Her voice was so weak.

"I'm here." The words barely passed the thickness in his throat.

"It came on suddenly."

"Shhh." He dipped water out of the pitcher and placed the dipper to her lips. "Drink a little."

She obeyed. "Did you... find the bear?"

"Aye." Hugh swiped at a tear rolling down his cheek. "We have enough bear meat for months."

"Good." Her eyes closed.

A strangled sob escaped him. *Lord, please, don't let her die.*

~~~~~

For the moment, Miss Clark slept. Miles was grateful for it since every time she awoke, she would moan in pain and grip her middle. He kept a pot near her for when she emptied the contents of her stomach and held her hair back as she did.

Constance had warned him to give her water even though she couldn't keep it down, but as much as he tried, she kept getting weaker. Then there were the nightmares where she kept calling out her own name.

Hannah was no better. Hugh hadn't left her side in two days, and Miles frequently heard his brother praying or sobbing in the middle of the night.

Miss Atwood and Constance had retired to the main house to get some sleep. It was taking a lot from Constance, nursing and caring for a babe and his sick wife... He took in a sharp breath. He meant servant, but not for long. When she recovered from this wretched illness, he would not wait another moment to make her his bride. If she would have him.

Lord, save her from this plague. He couldn't lose another woman he loved.

Miss Atwood had fallen ill as well, but she seemed to be faring better. Her energy was gone, and her forehead slightly warm, and she made frequent trips to the outhouse, but she still helped Constance with Miss Clark's and Hannah's care. He let up a prayer of thanks that she'd held off becoming John's wife for another month.
~~~~~

Miles heard the door open and knew they were back, but he didn't bother looking up to greet them. Instead, he wet a cloth and placed it on Miss Clark's forehead.

Constance walked to the fireplace and stood, arms crossed, until she had his and Hugh's attention. "You are doing these women no good by making yourselves sick. You haven't left their sides for two days."

Hugh protested. "I won't leave her."

"Nonsense," Constance said. "All your doting is getting in my way. I have enough of the sickly to care for. Be gone with you both. Stew is cooking in the hearth of the main house. Eat, sleep, then come back if you desire."

Miles glanced over at his brother. Hugh looked as horrified as he felt. "She's right." As much as he didn't want to depart, what Constance said made sense.

Hugh nodded and kissed Hannah on the forehead. Miles desired to do the same with Miss Clark but stopped himself. Even while she was ill, it would not be proper to kiss unless they were wed. He stood and followed his brother to the main house.

Later, as they were eating, Hugh pushed his plate away. "Mayhap, we should try to sleep as Constance suggested."

Miles agreed but doubted he would be able to. How could he when everyone he loved was taken away?

~~~~~

It had been three weeks of wetting cloths, holding buckets, trying to get the women to drink water, but no progress had been made. To Miles, it seemed they might have gotten worse.

Fortunately, Miss Atwood had already recovered and was able to help Constance care for Hannah and Miss Clark. They had taken turns sitting with the women while the other two took slept and prepared meals. It was his turn to sit with them.

Planting needed to start in the next week or two, or there wouldn't be a decent crop. It was already mid-June, and they should have started a couple of weeks ago. If that weren't bad enough, Hugh would have to meet with the council next week to get the supplies he needed in time, not only copper, but cloth as well, since Miss Clark was in no condition to weave.

No matter. Hugh wouldn't leave Hannah any more than Miles would leave Miss Clark. If nothing else, it had become clear that this woman he'd hired as a servant had filled a place in his heart that Mary's death had left empty. When she recovered, he would declare his affections for her and ask her hand in marriage.

If she recovered.

Miss Clark moaned, and Miles held her hand and stroked her hair. She opened her eyes. Every time she'd woken before, it was to be sick, so he grabbed the bowl.

"No need." Her voice sounded so weak. "I feel a little better. Could I
~~~~~

have some broth?"

His knees gave way, and tears welled up behind his eyelids. "Of course. I'll get it for you."

She closed her eyes, and he tried to convince himself he didn't imagine that she was beginning to recover. He ran outside to the main house and called to Miss Atwood. "Miss Clark, she's asking for broth."

"'Tis good news. I'll fetch it." She grabbed a cup from the shelf and filled it with broth from soup she was heating in the hearth. "What about Hannah?"

The giddiness that filled Miles a moment earlier dissipated, replaced by a knot in his stomach. "Still the same." He carried the cup of broth to the women's room.

Miss Clark was awake and had propped herself up against the wall.

He couldn't help the relief flooding him even if Hannah was still overcome. He sat beside her and handed her the cup.

She took a sip. "How long have I been sick?"

"Three weeks."

"And Hannah?"

"She's doing poorly." He wiped his hand over his face and deliver a slight smile that didn't reach his swollen eyes. "You're recovering. She shall also."

"Aye." Miss Clark took another sip of broth.

"When you've fully recuperated, I have something to talk about with you."

Miss Clark gazed in Hannah's direction. "And I you, but now is not the time."

Miles stood and poured her some water. "Rest. You need your strength." He strode to Hannah and felt her forehead. Still burning with fever. He glanced toward Miss Clark. She'd fallen asleep.

The door opened, and Hugh walked in and rushed to Hannah's side. "Miss Atwood told me what happened."

Miles placed his hand on his brother's shoulder. "No change with your wife."

Hugh wet a cloth and lay it on her forehead. "The council meets soon. I can't delay meeting with them."

Miles didn't say anything. He didn't know what to say. Hugh had to go. The colony's safety depended on it, but how could he leave his wife like this?

Hugh sat against the wall, pulled his knees to his chest, crossed his arms, and buried his head into them as he sobbed.

Miles silently prayed for Hannah. He knew the pain his brother was going through.

Hugh lifted his head, tears still in his eyes. "It was foolish, after what I've done, thinking I could find happiness, that God's mercy would cover all of my sin."

"Don't berate yourself. It only makes things harder."

Hugh kissed Hannah's forehead and sobbed again. When he was able to get himself together, he turned to Miles. "I'll leave two days hence. Take care of her while I'm gone."

"Miss Clark is recovering, and I shall accompany you. We'll leave your wife in Miss Atwood's and Constance's care."

"Lord, I put my trust in You." After uttering the prayer, Hugh leaned his head against the wall and let out a mournful sigh.

Miles wished he could do something, anything, to assist his brother. *Lord, we need a miracle.*

Hannah's eyes fluttered open. A good sign, but he dared not get his hopes up. Even with God's mercy, Mary had died. So had his brothers. Hannah's eyes opened completely, and she stood to her feet. Miles placed his hand over his chest, unable to speak. He couldn't believe it. Surely, he was dreaming. People weren't that sick one moment and standing the next. How could this happen?

Hannah placed her hand on Hugh's head, brushing back his dark hair. "Do not grieve, husband," Hannah said. "The Lord has heard your prayer."

~~~~~

Hugh's head jerked up, and his mouth gaped wide. He would have stood and immediately taken her in his arms, but he couldn't get his legs to move. He felt light-headed and wobbly inside. "'Tis a dream?"

His wife laughed. "Nay, I am quite well."

He laughed with her. When he had recovered enough to stand, he swept her in his arms and kissed her so passionately that he wasn't sure he could ever let go.

Miles cleared his throat.

Hugh's face heated. He had forgotten anyone was in the room. Then he laughed again and raised his hands in the air. "Praise be to our Lord."

At this point, his brother laughed too. The mirth filled the room until Hugh was not sure he would ever be able to stop, but if he was so destined to this hilarity for eternity, so be it. He took Hannah in his arms again, careful to give her a chaste kiss this time.

The mirth poured out of the bellies of each. How Miss Clark slept through all of it, he knew not. By the time Miss Clark woke, the laughter had died down, but Hugh enjoyed watching her astonishment as Hannah relayed the story of the Lord healing her. Then Miss Clark began to guffaw also, a belly laugh deep from inside of her that caused the others to join in her merriment.

For a time, none of them could speak except to utter praises. Hugh fell on his face, in awe of what the Lord had done for him, for Hannah. It was a miracle as great as the ones in Scripture.

After the titters calmed, Hugh motioned his brother outside so they
~~~~~

could talk. "With such a miracle in our midst, I believe I could face anything the council decides with the peace that the Lord brings. I don't want to delay. We'll go into town tomorrow."

"Agreed," Miles said. "I'll speak on your behalf. What about Hannah?"

"She'll want to come with us and support me, but I think it not wise. She has just recovered, be it so completely, and Miss Clark still needs her care. It's best we release Constance to return to her home with her babe."

"A wise decision." Miles said. "In a week or two, Miss Clark should be recovered enough to continue her chores. With your blessing, I'll tell your situation. We have need of her weaving skills."

"Tell her all of it if you like." Hugh chuckled. "Soon, the whole colony shall know my transgressions, and I welcome the truth to be revealed."

Miles set a hand on Hugh's shoulder and squeezed gently, a sign that his forgiveness was complete. Another miracle to be thankful for.

Chapter Twenty-Six

At dusk, Miles had Miss Atwood warm some broth. Pouring the broth into a cup, he left instructions for the girl. "I'll take care of Miss Clark this evening. You've been so busy caring for the ill, I'm sure you'll have tasks to keep you busy. I'll let you know when you can retire.

He took the cup of broth and his Holy Bible to the women's room and knocked.

"Come in," Miss Clark said.

Miles opened the door and smiled. The color had come back in her cheeks, and even though she had not made the miraculous recovery Hannah did, she was obviously well on her way.

He sat beside her and handed her the cup. "How are you feeling?"

"Weak but better. I'm still amazed at what happened with Hannah. It's like one of those miracles Jesus performed when He made lame men walk and the blind to see."

"Aye." His heart beat wildly in his chest. Suddenly, he was nervous around her. What did Hugh always say? *None but the brave deserve the fair.* How true. "I brought the Holy Bible. I thought it's been so long since I read to you..."

"I'd like that." Miss Clark took a sip of broth. "After the reading, could we converse? I have need to tell you something."

"Of course," Miles said. "I wanted to talk with you as well." He didn't plan to propose marriage yet. That could wait until they returned home from the Burgess, but he did need to tell her about Hugh. As soon as she had enough strength, she'd need to start weaving. "Shall we begin?"

Miss Clark nodded.

Because Hannah's miraculous recovery was still in his thoughts, he started with James five, verses thirteen through sixteen. "Is any among you afflicted? Let him pray. Is any merry? Let him sing psalms. Is any sick among you? Let him call for the elders of the church; and let them pray over him, anointing him with oil in the name of the Lord: And the prayer of faith shall save the sick, and the Lord shall raise him up; and if he have committed sins, they shall be forgiven him. Confess your faults one to another, and pray one for another, that ye may be healed. The effectual fervent prayer of a righteous man availeth much."

He gazed at Miss Clark, expecting to see the anticipation he usually found when he read Scripture, but it wasn't there. Instead, her eyes glistened with tears. "Pardon me. You have not yet recovered, and I've tired you."

"Please stay." She reached out and touched his arm. "I have a confession to make."

"A confession?" His heart started to race. "What kind of confession?"

She glanced at her hands, then back at him. "I have lied to you, and I wish to make a full account of it."

A heaviness came over him. Mayhap, this was the Lord showing him she wasn't the woman he thought her to be. He swallowed back the lump in his throat. "Go on."

She let out a sigh. "I only ask you to listen to my whole story before you respond. Then I'll accept your judgement."

His judgement? What had she done that judgement was necessary? "I'll wait."

"My name is not Honesty. She is my younger sister. I am Elizabella Clark."

The hair on the back of his neck stiffened. He suppressed the urge to berate her because of his promise, but the anger rose into his throat. What had she done that she had to take her sister's name to board the ship?

"My sister is fifteen years old. I'm twenty-three. 'Tis the truth we own a seamstress shop in the heart of London. Honesty had a heartbreak and planned to sail to Jamestown to marry another. I was against it. I refused to accompany her to the ship."

The muscle in his jaw twitched. He wanted to shout. *What does that have to do with you taking her place? Why did you deceive me?* But he remained silent, his hands grasping the arms of the chair.

Then she told the rest, how she had chased after her sister, how she'd seen a murder which led to her sister being stabbed, and how the murderers were at the dock when she went to the ship to inform them of the tragedy. With each new fact, his hold on the chair relaxed further.

'Twas an amazing tale, but why did she feel the need to lie? If she'd told it to the first mate, he would have surely dealt with the murderers posthaste and sent her on her way.

Miss Clark swallowed. "I know now I should have alerted the first mate, but I was so full of fear."

All the anger he felt about being lied to dissipated, and compassion overwhelmed him. He took hold of her hands and gazed into her eyes. "The way you chased off those ruffians with a pitchfork to save your sister is admirable, and I can understand your trepidation, but why didn't you inform the ship's captain of the error or tell Constance or me when you arrived in Jamestown? Surely, something could have been done."

Her hands trembled within his. A tear rolled down her cheek. "I wanted to, but I couldn't take the risk."

He squeezed her hands tighter to let her know he held no ill will toward her. "Why would they not believe you? Help me understand."

Another tear. "When my brother died, my father hauled me before the king's court and accused me of murder. He told them it wasn't an accident, that I didn't want to take care of Benjamin and Honesty anymore, so I started the fire on purpose."

He took a sharp breath as if he had been punched in the stomach. "Why would your father say that?"

"I don't know. The drink made him a cruel man." More tears. "The court ruled it an accident after hearing Honesty's account."

A warmth spread through Miles. He drew her toward him and embraced her. "I'm so sorry that happened to you. Some fathers can be cruel. I, of all people, know that." He pulled back and wiped a tear off her cheek.

"There's more." She said it so softly, he almost didn't hear her. "When the boy on the ship was caught, the captain told his men that the Burgess in Jamestown would hang him. Even so, when the ship landed, I had built up the courage to tell my story."

Understanding dawned on Miles. "That's when the boy was whipped."

She nodded.

It was right for her to be fearful, not only about telling the first mate, but about telling him. He'd allowed bitterness about his father to consume him. If she'd told him when she first arrived, God forgive him, he would have condemned her.

From this moment, he vowed to do anything to protect her. "You have been through a harrowing ordeal."

Even with her blond hair disheveled and her blue eyes wet with tears, she was so beautiful. His lips moved closer to hers, almost against his will. He shook his head to clear his thoughts. He wouldn't allow himself to kiss her unless they were wed.

The closeness of her made him dizzy. He backed away. No matter how much he loved her, he couldn't ask her to marry him. She had sailed to Jamestown against her will, and she wanted nothing more than to return to London. "Let me help you."

"How?"

His thoughts jumbled. If he took her away, he'd never see her again. Mayhap it would be better to convince her to stay. "How?"

"How can you help me in my plight?" Miss Clark stood and stepped toward him. "I wouldn't allow you to release me and pay my way to London. 'Twould be unfair to you."

Even in her distress, she thought only of him. Guilt gripped him. "Give me a moment."

He strode outside and looked to Heaven. A heaviness rested on his chest until he could barely breathe. There was no need for prayer. God had answered him, but he wanted none of it. He was to return Miss Clark to London, see his father, and return without her.

"Lord, is there any other way?"

~~~~~

Elizabella sat in the rocker, stunned. She had told him the truth, and he'd shown sympathy. Had there ever been a kinder man? When he'd embraced her, she could feel his vigor comforting and conveying his strength to her.

For a moment, he almost looked like he wanted to kiss her. If there was any chance for them, she might have leaned into the kiss, but he lived in Jamestown. He'd said himself he would never go to London again, and she had to. She needed to see if her sister fared well.

She dozed in front of the warm fire. For how long, she knew not. A door flew open and startled her awake. Slowly, she eased off the chair and turned around. Master Bonneville stood there, a sheen in his eyes.

"I'm going to London in my brother's place. When the *London Merchant* sails at the beginning of September, you shall accompany me."

Heat swept over her. She could barely believe it was that easy to gain passage to London. She should have told her master as soon as she arrived, but could she take advantage of him like this? "Nay, your brother desires to see your father. You had no such intention until I told my story of woe. I won't let you do this for me."

He motioned her to sit, and he sat in the other rocker. "My brother behaved shamefully before he married Hannah. A Native squaw he'd been with ended up with child, but she died in the birthing. So did the child."

Elizabella gasped. "Does Hannah know?"

"Aye, apparently he never hid it from her, but he is in trouble."

"How so?"

Master Bonneville's Adam's apple bulged. "The chief is demanding Hugh pay his debt to the girl's family. He must provide twenty woven cloths and five copper pans by the middle of August. Then he must stay in Jamestown and provide meat for the family until the youngest, a mere child, is wed."

She touched his arm. "You must be devastated to know your brother behaved thusly."

"I was at first, but his repentance is real, and I have forgiven him."

"Why would you make the trip to London only because he cannot? And why pay for my journey?"

Master Bonneville took hold of her hands. The touch was gentle, but it caused an excitement to course through her. "'Twas partly my fault. I have a tendency to be prideful and judgmental."

Elizabella chuckled. "Surely not."

"Shocking, I know." He cleared his throat. "The Lord has been showing me I am this way because I have never forgiven my father. I must see him again if it's not too late. Besides, the journey is already paid for."

A lightness overtook her, but she couldn't believe it yet. "'Tis too much.
~~~~~

I haven't fulfilled my contract with you for the first journey. Tis wrong to expect you to pay more."

Master Bonneville delivered a crooked smile. "You'll fulfill your obligation."

She placed her hand on her chest. "But how when the ship sails so soon?"

"Miss Atwood and Hannah shall do the cooking and other chores until Miss Atwood is released to marry. You'll use the thread you brought from London and work from dawn to dusk weaving the fabric we need. If you accomplish the task, I'll consider your debt paid. Do you agree to this arrangement?"

"'Tis a lot of work and only ten weeks away." She could easily weave a coverlet in a week if there weren't any fancy imprints or dying needed, but twenty in ten weeks? Even with the two coverlets she'd made since coming to Jamestown, she would be able to do nothing but weave, and then she wasn't sure she'd finish in time. "Most would not be able to complete such a task, but I might be able to if Hannah would help me warp the loom whenever I start a new piece."

"I'm sure Hannah shall assist however she's needed."

A laugh escaped her. "Master Bonneville, I vow to finish in time." God was answering her prayer, and she was so happy. She was going home.

"Miss Clark?" He cleared his throat. "I'll no longer be your master. Could you call me by my given name?"

She gave a faint smile. "You may call me Elizabella."

"Elizabella. 'Tis a beautiful name."

"Thank ye. We have a lot of work ahead of us in the next two months, Sir Miles, but I would still enjoy having our nightly Bible readings even if you have to read while I work."

Miles gave a slight nod.

She wanted to reach out and comfort him. She could imagine how hard it was for him leaving his brother during this trouble. He was as much of a protector for Hugh as she was for Honesty.

And she would miss him.

Chapter Twenty-Seven

Hugh took long strides on the path to the fort. He wanted nothing more than to put this behind him.

"Wait up," Miles said. "You're walking as if a bear were chasing you."

Hugh shrugged. "Not a bear. Perchance my own thoughts." He stopped to allow them both to catch their breath.

"Is there any way I can talk you out of the foolish endeavor?"

"Aye." Hugh stroked his chin. "I know you could, but please don't. The Lord is requiring me to face up to this. It is difficult enough tamping down my own arguments against it."

Miles gazed at him, a slight smile creasing his face. "I would do anything to spare you the consequences, but I am delighted by the change in you." His voice cracked. "Mary and I prayed you would come to a saving faith in the Lord."

Hugh swallowed back the lump in his throat. "I caused such a burden for so many years."

"No matter. It was worth it to see your transformation. Ready to start again at a slower pace?"

Hugh nodded. "What did Miss Clark say when you told her of my transgressions?"

"She has vowed to finish weaving the cloth in time for your mission."

"Wonderful news." It seemed all would be taken care of. He furrowed his brow. Except Father. Nobody would be with Father when he faced the king's court... Unless he already had. Miles had sworn he would never return to England, but dare he inquire? "I have a favor to ask of you."

"Anything."

"I can't leave the colony, but you can. Would you sail to London to be with Father? I vow to keep the plantation thriving while you're gone."

"You needn't ask. The Lord desires me to travel to London to forgive him. Elizabella has told me her story. I'll take her with me."

Relief washed over him. He raised an eyebrow. Miles had never used the given name of a servant before. "Elizabella?"

Miles blushed. "Miss Clark then."

"Does that mean she accepted your marriage proposal?"

"Nay, I never asked." The muscle in Miles' jaw twitched. "She is set on going to England where she says she belongs. My home is in Jamestown."

"How can she make that choice if you give her no other?"

Miles stopped and stared at a rock on the ground. "I don't wish to cause her distress about this, nor do I desire to go through another heartbreak."

Hugh placed his hand on his brother's shoulders. "Reconsider. Your heart shall break when you leave, whether you ask for her hand or not."

"True enough. I'll think on your words." Miles began walking again.

Hugh kept up with his pace, and soon they were at the fort. He wiped his hand over his face. *Lord, give me the courage I need.*

They entered the church and found the council already assembled.

"Greeting Masters Bonneville," Master Douglas said. "Do we have a new member of the council I didn't know about?"

"Hush," Captain Lawnes said. "I'm sure the younger Bonneville brother wouldn't be here unless he had urgent business about the Powhatans."

Hugh let out a deep breath. "Aye, I do."

Everyone started talking among themselves to the point where nobody could hear what anyone else had to say.

"Quiet!" Governor Yeardley pounded his gavel.

The men grew silent.

"What say the Natives?"

Hugh swallowed the lump in his throat but couldn't manage to speak.

Captain Lawnes stood. "If the Powhatan refuse to meet, we may be in more danger than we thought."

"I agree. You must know about my meeting with the chief as soon as possible."

Miles placed a hand on his shoulder.

Hugh was grateful for the support. He told the men everything, including the chief's response. "So, there you have it."

John let out a haughty laugh. "So, the high and mighty Miles Bonneville has a brother guilty of fornication. What say you, men? Surely, he should at least be publicly whipped."

Miles turned and grabbed hold of John's shirt.

"Stop it!" Hugh pulled him back. "He speaks the truth."

Miles let go and kneaded the back of his neck.

"Always loved to watch a good public whipping." Master Douglas stood and stomped his right foot.

Governor Yeardley glared at both John and Douglas. "We first have business to attend to." He turned to Hugh. "How much do you need to pay off Chief Opechancanough?"

"Five copper pots and twenty woven sheets of cloth. One of our servants is providing the garments, but we are in need of five copper pots and have no tobacco to purchase them until the harvest."

"I can sell you two of mine," Master Douglas said. "You can pay me after the harvest."

"We'll provide enough to purchase them out of the town's funds." Governor Yeardley turned his gaze toward Hugh. "I have all the cooper you need, but you shall pay dearly for it after you harvest your crop, say twice what it's worth."

Hugh nodded. "Agreed."

"Now, time to carry out the punishment."

Hugh squared his shoulders but couldn't stop the lump choking out the air in his throat.

"Why such haste?" Miles said. "My brother hasn't had a trial or been sentenced. You have no right."

"No need for a trial," the governor said. "He just confessed. Twenty strokes for adultery. If you remember, that's what Goodman Cooper received."

Miles' face turned red. "Hugh's crime is fornication, not adultery."

Captain Lawnes spoke, his voice low and menacing. "Goodman Cooper didn't risk the colony with his indiscretion. Or would you prefer we charge your brother with treason and hang him?"

Miles gasped.

A calm came over Hugh that surprised him. Nothing was required of him other than to surrender to the inevitable. Somehow, that revelation made it easier. "'Tis a fair sentence."

Governor Yeardley set his jaw. "All right then. Are we in agreement?"

The men shouted aye.

"I'm not in agreement with any of this." Miles pressed his lips together and glared at each of them. "I vote nay."

"Miles, please, let it be," Hugh said.

"The ayes have it," Yeardley said. "Men, take hold of Hugh and strap him to fence posts."

"No need." Hugh brushed aside the arms grabbing for him. "I'll walk there of my own accord."

~~~~~

It had been weeks since Elizabella had agreed to weave so much cloth in so little time. She had another four weeks before it was due, and she'd only finished ten sheets. Adding the two she brought with her, that left eight more.

Setting up the loom for the next piece would take hours. She and Hannah started the next piece by laying the warp thread across the loom. She was happy Miles had asked Hannah and Bridgette to carry out her chores, but Bridgette had left to marry, leaving Hannah with the brunt of the work.

If Elizabella didn't finish in time, Hannah's husband would be in grave danger. It was bad enough when he came home after being whipped by the colony for his indiscretions. She never understood why men in charge punished with such cruel methods.

Waves of gratitude to God and to Miles swept over her. Miles could have treated her thusly. Instead, he had compassion. He was even
~~~~~

cancelling her debt and sailing with her to England in five weeks' time. What other master would go to such lengths?

As she placed another row of thread on the loom, her stomach felt as if a flock of geese had taken residence in her stomach. It would be pleasant to have him with her during the journey, but she wasn't looking forward to the day of their parting.

Their nightly Bible readings had somehow turned into something more. A fondness for him grew within her no matter how she tried to tamp down those feelings. Honesty needed her, and she'd promised her mother she would protect her. She would return to London where she belonged, and Miles would sail back to Jamestown to protect his brother and work his farm.

Enough of this. She needed to concentrate on her work. She turned, bumping hard into the loom, and dropped the yarn. "Owww."

"Are you all right?" Hannah asked.

"Aye." Elizabella rubbed her thigh where she'd run into the loom. "'Tis a clumsy oaf who doesn't look where she's going."

Hannah let out a chuckle. "I'll finish the row. Why don't you take a walk and get some fresh air?"

"Nay, time is not on our side."

"And if you keep making mistakes, it will take twice as long." Hannah stood with her hands on her hips. "I'll work on setting the warp while you're gone. Then you can come and take over with your vigor restored."

Elizabella hated to admit the soundness of the advice with so much work ahead of her. She let out a sigh. "Only for a moment. I'll return soon."

She strolled outside toward the field where the men were seeing to the crops. They had started planting as soon as the men had returned from the fort, although Hugh had taken a couple of days to recover before he'd joined them.

Now the crops were sprouting, but there was still plenty of work for the men to do. They cultivated the soil daily to keep the weeds and cutworms at bay. Soon, the cultivation would stop and the daily inspection for worms and insects would begin. Then the plants would be primed and topped in preparation for a fine crop's harvest.

Miles raked the ground, his arms bulging. His servants were loyal to him and gave him a full day's work, but Miles worked harder than them all. Her stomach fluttered. If only there were a way to stay here with him.

She shook her head. 'Twas folly to think that way. She needed to travel to London to take care of her sister. What must Honesty think by now? Perchance she'd given her up as dead. Her sister would have never considered that she had sailed for Jamestown. She had to return and reassure her as soon as possible.

Besides, she had no reason to believe Miles cared for her in the same way she did for him. He had been a kind master and had shown her the way to her Lord, but wouldn't he do that for any lost soul? Even if he had some affection for her, he could never leave this place for long. He also had a younger brother to protect.

Why would anyone willingly leave this paradise forever unless they had no choice? She let out a sigh. If only she had a choice.

Jamestown, the colony she dreaded, had taken root in her heart. There was room to breathe here without the stuffiness and the foul smells of the city. She took a whiff of air and smelled flowers and fresh dew, not the butchered pigs and sewage that assaulted her senses in London. Here, in the middle of the night, there wasn't yelling and horse carriages crowding the night sounds. Instead, night birds, crickets, and frogs serenaded her.

She wiped a tear falling down her cheek. *Lord, help me to forget Jamestown and Miles. Help me to love my old life in London as I once did.* The peace she normally felt when she prayed didn't come to her this time. Perchance the Lord required obedience first. The peace would come when she returned to London.

She walked back into the house. Hannah had made great progress with the warp. She hurriedly set about helping Hannah finish.

It took until noonday to set the pattern. She stepped back and took a look at it. "Thank ye, Hannah. Why don't you take nourishment? I'll get started on this."

Hannah nodded. "You should take your own counsel."

Elizabella's stomach rumbled. Dare she take time to eat? Nay, there weren't enough hours of daylight as it was. "I'll take my midday meal after I begin the weft."

Hannah left, and Elizabella pulled out her weft thread and began threading it into the warp. At least, there was no need for a complicated pattern. She would have never finished in time if that had been required.

Time passed, and the weaving started going faster. She might be able to finish this coverlet by tomorrow evening, thanks to Hannah. She started another row.

A knock on the door interrupted her. "May I come in?" Miles' voice.

Her stomach fluttered, and she set her threads down carefully. "Enter."

Miles opened the door. He wore a good amount of dirt on his face and clothes and carried a plate of stew in one hand and a cup in the other. He set them on the small table in front of the hearth. "When you didn't come for the midday or evening meals, I thought you might be deep in your labors with no time to fetch food."

"Aye, 'tis true." She looked out the window. It wasn't dusk yet, but the sun was low in the sky. Her stomach growled to remind her she'd been too long at her task without paying it mind.

"Wouldn't hurt to take a moment to eat, so I brought this feast to your domicile."

She smiled and sat at the table. "A feast indeed. Would you like to sit with me?"

He glanced at the door. "I suppose it would be all right."

"Don't allow me to keep you from your work."

A crooked grin caused his dimples to deepen. "My work is almost finished for the day, but I daresay you will continue into nightfall by candlelight." He sat across from her. "That is why you must take nourishment."

She started eating, suddenly realizing how hungry she was.

"I suppose you'll be pleased to start your journey to London."

"Aye, I miss my sister."

His dimples faded. "Aye, your sister. And England. I'm sure you miss your home."

If only he knew how much she'd grown to love this land. "Of course, I'll miss Jamestown. If there is a more bountiful land, I have yet to know it." She wiped her hand across her mouth. "But as you say, London is my home. My sister is there... and my sewing shop."

"Aye, well..." Miles stood and headed to the door. "I shan't keep you any longer. Hugh shall wonder where I've been off to."

"Thank ye." She stood, an emptiness taking over despite the hearty meal. "For the food, I mean. Shall we meet here for Bible reading again tonight so I can work as I listen?"

Miles gave a crisp nod. "Until then." He walked out the door.

If only she could find a way to tell him how much he meant to her and how much she would miss their time together. Nay, she couldn't. No matter how beautiful Jamestown was, she would never leave her sister in London. Some things were best left unsaid.

~~~~~

Miles reached down to grab his rake, but he couldn't stop thinking of Elizabella and how he would have to leave her in London. He wanted to tell her the truth about his feelings for her, but it would only make the parting more difficult.

"Did you speak to her?" Hugh asked from the next row.

"Speak to who?"

Hugh dropped the rake, crossed his arms, and delivered a glare so dangerous that Miles had to forsake what he was doing or risk having his brother's dagger eyes cutting his flesh.

He dropped the rake. "Aye, when I brought her the evening meal."

"And?"

Miles shrugged. "She's looking forward to her journey to London and to seeing her sister again. She is adamant about it. I shan't act the fool by proposing to a woman who doesn't want me or my land."

"How do you know if you don't ask her? You love her. Declare it, or you're a fool."

"She has an obligation to her sister. If I told her the truth, it wouldn't
~~~~~

change things, but it would make both of us miserable. I shan't be the cause of her unhappiness."

Hugh let out a gusty sigh. "A good woman makes a man, but a fool remains a fool." He continued raking his row. "I've never known you to intentionally deceive."

Cords tightened in Miles' neck in the same way Elizabella's loom pulled on thread. He didn't bother to answer. Instead, he took out his frustration on the ground with his rake. He'd almost wished he hadn't told his brother how he felt about her.

The honorable thing to do was journey back to England with Elizabella and then say farewell, but his brother's comment made him unsure of what was best. He wasn't in the habit of deceiving. He was trying to help Elizabella by sacrificing his happiness for hers. That was the honorable thing to do, but the thought kept nudging him.

The truth was an honorable thing also.

Chapter Twenty-Eight

Hugh finished loading the copper, cloth, another buck, and a couple of turkeys onto the raft at the river's edge. The turkeys were not required, but it didn't hurt to make a gesture of good will. It amazed him that Elizabella was able to finish all twenty pieces. She hadn't completed the last one until this morning, causing his journey to be later than he planned. It would be a relief to deliver the goods and be done with it. Not exactly true. He would deliver more game three months hence and continue to supply it for a long time to come.

All that was left was his farewell to Hannah. He swept her in his arms and kissed her deeply, hoping it wouldn't be their last. "I'll return as soon as I can. Perchance a day or two."

"I'm fearful." She buried her head into his shoulder. "What if the Powhatan decide to take the bounty and slaughter you as well?"

He pulled her chin up until she faced him and did his best to hide his own trepidation with a false smile. "They shan't harm me as long as I provide meat for Wupun's family. Do not fear. I'll return unscathed."

Hannah nodded, but a tear rolled down her cheek.

He wiped the tear and gave her a wink. "Your fears are unwarranted. With the bounty I'm delivering to them, they'd be foolish to harm me now." He gave her a tender kiss and a quick hug he hoped would reassure her. "Take comfort. I'll return soon."

Miles ran toward them. "Brother, wait."

Hugh gave his wife one last peck on the cheek. "Perchance you should return to your cooking."

Hannah glanced in Miles' direction, nodded, and headed to the main house.

Hugh watched Miles rushing past her on the way to the river. What was he about? Miles had told Hugh he wanted to go with him to the village, but Hugh had refused. The Powhatan would only be expecting him.

Miles soon reached him. "I'm accompanying you." He climbed onto the raft.

"We've already been through this." Hugh climbed on beside him. "Tis best if I go alone."

Miles' brow furrowed, and his jaw set. "I'm going with you." The determined glare showed there was nothing to be done.

"It's too dangerous." It was hopeless to convince his brother to stay, but Hugh had to try. "This might anger the chief. What then?"

"He won't concern himself with me if you have the bounty he asked for. It's not like we're going there with an army. We're two men."

"I still don't like it," Hugh said.

Miles grabbed the pole and pushed them offshore. "I'm going, and there's nothing you can do to stop me."

Hugh let out an exasperated grunt. "You're a persistent man." He grabbed for the pole. "I'll at least guide the raft."

Miles nodded and sat, causing it to shift slightly.

"You used to be the wise brother," Hugh said. "Following me to the lion's den is not prudent. What happens if they decide to slaughter us both?"

Miles grabbed his musket. "I'll fight alongside you."

"There's nothing you can do to stop it. We have two muskets and a hunting knife between us, and there are over a thousand braves waiting to meet us. What about the women if something happens to both of us? How shall they fare?"

"Nothing will happen." Miles kneaded the back of his neck. "If we don't return, I've instructed Elizabella to release the men and sail with your wife to England next month."

Hugh threw his hands in the air and strode to the other side of the raft, as far away from his brother as he could get in that small space. Miles would not let him face this alone any more than he'd allowed him to suffer the beating from the council without speaking on his behalf.

"Thank ye." Hugh barely huffed out the words.

Miles didn't say anything, but an insufferable grin crossed his face.

They kept quiet, each in their own thoughts, until they reached the shore of the Native village. Miles helped Hugh pull the raft onto the sand. A dozen braves surrounded them and started unloading the raft. Hugh didn't bother to help them. He wasn't sure they'd accept the assistance.

When the warriors were finished emptying the raft of the supplies, they led Hugh and his brother to the center of the village where Chief Opechancanough sat waiting for them. Wupun sat at his side.

Nobody spoke, and Hugh decided it was best to remain quiet until they did.

"Did they bring everything?" Opechancanough asked one of his braves.

The man nodded. "Aye, and turkeys as well."

"Very good. Wupun, are you satisfied?"

Wupun stood. "My daughter lies in the ground. How shall I ever be satisfied?"

Hugh swallowed hard but still kept his peace.

"Quiet, woman." The chief snapped his fingers.

Wupun sat back on the ground.

The chief placed his hand on Hugh's shoulder. "Who is this?"

"My brother." Even though the chief didn't squeeze, Hugh couldn't help but remember the bruise from last time. It took as long to heal as the beating he'd received at the fort. "I needed his help with the supplies."

Opechancanough stood in front of Miles with his arms crossed. Miles didn't speak, and soon the chief grew tired of intimidating them and stepped back. "You have fulfilled our agreement. Go, but be back in three moons with another buck."

Hugh nodded. "What about the meeting with the Jamestown council? When shall I say they can see you?"

"No need for a treaty," Opechancanough said. "We'll remain at peace unless you leave this land or until I decide we can no longer tolerate the white man's ways. Tell them to consider my words."

The lump in Hugh's throat grew larger. Opechancanough had made up his mind, and he was using Hugh's transgression with Suleta as an excuse. The random attacks on colonists would continue. Sooner or later, the Natives would declare war. It was only a matter of time. All Hugh could do was appease him for as long as he could and hope it extended the time they had to prepare. "I'll repeat what you have said."

Miles didn't respond in any way, and Hugh was grateful. No matter what his brother had said, the chief would have considered it an insult.

Opechancanough waved his hands toward the raft. "Go while I allow it, and do not bother us with your talk of a treaty again."

Warriors surrounded them and escorted them at a hurried pace toward the empty raft.

Miles grabbed the pole and pushed them out into the river.

They traveled until they could no longer see the village before Hugh managed to speak. "We have to get word to the Burgess. Someday they'll try to massacre the colony. How long that shall be I can't say."

"We'll attend to it soon. They've planned one more meeting before I sail away. We'll tell them then." Miles' brow furrowed. "I hate leaving you with this trouble brewing."

"'Tis trouble I created. I'll appease them for as long as I can."

"Mayhap, I should stay."

"And what could you do but see to it our father has no one to speak for him? I can't go. Please don't make things worse by refusing to sail."

Miles nodded. "I won't be in London long. After I see to Father's fate, I'll charter a ship across the great sea if I have to sail it myself. You shan't face them alone."

"Stay in London as long as you wish. Marry Elizabella, and build a life there."

Miles placed his hand on Hugh's shoulder, the same one the chief was fond of. "I'll return. I pledge it."

As much as he wanted Miles to return to the colony, it was best he remained in London. "Know one thing, Brother. That is one vow I don't desire for you to keep."

Miles snorted. "And yet, I shall."

Hugh let out a deep sigh. He would miss his brother. As much as he had fought with him and done everything he could to vex him, Miles had forgiven him and supported him when he needed it the most. He'd become his closest friend, closer than a brother.

Keep Your hand on him, Lord. Do what You must to make him realize his place is with Elizabella.

~~~~~

Miles had worked hard over the last month. The entire crop of tobacco wasn't ripe yet, but he'd been determined to harvest everything he could. He wouldn't leave it all on Hugh's shoulders. He had even insisted on working until they left for the fort.

Even so, he still took time with Elizabella to read God's Word. He knew he was making the parting, when it came, more sorrowful, but he couldn't help it. He needed to spend every moment with her until the day they must part ways.

Should he tell her the truth about his love for her even though she couldn't return to Jamestown? He couldn't stay in London even if he wanted to, not with this trouble brewing and his brother in the middle of it.

Which was more honorable? To let her happily depart because of his deception or to declare the truth and let her depart in misery? He knew not.

Now they'd come to Jamestown for a final meeting with the Burgess. They wouldn't return to his farm since the ship intended to leave two days hence. He and Elizabella would stay at the fort until they sailed.

Hugh had insisted he accompany Miles to the meeting. He wanted to tell them what had happened with his own words, even if they reproved him for it. He had changed so much in such a short amount of time. Miles couldn't help being proud of him.

After the meeting, Hugh and Hannah would remain at the fort until the departure. Another thing Hugh had insisted on. When they stepped into the church, everyone else was already there and waiting for them.

"Good day, Masters Bonneville." Governor Yeardley's sarcasm was evident. "So glad you decided to join us."

"I'm sailing in two days," Miles said, a bit irritated at the governor's sharp tongue. "As you well know, there's much to attend to." He bowed slightly and waved his hand with a flourish, knowing it would annoy them.

"Well..." The governor cleared his throat. "You're here now. Sir Hugh, what have you to say? When can we meet with Chief Opechancanough?"

"You won't."

The murmur filling the room caused Hugh to delay before saying more.

Governor Yeardley called for quiet. "Go on."

"The chief says he won't agree to any treaty. He says he'll keep the peace unless I leave the colony, or until he loses his patience with us."
~~~~~

"There must be something you can do to convince him," Captain Lawnes said.

"I don't have his favor at the moment." Hugh leaned against the wall and crossed his arms. "If I go back there before it's time to deliver more game, I might not come out alive." He unfolded his arms, took a couple of paces away from the wall, and wiped his face. Angry mutters erupted as he made his way back to the wall and crossed his arms again.

Miles pressed his lips together. The Burgess was not taking this well, but he'd promised not to interfere with his brother's account of it. Still, Hugh was obviously distressed. If their accusations continued, he would intervene.

"I was against this from the start." Master Douglas stood and stomped his foot. "Didn't I tell you all we'd be slaughtered in our beds if we don't do something? Now's the time before the chief decides to attack."

"And what action shall we take?" Captain Lawnes stood and started pacing. "There are thousands of them."

Master William Capp stood. "We wouldn't be facing this now if the younger Master Bonneville hadn't betrayed us. He should hang."

The others roared agreement and, as one, started toward Hugh.

Hugh just stood there, a blank expression on his face, as if he hadn't heard their ugly words.

Miles stepped in front of him. "My brother paid dearly for his sin. How many others in this colony have sampled the charms of Indian maidens? I daresay more than him."

John Cooper and a few of the others blushed and stepped back.

"Because of him, the Natives might attack at any moment," Master Capp said. "Shall we ignore the harm he has caused to the colony?"

Governor Yeardley, William Capp, and some others continued toward Hugh.

Reverend Cochran, Samuel Jorden, and John now moved to Miles' side. Miles swallowed. After the way he had treated John, he had some apologizing to do.

Reverend Cochran extended his hands as if he could stop them all with a slight shove. "Gentlemen, let us have cooler heads prevail here."

Captain Lawnes now moved to the reverend's side. "Do you plan to hang the younger Master Bonneville and make the Powhatan even angrier when he doesn't show up with game? Come now."

Master Douglas and some of the others joined Miles and the men guarding Hugh. The tide had turned.

The governor stepped back. "Perchance you do show wisdom here. Better to keep him alive and reporting to us after his visits to the village than risk hanging him and having the chief carry out reprisals."

Miles let out a breath. If nothing else had, this incident convinced him he had to return to Jamestown as soon as he saw to his father. He wouldn't leave his brother for long to face the angry horde in the colony or in the Native village.

Chapter Twenty-Nine

Elizabella hugged Hannah, who had insisted with Hugh on accompanying her and Miles to the ship. "I'll miss you."

"And I you." Hannah's eyes were moist with tears.

Hugh took Elizabella's hand. "Take good care of my brother."

She nodded. "I'll see he finds his way back to you."

A pained expression crossed Hugh's face, but it was replaced quickly by a large grin.

"Come now, Brother." Miles slapped him on the back. "Nothing shall delay my return before the spring planting."

"Not on my account." Hugh brought him in close. "Tell Father I love him, and I'm praying for him."

Miles gazed at him a moment longer. "I shall. Take care of yourself and Hannah."

"I'll do my best." Hugh glanced toward Elizabella. "Don't return on my account."

Elizabella raised an eyebrow at the odd comment.

First Mate Rogers strode to the gangplank. "Time we leave. Finish saying your farewells, or we'll sail without you."

Miles embraced his brother and slapped him on the back. "See you soon." He looped Elizabella's arm in his and escorted her up the gangplank.

They each rushed to the side of the ship and waved goodbye as the sailors brought in the gangplank and raised the anchor.

Elizabella took one last look at the colony. It had seemed like a jungle when she had first arrived. Now it was more like utopia. She longed to see her sister again, but she would miss this untamed land.

Miles stood by her side and watched as they rowed out of the channel. Soon the sail raised with a whoosh and the colony faded from view.

"I'll miss Jamestown," Elizabella said. "When I came here, I never thought there could be a more dreadful place. Now it feels more like I'm leaving a paradise."

"A paradise, mayhap." Miles said. "But with the Native trouble and the seasoning, I dare say, it has snakes."

"All paradises do."

~~~~~

They stood at the railing, watching as the ship drifted farther away from the shore. Nothing but blue skies and thud of the waves rolling against the ship.

Miles wanted to tell her how much she meant to him, but since they
~~~~~

were going their separate ways when the journey was over, some things were best left unsaid. The last time he was on a ship, he had dreaded the journey Now, he wished it wouldn't end because, when it did, he'd never see her again.

Mayhap, there was a way. Once Elizabella saw her sister was safe, she might be willing to marry and return to Jamestown.

He cleared his throat. "The last time I was on a ship, tragedy struck."

She placed her hand on his arm. "Do you wish to talk about it?"

He didn't say anything for a few moments. The memories of past torments mixed with the pain he would feel when they arrived in London, and he wasn't sure he could speak without betraying the stirring within him.

Slowly, he took a breath and let it out. "My mother insisted I take my three brothers and sister to Jamestown. After the incident with the wine, she wanted us as far from the scandal as we could get. I wanted to wait until she could come with us, but she..." He swallowed at the lump in his throat. "She was a determined woman. So, we set sail."

"Since only Hugh remains, I assume something happened to the others."

He nodded. "Henry and Thomas died during the seasoning, but Mabel never saw land."

"What transpired?"

"She became ill shortly after boarding." His voice thickened. "She never recovered."

Her blue eyes showed her compassion. "I'm so sorry for your pain."

"We all have suffered loss." He tried to make it sound casual, but it didn't come out that way. He took hold of her hand. "Your first journey wasn't pleasant either, I daresay."

She didn't pull her hand away. Instead, she leaned slightly closer. "Nay, but had I known the beauty of Jamestown..." Tears formed in her eyes. "And if I'd known the companionship I'd find there, I wouldn't have fretted so."

He squeezed her hand and took a step closer to her. "And who did you find this companionship with?" Heat coursed through him, and her touch filled him with tingles. He knew he should depart now, but like a moth to a flame, he could never walk away.

"You." Her lips parted slightly. "If only I could have stayed, but..."

He took her in his arms, and their lips seemed to join without their consent, as if they could no longer remain apart. He leaned into the kiss, the headiness of her overtaking him.

She pulled back, breathing heavily.

He released her, his shame at kissing her mixed with the desire to do it again. "Forgive me. I shouldn't have done that."

She lowered her eyes. "I was as much to blame."

Every nerve within him was on fire. He could not deny his love for her a moment longer. After kissing her as he did, there was only one honorable thing left to do. "Do you remember when you first came to Jamestown? I asked if you would marry, and you said you'd be more likely to see a bird in last year's nest."

"I remember," Elizabella said. "Now you know why I was so adamant."

He ignored her words. "The bald eagle that resides in Virginia doesn't abandon her nest once her eaglets are hatched. She adds to it and uses it for years."

She tilted her head. "What are you saying?"

"I care for you deeply." He knelt on one knee. "Marry me."

Tears welled in her eyes, and she blinked them back. She reached out to touch his arm but pulled her hand away before it reached him.

He rose slowly to his feet, an ache gripping his heart. "I know you can't give your answer until you see your sister safe, but I desire you to become my wife."

The silence between them spread like the sea surrounding the ship. With each moment, it grew until he was sure they were an ocean away from each other with no vessel to traverse the expanse.

"I do care deeply about you." Her voice was soft with a tone of regret. "If things were different, I'd be honored by your proposal, but I can't." The tears welled up again. This time, one escaped onto her cheek.

His stomach tightened as if he'd been punched, and a slight moan escaped him. "Not now. Of course, not now." His words had a pleading quality, but he couldn't help it. "After you see your sister. After you make sure she's safe."

She turned away and stared at the endless blue waves thudding against the side of the ship. "I can never leave my sister. I vowed to my mother to take care of her and keep her safe. I'm already responsible for Benjamin's death. I can't desert her even for you."

He took hold of her shoulders and turned her around to face him. Her tears almost made him gasp. He would do anything to wipe them away. "We'll take her with us when we return. She'd already planned to become a Jamestown bride. Marry me, and I'll see she finds the worthiest of husbands."

She pressed her lips together. "And how shall I keep her safe in Jamestown? I was one of the fortunate ones. I didn't die at sea or during the seasoning. Then there's the trouble with the Natives. They might attack at any moment. How can you give assurances she wouldn't succumb if I was foolish enough to agree to this?"

"You ask too much. Am I the Lord who has power over life and death? There are perils in London, as you can well attest."

She turned away from him and stared at the ocean.

"My pardon." If only there was a way. He should have kept from speaking. It had only made things worse. "I can't stay in London. Not with the trouble my brother has put the colony in."

She dabbed her eyes with her handkerchief but wouldn't look his way. "I don't want to part from you, but I must. You can't leave your brother for long, and I shan't break my vow to keep my sister safe. The Lord has ordained our separate paths."

"Nay." He turned her around and took her in his arms, and she didn't resist. "I cannot believe the Lord would bring us together like this unless He meant for us to marry."

She paused for a moment then shook her head. Then a sob escaped. His heart crumbled for both of them as she buried her face in his shoulder, her body shuddering.

"We'll find a way." He stroked her hair. "We have to find a way."

She pulled herself from him and hurried to the other side of the ship. It might as well have been the great sea between them.

He was more resolute than he'd ever been that he couldn't leave her, but he couldn't stay in London. *Lord, what do I do now?*

~~~~~

Elizabella ate her midday meal in the hold since Miles was eating on the open deck. For the last week, she'd done everything she could to evade him. It did little good. Every time she went on deck to watch the ocean and get fresh air, he was there, and she would turn to walk away. At least he didn't follow her, but no matter how hard she tried, the ship was too small to avoid him forever.

He climbed down the ladder and nodded to her.

She didn't respond to him. Instead, she walked past him and climbed on deck, anywhere he wasn't. She strode to the side and gazed at the ocean. The wind had picked up, and the waves had grown in intensity, mirroring the conflicting emotions gripping her heart.

What was she to do? The thought of letting Miles leave her in London and sail back to Jamestown made her stomach roil. She loved him, but she couldn't break her vow. She had to care for her sister.

Lord, take away this affection we have for each other.

She'd prayed this same request often since he'd declared his love for her. If anything, her feelings for him grew stronger.

The sky was no longer blue even though it was midday. Dark clouds obscured the sun, and the wind blew heartily. The fury of it matched her emotional torrent. She wrapped her cloak tighter around herself.

Prayer didn't help. Nightly she had prayed and asked the Lord to take away this intense closeness she felt toward Miles. God had answered her prayer to return to London. He'd even miraculously healed Hannah of the seasoning. Why was it that He couldn't give her the peace she needed when it came to this?
~~~~~

First Mate Rogers called out commands. "Put the ship in irons."

The sails turned into the wind, and the ship slowed in speed.

The more she prayed, the stronger her feelings for Miles grew. A large wave rocked the ship, and she grabbed hold of the side to keep from falling. Icy water sprayed her face.

"Miss, get below," Rogers bellowed toward her.

She wanted to obey, but the waves crashed over the sides, and she grabbed hold to keep from being tossed. Her heart raced, and she couldn't bring herself to let go.

"Douse the sails!"

The sails lowered quickly with a *whoosh*, but the waves drowned out the noise as they beat furiously against the sides. The ship rocked from side to side making her unsteady on her feet. She had to get below, but she was afraid to let go of the handhold she'd found on a beam on the side of the ship. How could a storm grow so fierce in such a short time? A wave swept over her and drenched her clothes.

"Drop anchor!"

She let go, but before she took two steps, another wave swept over her, causing her to grasp the beam again. As loud as the wind had now become, her heart thrashed louder in her ears.

"Lord, help me."

The gale swallowed up her prayers.

An arm wrapped around her stomach, and she felt herself being pulled away. She knew she was being rescued, but she couldn't bring herself to let go. Another wave swept over her. She heard herself screaming, "Nay, I'll drown."

"Release your hold," Miles shouted over the wind.

She clung tighter the beam.

"Trust me. I've got you."

She surrendered and let go. He pulled her to him, and she wrapped her arms around his neck, clinging to him to keep from being swept away. Only then could she feel the rope tied around him.

"Hold on tight. I have to let go of you."

As he did, she clutched him tighter. He grabbed the rope and pulled them toward the ladder going below deck. He helped her down then joined her.

She crumpled to the floor and tried to stop trembling. He sat beside her and wrapped his arms around her. The storm and wind still battered around them, but the sound was muted as if they had pillows over their ears.

Only then did she notice how cold she was. Her body shook uncontrollably, and she couldn't stop her teeth from chattering.

Miles pulled away. "You must get out of those wet clothes."

She stared at him, not sure what he was saying.

"You can change behind there." He pointed toward the side where barrels had been stacked. "Call to me when you have changed your clothing."

She removed her cloak and outer clothing and pulled a fresh tunic and skirt out of her chest, then made her way to the barrels. She tried to dress quickly, but her shivering made it difficult. She'd never been so cold even during the Great Winter of 1608. When she had managed to clothe herself, she called out, "It's done."

He grabbed a blanket and wrapped it around them both, then had them sit and lean against the barrels.

Even with the warm blanket, dry clothes, and his arms around her, her teeth still chattered, and she couldn't stop shivering. "Are we going to die in this storm?"

He rubbed his hands up and down her arms to warm her. "Nay, it will soon pass over. Sailors are well acquainted with these squalls."

She wasn't sure she believed him, but it still made her feel more secure. His arms around her made her feel safe. Soon the chattering stopped.

"I've been such a fool."

"How so?"

"We could have spent every moment on this journey with each other. Even if we have to part in London or death takes us, I don't want to waste the time we have together."

He kissed her forehead. "It'll make the parting more painful when it comes."

She gazed into his eyes. "I'm in love with you. I can't leave my sister and break my vow, but the sorrow I'll feel at our parting can be no less than if I hadn't spent this precious time with you. I won't be able to retrieve it again."

Neither of them said any more. They sat together with the blanket around them, listening to the storm. After a while, water started pouring through the entrance to the hold, and they had to move behind the barrels to keep from getting wet.

A half dozen men passed through to the lower decks and bailed water. They made a chain, passing the buckets of water from one to another until they could get them to the top deck and dump them over the side.

The storm was getting worse. The wind grew louder even below deck where they were sitting. The ship rocked so violently she didn't know how it stayed above water. More men were climbing down to bail water. Only her silent prayers and Miles at her side kept her fear at bay.

He took hold of her hand. "Marry me as soon as this storm passes."

She laid her head on his shoulder. "I wish nothing more, but I told you why I can't. You must return to Jamestown to help your brother convince the Natives to make peace, and I cannot leave my sister and break my vow."

"I've not ceased to pray about this since you rejected my proposal. I believe God wants us to marry."

"Are you mad? How could a marriage survive such separation?"

He gazed into her eyes and touched her cheek with his hand. "We don't know what is to come. We may only have tonight, but I know I'll wed no other. I'm asking you to trust the Lord with our future since He is the one who brought us together."

For the first time since the storm began, warmth flowed through her. A peace came over her. This was foolishness, but she couldn't shake the feeling inside of her that this was what God wanted. "What happens when we have to part?"

"We'll trust the Lord to bring us together again." Miles kissed her hand. "Situations may change. By the time I return to Jamestown, the Natives might have decided to make peace, or your sister might have married, or she could insist on still becoming a Jamestown bride." He raked his fingers through his hair. "I don't know how He will manage it, but I trust the God who walked on water, calmed the seas, and so miraculously healed Hannah. He brought us together, and He'll work His purposes."

Lord, what do I do? She already knew God's answer. "How can we do this? There is no preacher aboard."

Miles grinned as if she'd already given her hand. "Aboard ship, the captain can perform weddings."

"If we survive the night."

"Aye."

This was insane, yet... "Do you really believe we should marry when there are so many reasons not to? Is it right to do so?"

He touched her face. "I only know that I love you desperately, and I can't bear us parting. With the way I feel about you, marriage is the only honorable and right thing to do."

"I'll marry you." A warmth swept over her.

He leaned toward her and kissed her, gently at first, then with a passion that swept over her. She couldn't allow this with one who wasn't her husband. She pulled away.

He lowered his eyes. "My pardon. I'm behaving shamefully. I must learn to save our kisses for after we are wed."

"Mayhap, we should do something other than sitting so close under this blanket together."

He stood and held out his hand for her. "Come, let us celebrate our engagement by joining the bucket crew. They could use the help."

She took his hand and allowed him to lead her to the line passing the buckets.

The storm raged on, the ship continued to rock, and they kept bailing water. The wind was so loud and so fierce that it reached them below deck. She was chilled, exhausted, and didn't know how she kept standing, but she kept bailing through the night.

If they survived, she would marry Miles as soon as she could.

Chapter Thirty

Miles watched Elizabella sleep. After the time they'd had, he didn't want to wake her. Even with her hair askew and matted and her face chapped from the wind, she looked beautiful. The storm had raged until after the sun had risen, and they'd bailed water until dusk the next evening. Finally, they ate and slept while the crew secured the ship and repaired damaged planks.

He'd risen with the sun and had gone about making arrangements for their wedding. The captain not only had agreed to marry them, but he offered them the captain's room for their wedding night, saying he could bunk with his first mate for one evening.

Miles had grabbed some ship biscuits and brought them to where Elizabella lay sleeping. When she awoke, they would eat breakfast together and join in matrimony. His throat tightened. Unless she'd changed her mind.

That was why, even though they'd been awake for almost two days, he'd been unable to sleep since daybreak. She'd agreed to marry him only because they were in danger. Now, in the light of day, would she reconsider? The thought terrified him.

Why was she being so obstinate about her sister? He understood why she would want to go to England to make sure her sister was well, but the girl would be sixteen by now, a full-grown woman with a business to sustain her.

Even if the sister didn't want to run their sewing shop, she'd already shown her desire to become a Jamestown bride, and he could give her the means to do so without having to indenture herself. Jamestown did offer many dangers, but it also offered great joys and room to breathe. He let out a gusty sigh. People died in England too.

What if Elizabella hadn't changed her mind? Would she marry him and still stay in London to nursemaid her sister? How could he leave her? He let out a gusty sigh. How could he stay?

If they wed, he could order her to go with him. He would be her lawful husband, but could he make such demands on her? Nay, he loved her too much.

He loved her.

That was the only answer he had. He loved her enough to marry her and trust God with the future. There were no promises things would work out well, they hadn't with Mary, but he would step into the raging sea and see what God would do.

Elizabella stirred, stretched, then opened her eyes. When she saw him, she smiled. A good sign. "Good morning, my love."

"I brought you breakfast in bed." He handed her a biscuit.

She sat up. "My, I feel like a fine lady indeed being served such a magnificent feast on my wedding day."

Miles couldn't help the sigh of relief that went through him. She hadn't changed her mind. "I talked to the captain. He'll not only perform the ceremony, but he's allowing us to use his quarters for our..." His face grew warm. "...wedding night."

"What a kindness." A blush reddened her cheeks as she delivered a soft smile.

They ate together without saying another word, but it was a comfortable silence, the silence a married couple would have together in the morning. He couldn't help but feel everything would work out. God would make a way for them to remain together.

When they'd finished eating, she rose to her feet. "Off with you now. I must change. I won't be wed in clothes that look like I've been bailing water for hours."

"You look beautiful to me." He wanted so much to touch her, to kiss her, to surround her with his arms, but he didn't dare. He'd already succumbed to the temptation twice, and he wasn't sure he'd be able to stop if he allowed himself free rein. Best to wait until tonight when he could show her his love with God's blessing.

He climbed the ladder and strode to the edge of the ship. Hard to believe a tempest had almost sunk the ship so recently. The sun shone bright with no clouds to shield it. Waves rolled gently against the side, not causing much movement aboard. God had blessed their union with a beautiful day. Hopefully no more fierce storms were beyond the horizon.

Elizabella soon made her way to the top deck. Her hair had been thoroughly brushed and had been pinned into a simple style. Her gown was silk with pink embroidered flowers. She couldn't have been more lovely.

He took her hand and hurried to the captain's quarters. He knocked but did let go of her hand, almost afraid if he did, she would think better of their nuptials. The captain finally answered.

"We're here to be married."

"Then let's be done with it." The captain grabbed his Prayer Book and led them to the open deck where First Mate Rogers could witness the ceremony. First, he read the marriage Banns, and they both swore they were not encumbered by any other marriage contract. The reading of the Banns was a simple matter aboard ship and required no prior reading since ship weddings were regulated by handfasting laws.

Miles took Elizabella's right hand with his.

"Make your declarations," the captain said.

"I, Miles Bonneville, Lord of Worthington, take thee, Elizabella Clark, to my wife, 'til death us part, and thereto I pledge thee my troth."

She blushed and said, "I, Elizabella Clark, take thee, Miles Bonneville, Lord of Worthington, to my husband, 'til death us part, and thereto I pledge thee my troth."

"I pronounce you husband and wife by my authority as captain of this ship. Master Bonneville, you may kiss your bride."

Miles kissed her tenderly for the benefit of the sailors around them, but when they were alone, he would embrace her more fervently. He only wished he had protected her honor in a greater way before and that this had indeed been their first kiss, but it would not be the last. He led her to the captain's quarters.

~~~~~

Elizabella stared at the ocean. It had been over a month since she had wed. Miles, her marriage, everything felt so right, but the closer they traveled to London, the more she worried about what she would find there. Was Honesty even alive? If she was, how could Elizabella leave her alone? Miles would return to Jamestown with or without her. With his brother and the colony in danger, he had no choice.

"A penny for your thoughts." Miles came behind her, his warm breath blowing on her neck.

"Not sure they're worth that much," Elizabella turned and smiled at him.

He wrapped his arms around her, making her feel safe. "Come now. The closer we get to England, the more time you spend staring at the sea. What's troubling you?"

She shrugged. It was tempting not to answer, but he was her husband. He had a right to know. "What will we find in London? I'm anxious for my sister's health. If she is well, what am I to do about her? I can't break my vow to my mother."

Miles stepped back and wiped his hand over his mouth. "A predicament indeed, but you made vows to me as well."

Elizabella turned back toward the sea. "I know."

Miles stepped beside her and held her hand. "I'm also concerned my father might have already been executed before I have a chance to make things right, but Scripture tells us to give our anxieties to God, for He cares for us."

"I know that too. It's easier said than done."

His brow furrowed. "Are you regretting our marriage vows?"

"Nay, never." She placed her head on his firm chest. "I refuse to regret what we've had together."

"But..." He kissed her forehead.

"What if I can't return to Jamestown with you?"

"There is no you or me." He embraced her in his strong arms. "There's only us. We are one now."
~~~~~

She struggled to make sense of this. His nearness comforted her, but that wouldn't help them solve their dilemma. "I won't leave my sister. You know that."

He turned her toward him and kissed her lips softly, the way he did when sailors were around. "God has a plan. When the time is right, I'll return to Jamestown... with you." He kissed her again with a little more intensity.

She started to lean into the kiss but stopped herself. He was distracting her, but his kisses wouldn't solve anything. She pulled back from his arms and touched her lips where the pressure of his love still lingered. "I want to believe that, but we have to be reasonable."

He groaned. "Wife of mine, when we wed, we weren't being reasonable. We made a leap of faith. There is no practicality in that. We only need to wait and see what God does."

Her chest tightened as if an anchor rested on it. "How can we do that?" She took a couple of steps away from him and crossed her arms, guarding her heart from the emotions he stirred within her. "If my sister lives, I'll have to stay and take care of her. You have to return to Jamestown."

The muscle in Miles' cheek twitched. "You're my wife. Think you not that I'll do what I can for your sister? If she wishes, we'll take her with us. If not, you have provided for her with your shop. Either way, you must return with me."

Tears threatened to stream down her warm cheeks. Even if he was her husband, he had no right to order her to break her vow to her dying mother. "So, you plan to carry me aboard without my consent? I think not."

"Of course not." Miles let out a noisy sigh. "Let's not quarrel. As I said, the Lord has a plan. We need to place our trust in Him." He stepped toward her and tried to take her hand.

She pulled it away. "You know not what I'm suffering. You expect me to put my sister in danger so you can keep me under your command as my father did to my mother?" The tears flowed freely now. "If I'd known you would do this, I wouldn't have married you."

"Elizabella, please." He reached out his hand.

"Don't touch me." She ran to the ladder going below deck. Hopefully he wouldn't follow her. She needed to get away. Deserting her sister was out of the question, no matter what he said or did, even if she had to run away from him.

When she reached the end of the ladder, she looked up. He wasn't there. As much as she didn't want him to follow, his absence left her with an empty feeling.

Lord, what am I to do?

~~~~~

Miles' heart sank. He loved her so much. Why couldn't she understand that? He would do anything for her. A lump formed in his throat. Not
~~~~~

"anything." He wouldn't stay in London indefinitely when his brother was in danger. How could she expect him to do that?

It hit him harder than a punch to his middle. That was what he was expecting her to do, leave her young sister or bring her along when it might put her in danger. Still, she was his wife. It was his responsibility to care for her and her sister. If only she trusted him to do that. She had survived the seasoning. Her sister would as well. He paced the deck, trying to find a way to reason with her.

When the sun was beginning to set, he found no solution to his troubles, but a realization came to him. He missed her in his arms. He hurried to the lower deck to find her. They needed to resolve this, at least for now.

She sat behind one of the barrels, sniffing. A lump formed in his throat. She'd obviously been crying. He lowered himself to sit beside her. She glanced his way for a moment, then stared at her hands. He didn't speak for a while. He didn't know what to say.

Finally, he took her hand in his. "You know I adore you."

She didn't say anything, but she didn't pull her hand away.

He let out a soft sigh. "I want nothing more than to be your devoted husband, to care for you and your family."

A sob escaped her.

His heart melted. "Forgive me."

She buried her head in his shoulder and cried.

He wrapped his arms around her. "I would never use my position as your husband to force you to do something against your better judgement. Tell me you know this is true."

She wiped her eyes and gazed at him. "Even if it means me staying in London without you?"

Lord, what am I to do without her? The irony that it was his turn to doubt God's plan didn't escape him. The lump threatened to choke him, but he forced the words out. "Even then."

Chapter Thirty-One

England, October 1620

Elizabella stood beside her husband as the gangplank lowered. They had arrived late, and the sun was already beginning to wane. On the journey here, her love for him had grown into a tangible thing. Now that they were in London, that love felt like an anchor on her chest. Unless the Lord performed a miracle, they were closer than ever to the day they must part from each other.

Miles offered his arm. "After I make arrangements for the ship to keep our trunks until the morrow, we should go to your sewing shop to make sure your sister fares well."

She nodded and linked her arm with his. After making the arrangements, they linked arms to walk off the ship. He waved his hand to signal a carriage for hire. She told the driver where she lived, and he helped her as they stepped into the carriage.

"Where shall we stay while in London?" Elizabella said. "I mean, with your father's whereabouts unknown, perchance we should stay at my home."

"Agreed. I'm not even sure if King James has seized my father's estate. I'll see about him tomorrow."

She nodded.

"Elizabella." He took her hands in his. "I must tell you... I adore you. I love you with every fiber of my being. Going back to Jamestown without you would be a lonesome venture I'm not sure my heart could bear."

She looked at her hands in his, and heat rushed to her cheeks. "I feel the same."

He kissed her hands and moved closer and kissed her lips tenderly. "Then you'll go with me?"

"What can I say?" A wave of heaviness swept over her. "I can't leave my sister." Her eyes burned with unshed tears. "And you must return to your brother."

The color drained from Miles' face.

Elizabella wished she could take back the words that hurt him so. She really did love him, but she couldn't leave her sister after God had provided a way back. Her brother had died because of her, and she couldn't betray her promise to her mother. The guilt would be unbearable.

If only he could stay in London with her, but he would never be happy here. Jamestown was his home, and his brother was in danger. He would eventually feel contempt for her if she convinced him to stay.

The carriage stopped. He opened the door and helped her out, then paid the driver.

"Are you certain this is where your shop was located?" His voice was thick.

She looked at the storefront and gasped. The sign on the front said *Johnson's Clockmakers*.

A wave of nausea swept over her, and she felt as if she might swoon. What could this mean? Miles caught her by the arm and held her upright.

"What happened?" she asked.

"Let's find out." Miles tried to open the door, but it was locked. He pounded on it until a short man with curly gray hair answered.

"What is this?" the man asked. "We're closed. Why are you knocking on my door at this late hour?

Miles placed his hands out in a conciliatory gesture. "Forgive us for disturbing you. My wife is searching for the former proprietor of this property, a seamstress named Miss Honesty Clark."

"I know of no seamstress by that name. I bought this store from a Welsh baker name Bassford just last month.

"You must know her." Elizabella took a deep breath and let it out slowly as she tried to make sense of the scene before her. "She's my sister. She's about my size and looks a lot like me except she's younger." She knew she was rambling, but she couldn't help herself. "The baker must have told you about her. She and I owned this shop. Surely, you at least have heard of her."

"No, Miss, I have not."

The clockmaker started to close the door when Elizabella placed her body in front of it. "Our gold. It was hidden behind a brick in the shop." She turned to Miles. "Please, make him open his shop so we can at least check."

"I haven't stolen any gold of yours," the clockmaker protested. "Now off with you."

Miles shrugged. "Goodman Johnson, I implore you. My wife is much concerned. We've sailed from Jamestown and expected to meet her sister at this very shop. You can understand how distraught she is no find no sign of her. Could we come in for a moment and look around? We shan't disturb anything."

"I assure you, I know nothing of this woman you speak of." Goodman Johnson sighed heavily. "I suppose it won't hurt." He opened the door wide so they could enter.

Elizabella ran past the clocks lining the walls and pulled out a loose brick on the hearth. "We keep it in here." She stuck her hand in the open space. The metal box was gone. She felt around, hoping it might have been pushed aside. Nothing. Her heart beat so hard she thought it might burst out of her chest. She turned to the clockmaker. "What did you do with it?"

Miles grabbed her by the arm and escorted her toward the door. "Goodman Johnson, thank ye for your time."

Elizabella tried to pull away, but Miles placed a finger to his lips and gave her a warning look. She didn't trust this clockmaker, but she trusted her husband and allowed him to lead her away.

When the clockmaker closed the door behind them, Elizabella turned to Miles. "What are you about? He stole my gold."

"Mayhap not." Miles wrapped his arms around her. "It could have been the baker, or the one who sold this shop to the baker. We can't accuse this clockmaker until we find out what happened."

"What did happen?" Elizabella swallowed hard. "Did Honesty die? Was the shop turned over to the king?"

"You don't know that's what happened. Don't lose hope yet."

"What other explanation is there?" She trembled and laid her head on his shoulder. She struggled to slow her breaths.

"Where did you leave her when she was injured?" Miles asked.

"The surgeon." He, above all others, would know what had happened. Wiping her face, she struggled to calm herself. "He's in Pudding Lane."

"Not a place to wander at night." Miles pulled back and furrowed his forehead in thought. "The Seven Stars Inn is a short distance from here. We can stay the night there. In the morn, we'll find the surgeon. He'll let us know all is well."

Elizabella nodded. "Please, Lord. Let it be so."

~~~~~

Elizabella rose from her slumber before dawn broke. She hadn't slept well. Every time she started to doze, questions about what happened to her sister assaulted her. If Honesty were still alive, why would she sell their shop? Who took the gold? Was it her sister? Was she even alive? Finally, when the first light shone through the window, she gave up trying.

Miles was still sleeping, so she slipped her petticoat over her linen smock and pulled her silk stocking over her legs as quietly as she could. Then, she pulled her gown over her petticoat and attached the linen cuffs and ruff. It was too early to call on the surgeon unless it was an emergency, so there was no reason to wake her husband. She added some logs to the hearth and replenished the fire from the night before.

Her stomach grumbled. Their last meal was onboard the ship, and it consisted of hardtack. Not very appetizing. As soon as her husband woke, they would break their fast in the dining room.

She sat in a chair by the fireplace and tried to warm herself by the fire. Today, they would need to find a carter to deliver their trunks. If she'd known what she would find, she would have insisted they do so when they left the ship, but it was so late.

Lord, please help me. Give me wisdom to know how to find my sister.
~~~~~

"Why didn't you wake me?" Miles rose from their bed.

"No need," she said. "Tis too early to search the surgeon out."

"Aye." He took her hands in his. "Tis not too early to break our fast. After we eat, we can search for your sister's whereabouts."

Elizabella pressed her lips together.

"What troubles you?"

"I'm not sure where the surgeon resides," she said. "'Twas a year ago, and I was most distressed at the time."

Miles wrapped his arms around her. "After we have been fortified with a good meal, we'll retrace your path from your sewing shop to the ship. If we have to, we'll search every house and building. We'll find the surgeon and your sister."

Unless Honesty was dead.

Nay, she couldn't allow herself to consider it, or she'd go mad.

Miles dressed, and they arrived at the dining room to eat. After they'd eaten a hearty meal, they started at the sewing shop and headed to the wharf as she had that day. They approached Pudding Lane where the murderous ruffians had stabbed her sister. The stench assaulted her. She'd forgotten how foul the city odors were. It wasn't only the smells. The buildings were crammed together with no room to breathe. So unlike Jamestown.

She shook her head. No use thinking about what could not be. If Honesty was alive, she would stay in London to care for her sister and die away from grief at being parted from her husband.

The oddness of it struck her. When she was taken to Jamestown, she wanted nothing more than to sail back to London. Now that she was in London, she longed for the beauty of the colony.

As they strode toward the alley where Honesty was attacked, Elizabella examined every storefront. Butcher shops, launderers, cookery, weavers, bakers. She recognized them, but none looked like the area she'd been in almost a year ago. Perchance they were on the wrong road?

They passed another crossroads, and she saw it. Cool beads of sweat dotted her forehead. The alley where it happened was straight ahead. She ran into it and stopped.

Miles rushed in beside her. "Is this the place?"

"Aye, my sister was stabbed here." The dark stain of her sister's blood had washed away, but it was buried deep in her memory. Her head felt dizzy, and she was sure she was about to be sick. It all came flooding back.

She went to the barrel in the corner. "This is where I hid until I saw her." Tears rolled down her cheeks. "I couldn't keep her safe." It was her fault if Honesty was dead, just as the blame had been hers for Benjamin's demise. A sob came from deep inside of her.

Miles took hold of her hand. "We'll find her."

She nodded. *Lord, I asked You to heal the other memories of things I've done or things done to me, but how can I go to You with this? I let this happen to her. Forgive me.*

A familiar peace swept over her. Whether the Lord was healing her or preparing her for what was to come, she knew not, but they had to go on. They had to find her sister.

"The king's guard came to assist me," she said. "He carried Honesty out of the alley and to the right." She pointed down the road.

Miles squeezed her hand. "Then let's see where it leads."

She accompanied him. "There was an apothecary up ahead." She searched each building to see if it looked familiar. A butcher. She remembered the smell of roasting pig. Then the glassworks shop. There it was. Relief swept over her, and she pointed to the wooden sign hanging above the surgeon's door.

Miles knocked.

The surgeon opened the door. "What can I do for you?"

Elizabella's legs grew weak under her. It was the same man who had treated Honesty. She would have crumpled to the floor in the doorway if her husband hadn't been supporting her. He helped her to a bench inside. She nodded her gratefulness but still couldn't find words.

"Are you ill?" The surgeon gave her some water and felt her head.

She swallowed, allowing the cool water to loosen her throat. "Nay, I am well. I desire information. Do you remember me bringing my sister here about a year ago? She was stabbed."

His brow furrowed. "I can't recollect every patient I've seen over the last year. I'm a busy man."

"She looked a lot like me. We were both wearing dark blue cloaks."

His features softened. "Aye, I remember. You never came back to fetch her."

Elizabella swallowed another sip of water, almost afraid to ask. "Is she well? What happened to her?"

The surgeon raised an eyebrow. "If it's information you want, I must be paid what you owe me."

"What are you about? I paid you handsomely."

"Nevertheless, I require at least two more pounds."

Heat rose to her neck. "A fine healer you are. You wish to fleece me, do you?"

The surgeon grinned. "I care not for your insults. You'll pay if you wish me to speak."

Miles squeezed her hand and reached into his purse. "I'll give you a half pound. If that's not sufficient, we'll find what we're looking for elsewhere."

She let out a sigh. It wasn't right, but what could they do? She had to know what happened to her sister.

The surgeon shook his head. "I must have at least two pounds."

Miles helped Elizabella to her feet, turned his back to the surgeon, and gave her a wink. "Come, Wife." He started to lead her out the door.

She wanted to refuse, but she didn't.

"Wait," the surgeon said. "I'll take a pound."

Miles smiled. "My price hasn't changed. Take it, or we'll be on our way."

The surgeon pressed his lips together into a hard grin. "All right then. Half a pound."

"Done and done." Miles gave him the half pound he still had in his hand.

The surgeon took the coin and threw it in a wooden box on the table. "She's alive and well. At least she was a year ago when she departed to look for you. I know not what happened to her since then."

Tears watered Elizabella's eyes, but she held them back. At least, Honesty was alive, although she knew not where to look for her.

"Fare thee well." Miles took hold of her arm and led her out the door.

When the door had closed, she scoffed. "A thief would be a better profession for him."

"Aye."

"What do we do now?" She swiped at a tear running down her cheek.

"Don't fret. I have resources you know not of." Miles waved his hand and hailed a carriage.

After they climbed in, Elizabella turned to him. "Where are we going now?"

Miles patted her hand. "The Weathersby House. Sir Robert is a friend of mine. He'll help us."

Elizabella gasped. "Sir Robert is the man who broke my sister's heart."

Chapter Thirty-Two

They arrived at the Weathersby house an hour later. Even though Miles had spent most of the carriage ride trying to convince Elizabella of the good sense of going there, she wasn't sure she wanted to see the man who broke her sister's heart.

Miles helped her out of the carriage. She stood, staring at the house, reluctant to go any further. It was a typical manor home for the titled. She'd seen many of them while delivering gowns. Many lords and ladies now wintered in London instead of their drafty castles at their estates. They often left the management of their lands and seeing to the needs of their people to servants so they could be included in the festivities of the King's court. The need for dresses for these parties had made her wealthy, but she still felt disdain for these privileged people.

"If anyone knows where your sister is, it would be Robert." Miles offered his arm. "Even if he doesn't know, he might at least know what happened to my father."

"Of course." Elizabella took his arm. "I wasn't considering your concerns."

He shrugged. "I was only thinking if his estates haven't been taken away, we could use the resources to find Honesty."

Heat rose to her face. She had only been thinking of finding her sister, not of Miles' difficulties, and it appeared her husband was doing the same. If there was a more considerate man, she knew not who. "Lead on."

Miles escorted her to the front entrance and banged the bronze door knocker.

A butler opened the door. "Good evening." He didn't bother to invite them in. "May I be of service?"

"I desire to see Sir Robert," Miles said.

"Sir Robert and his wife are occupied."

Wife? Every muscle in her body tensed. Surely, after breaking the engagement with her sister, he wouldn't have married another so soon. If he had, she would give him the tongue lashing he deserved.

Miles cleared his throat. "Tell Sir Robert that Lord and Lady Miles Bonneville have just arrived from Jamestown. I'm sure he'll see us."

The butler escorted them into the foyer. "Wait here."

Waiting in the foyer was appreciated. She was well used to waiting outside while measuring for dresses until the lady of the house deemed her worthy of entrance. Her pulse raced. At least in the colony, titles meant nothing. Every man had an equal footing.

The door opened, and the butler reappeared. "Sir Robert shall see you now. Follow me."

They walked through the large wood-paneled hallway, with an ornate staircase traveling to the second floor, until they reached the parlor. It had bright green walls with paintings hanging everywhere. She'd been in many homes like this, but their four-room wattle and daub house in Jamestown felt more like a home. She sat on the nearest flowered settee to wait, and Miles sat beside her.

She rolled her shoulders to try to relax her corded muscles. "I am horrified he didn't have enough decency to wait to marry after jilting my sister."

"Would you prefer to wait in the foyer?" Miles asked. "I'll confront him alone about your sister's honor and find out what we need to know."

Elizabella shook her head. "I want to hear how he gives an account of his actions."

"Sir Miles." Robert burst into the room and reached to take Miles' hand to shake it. "I can't believe it. I thought you were in Jamestown. Good to see you've left that dreadful place and have arrived back to civilization."

Miles stood. "Sir Robert, I wouldn't have bothered you, but—"

"Nonsense, it's no bother." Robert turned to Elizabella. "Miss Clark, I am astonished to see you waltz into my sitting room. We've looked everywhere for you."

Elizabella tilted her head and glanced at Miles. He looked as confused as she felt.

Miles motioned toward her. "This is Lady Bonneville, my wife."

Robert's brow furrowed. "I'm perplexed. Do you mean to tell me Miss... Lady Bonneville was in Jamestown all this time?"

Elizabella stood. Heat rose within her, and she couldn't remain silent another moment. "Aye, 'tis so." She pointed her finger at his chest and spit out her words. "Honesty was the one who wanted to journey there because of you. She would have if she had not been stabbed, and now she's missing. Mayhap you should have considered her before taking a new wife."

Robert placed his hands on his hips. "Missing... A new wife... What are you about?"

"Elizabella?" The soft woman's voice came from the doorway. "Is it really you? I thought you were dead."

Elizabella turned and stared at her sister, but no words came out. She collapsed into Miles' arms. He helped her sit in a nearby chair.

Honesty ran to her and patted her hand. "Fredrick," she shouted, "get some smelling salts."

"No need," Elizabella squeaked out. "I'm well."

Miles stood and faced Robert. "What the devil is going on?"

Robert grinned. "Meet my wife, Miss Honesty Clark, now Lady Weathersby."

Miles' mouthed opened wide, and he sat on the chair beside Elizabella.

"Thank the Lord. I thought I was dreaming," Elizabella said.

Honesty touched her cheek. "'Tis real enough." Tears rolled down her cheeks. "Where have you been? We thought you were dead."

Elizabella stood and embraced her sister.

Robert turned to Fredrick. "Bring us some dancha and wafers." He patted Miles' back. "I remember you don't abide stronger drink or ale."

The butler left to do his master's bidding.

Miles stood. "I desire to hear everything, but could I inquire of something first?"

"Of course," Robert said.

Miles cleared his throat. "I heard my father was under arrest in the Tower of London and that his property had been confiscated by the king. 'Tis the reason I returned to London."

Robert set his hand on Miles' shoulder. "'Tis old news. The charges have been dismissed, and your father's estate has been returned to him. All is well."

Miles shook his head. "I must go to visit him on the morrow."

Fredrick came into the room with refreshments.

Robert stood. "Fredrick, prepare one of the bed chambers. Our guests shall stay overnight."

"We couldn't impose," Miles said.

"Balderdash. You're family. Stay here as long as you wish."

Miles nodded. "Thank ye."

"I can't wait another moment," Elizabella said. "Tell me, Honesty, what happened after I left you at the surgeon's."

"After I recovered, I looked everywhere for you," Honesty said. "I knew something must be wrong when you didn't come to see about me. I never considered you'd sailed. You were so set against me going to Jamestown. How did you describe it? A savage land full of death."

Elizabella smiled, remembering how she felt when she first saw the New World. "I was wrong. 'Tis a beautiful land full of wonders. I've seen flowers and trees I never knew existed. The temperature is pleasant compared to London."

"You sound like you're describing a paradise," Honesty said.

"Aye." Miles cleared his throat. "'Tis that and more."

"When you couldn't find me, what did you do?" Elizabella asked.

Honesty blushed.

"She came to my door." Sir Robert took her hand in his. "I endeavored to give her the resources she needed to search, but to no avail." He turned to Elizabella and gazed into her eyes. "I was a fool and a coward when I broke off the engagement. Assisting her made me see the error of my ways. I told my father he would accept her as my wife, or I would sail to Jamestown and give up any fortune I was set to inherent."

Elizabella drew her hand to her mouth. Was it possible she was that wrong about Robert's character? Mayhap, but she wasn't ready to trust him completely.

Miles let out a chuckle. "I would have liked to be privy to that conversation."

"Aye, the servants made themselves scarce, but in the end, he agreed. He said if I wanted her that badly, I must have her."

"Since then, Robert's parents have been wonderful," Honesty said. "They've treated me as a daughter. I've been happy, but your disappearance had cast a cloud over me. I was sure you'd been murdered by those horrible men. I'm so relieved you're safe, but how did you come to end up in Jamestown of all places?"

Elizabella told them what had happened up until arriving at their doorstep. "I'm so grateful to find you well."

For the rest of the evening, Elizabella and Honesty shared stories of their time away from each other. Honesty seemed content, but Robert had betrayed her once. What would happen if Elizabella returned to Jamestown and Robert showed his true colors again? She wouldn't be there to help her sister. She needed to stay in London until she was sure he wouldn't desert her sister again. She'd promised her mother to protect and care for her.

After dinner, they retired to their room. Miles took Elizabella in his arms and kissed her. She responded easily, but how would she tell him she needed to stay in London?

He pulled back. "I love you."

She held back the tears that threatened to spill. "I love you too, more than you could know."

He kissed her again, this time more passionately, and warmth spread throughout her entire body. He wiped her cheek. "Why the tears? Your sister is safely married, and our prayers have been answered."

"Aye, she is safe." She couldn't tell him now. Better to wait until it was closer to time to sail.

Chapter Thirty-Three

Jamestown

Hugh carried a buck into the Powhatan village. Even though the chief and he had worked out the terms of their agreement, he still felt dread when he made another delivery. At any moment, Chief Opechancanough might change his mind and decide meat for Wupun's household wasn't enough to appease him.

Hannah had expressed her misgivings before he'd left, and he assured her that the meat he delivered would keep him safe. He wished he had the confidence he'd tried to show her. He headed to the center of the village.

The men were not hunting and had gathered around the fire to tell stories. Hugh let out a sigh. He'd hoped the warriors would be gone and he could deliver the deer to Wupun's longhouse without meeting up with them.

Chief Opechancanough glared at him as he approached. Hugh wasn't sure if it was because of the chief's disdain for all white men or him in particular, but the glower made him nervous. Something had shifted. He could feel it in the leader's stance.

Opechancanough nodded to one of the warriors, and he took the buck from Hugh and delivered it to Wupun's longhouse. Shortly after that, Wupun and Kimi, Suleta's younger sister, joined the warriors around the fire.

"Come closer, Hugh," the chief said. "I have good news to share."

He drew closer, but the pronouncement did nothing to ease his tensions.

The chief put his hand on Hugh's shoulder. "Wupun has found a brave to agree to wed her youngest daughter."

"That is good news," Hugh said, still suspicious of what the chief was about. "When is this to happen?"

"Not for another year." The chief squeezed slightly, not enough to hurt, but enough to alert Hugh that something was wrong. "The girl won't be old enough to marry until then."

"I'll still provide for Wupun until then," Hugh said, hoping that would appease him.

"Do you really believe I'll let you off that easily?" The chief squeezed a little harder.

Hugh jutted his chin to keep from wincing. What was it about the Powhatan that caused them to use a friendly gesture like this as a warning or a weapon? "I've done everything required of me. What more do you want?"

"A wedding gift." Opechancanough laughed heartily, and the other warriors chuckled as if he'd told a funny jest. "Kimi's warrior has agreed to provide meat to her family. Once you give what Kimi requires, your obligation to Wupun's family shall be over."

Hugh wasn't sure what they were laughing about, but he knew it would be dangerous for him and the colony. *Lord, help me.* "What gift do you desire from me?"

"What gift indeed? Mayhap you have met the man pledged to be Kimi's husband since he had also pledged to marry Suleta before she died in birthing your babe." The chief removed his hand from Hugh's shoulder, but the pain remained. "Perchance, Kimi and her future husband would enjoy seeing the man who was responsible for her sister's death clubbed to death by our warriors. It would be a fine gift to them."

Hugh's throat grew dry, and he held his breath to keep from gasping. If they'd decided to execute him, there was nothing he could do or say to stop them.

"What do you say, Kimi?" the chief asked. "What wedding gift would you like?"

Suleta's sister came closer. "There are a few other things I would prefer over his execution."

"I'm sure Hugh will gladly provide them to escape his death." The chief motioned to Kimi.

"Three iron pots, some beaver pelts, maybe ten, two iron axes, two hoes, and half a dozen woven blankets."

Hugh took in a huge breath. Until then, he hadn't realized he'd forgotten to breathe. The beaver pelts, blankets, and pots wouldn't be troublesome, but he couldn't secure the farm tools easily even with the prosperous tobacco crop he'd harvested. Half of the crop had already gone to pay for the copper pots, and farming tools were sparse and dear. If he sold a few of the servants, he might be able to pay for them and order them when the next ship came, but it was unsure if they would arrive within a year. Ships were often late, and sometimes they never made it.

He had an idea. "If I'm able to provide this wedding gift in time, what will you provide in return?"

"Other than your life?" The chief cackled and all his warriors laughed with him. "What do you want?"

"My people want a peace treaty with Powhatan."

The chief rubbed his chin. "I'll agree to holding a council with them if you present everything in time."

Thank ye, Lord. That would be enough to get the entire colony to help Hugh obtain the goods. Perchance there was hope.

The chief waved his hand for Kimi to continue.

It was obvious she had rehearsed the list. "I'd also like a polished glass, a pair of scissors, some glass beads, and two barrels of rum. Oh, and a musket for my husband."

Hugh tried to protest, but all he managed was to sputter. He already had the rum, beads, scissors, and musket, but how could he possibly manage to get a mirror? Finally, he found his voice. "Polished glass? I don't believe there is one in all of Jamestown, and even if I could have one shipped, it would be too costly."

"Aye, there is," Kimi said. "Amonute told my mother about it before she sailed away with Lord Rolfe." Amonute was the given name of Lady Rolfe, also known as Pocahontas. Lord Rolfe had presented her with a mirror on their wedding day.

"She took it to England with her." Hugh tried to calm his tone. It wouldn't do him any good to shout at the Powhatan. "Be reasonable. Most of what you ask for is not possible for me to obtain within five years, let alone one."

"Silence," the chief bellowed. "You'll present these things to Kimi within six moons, or we'll have you entertain at the wedding by shedding your blood."

A shiver went through him. The only reason Kimi asked for these things within such an impossible time was because they planned on him failing. They had no interest in a treaty. They had decided to kill him.

"I'll do what I can, but it'll take years to obtain all you desire."

"Then you'll die," the chief said.

"You can't expect me to give myself over to be beaten to death."

The chief took a step toward Hugh. "You'll provide all the items Kimi wants, and we'll meet with your council. If not, your life is forfeit. If you don't return within six moons or try to depart this land, I'll take my revenge on the colony, and I won't spare your wives or your children."

Pain overtook Hugh's chest and lungs as he gasped for air. He took a step back. "I'll return and provide everything I can, but you have given me an impossible task."

The chief stepped close enough for Hugh to smell the fish he'd recently eaten. He squeezed Hugh's shoulder so hard that Hugh fell to his knees and let out a moan. "Then we'll enjoy the entertainment you'll provide."

~~~~~

London

Miles stood in front of the house where he'd grown up. He never thought he'd step through those doors again. He still didn't want to, but the Lord urged him on. He had to find some way to forgive his father if he would ever be able to change his judgmental ways.

He paced the road in front of it seven, eight, nine times, before he squared his shoulders and walked to the door. Placing his hand on the
~~~~~

knocker, he paused. Should he knock and walk right in? After all, it was his house too. Caution might be the better route since he wasn't expected. He banged the knocker twice and waited.

Nobody answered.

He knocked again, more forcefully this time.

Nothing.

Checking the door, he found it unlocked, turned the latch, and stepped inside. The window coverings were closed, and the candles remained unlit.

"Father," Miles called out. "Anyone home?"

"Miles?" A weak voice reached him from a room on the far end of the hall. "Is that you?"

He peered down the hall and tried to make the shadows come into focus.

"I thought you were in Jamestown." His father came into view and slowly walked toward him.

Miles' chest tightened. Was this really his father? The man he knew was handsome and well-built, and clean-shaven except for a well-kept mustache. Except for his facial features, he looked nothing like the man Miles had disdained.

Father had lost a great deal of weight, and he looked weak. His clothing was not kept up, and his stockings were dirty and torn. The facial hair sprouted on his face as if he hadn't seen a razor for a week and didn't care to. The attractive and charming features that had lured ladies to be unfaithful to their husbands had faded. He made it to where Miles was standing.

Miles struggled to find his voice. "I was, but we heard of your difficulties and..."

Father let out a snort. "Difficulties? That's one word for it."

Miles' chest now felt as if a log resided on it. This was not what he expected. "What happened?"

"You should know." Father's breath came out in gasps as if walking down the hall used all his remaining energy. "Don't you remember what you said when you left?"

Miles did remember. Father had tried to block the door to keep him and his siblings from leaving. He had taken Father's shirt in his hands.

"Do not impede our exit, or I'll give you the thrashing you deserve."

"You would dishonor your own father?"

It had been the only time Miles had seen fear in his father's eyes, but that didn't stop him from his anger. "You're not my father. You gave up that right long ago. May God curse you. If there is any justice, you'll end up wretched and alone." He had let go of his father and pushed him aside as he walked out the door.

"Well," Father said as he plopped into a nearby chair. "You have your wish. I am well and truly wretched and alone."

Heat swept over Miles. What had he done? His father had acted shamefully, but he'd cursed his father and left his mother and sister to suffer the consequences of his actions. He'd considered himself the one in the right, but they both had sinned. He reached out to place a hand on his father's shoulder but thought better of it. Instead, he pulled out a chair and sat across from him. His throat thickened.

"Where are the servants?"

Again, his father laughed. "I was accused of treason. My servants deserted me when I was arrested. Even though the king released me, I can't pay anyone enough to work for me except a housemaid that comes in a couple of hours a day to care for my needs."

"I thought you were back in the king's good favor."

"Nay, he tolerates me at best. He knows I didn't betray him, but I've gone too far to ever be in his good graces again."

"I..." Miles wiped his hand across the back of his neck. "I didn't know."

"Would you have cared if you had known?"

Miles' body slumped at the truth of those words, but he didn't say anything.

Father sprang from his chair, grabbed a bowl from the table, and vomited blood. Miles, shocked by how sick his father had become, went to him and placed his hand on his father's shoulder until he was done, then helped him to his chair.

"What ails you?" Miles asked. "Have you seen a surgeon?"

Father wiped his mouth. "Many. My stomach has stopped. I haven't been able to eat or drink. The last surgeon says I'll be dead within a week, so you don't need to bother yourself with me. Go back to Jamestown where you belong."

The pressure in Miles' chest felt as if it might explode. He tried to take a breath, but it caught. "I won't leave you like this. You're my father."

"You didn't stay to take care of your mother, and you loved her."

Miles wiped his hand over his face. His father always knew how to wound where it hurt the most. "We left Gladys to care for her needs."

"Gladys," Father said with a disgusted tone. "As soon as your mother died, your sister couldn't wait to marry and leave me alone. I haven't seen her since."

Anger rose up in Miles, and his hands fisted at his side. "That was not my doing. You were the one who should have seen to Mother's needs." He pressed his lips together. *Lord, keep me from getting angry.* His anger gave way to a love and concern he hadn't felt for his father in a long time. "All of that is in the past. I'll see to you until your passing."

"A little late for that. I'll be in Hades soon enough."

Miles sat beside him. "Forgive me for my harsh words toward you. I shouldn't have dishonored you."

"I'm going back to bed." Father stood and headed down the hall.

Miles lent him his arm. "I'll help you."

Father glared at him for a moment before accepting his help.

After getting him to his room and settling him in bed, Miles considered what he should do. "Who is the surgeon treating you? I wish to speak to him."

"He'll be by in the morning."

Miles nodded. "I'll gather my things and be back within the hour."

"No need."

"I'll be back soon." Miles headed to the door. He wasn't sure if he wanted Elizabella to stay with him, but he needed to care for his father until the inevitable happened. Mayhap God brought him here to lead his father to redemption. That would be an answered prayer indeed.

Chapter Thirty-Four

Elizabella listened intently while Miles told her about his father.

"I would never ask you to attend to him," Miles said. "Especially since you've just been reunited with your sister. I did hire someone to nurse him before I came here."

"Of course, I'll help. You're my husband." She would have plenty of time to visit with her sister after Miles returned to Jamestown without her. Until then, she wanted to spend every moment she could with him.

He embraced her and buried his head in her shoulder. "Thank ye. You don't know how..." He cleared his throat and gazed at her. "My father is still the reprobate he always ways, but I now see I was at fault too. I said some dreadful things to him the last time I saw him. If I could show kindness to him these last days he spends on Earth, I might be able to lead him to the Lord's grace."

"A worthy ambition." Heat flushed Elizabella's face. She hated deceiving Miles, but she would not add to his grief by telling him her intentions. On the other hand, she had put away deception when she told him about her accidental journey to Jamestown. How could she not tell him?

Elizabella disentangled herself from his arms and took a couple of steps back. "Before we go to see to your father, there's something you must know."

Miles' brow furrowed. "I promised my father we'd be there within the hour. Whatever you have to say, couldn't it wait?"

"I wish it could." She blinked to keep tears from being shed. "I can't leave my sister and return to Jamestown, at least not yet."

"I can see your reluctance, but the ship doesn't sail for another month. That should give you the time you need to visit with her and say your goodbyes."

A heaviness lodged in her throat. "I couldn't possibly depart for at least a year. I vowed to protect her."

The muscle in his jaw twitched. "What you say makes no sense. Your sister has a husband to care for her."

"Until I'm sure of his worthiness, I must wait here in London."

"This is foolish. You've fulfilled your duty to her, and I can vouch for Robert's character." He grabbed hold of her arms, pulled her to him, and kissed her with intensity. "Now, you have a duty to me. You're my wife."

She lay her head in his shoulder and sobbed. He embraced her despite his obvious anguish.

When the sobs subsided, she stepped back, determination set in her jaw. "When my mother died, I promised I'd care for and protect Benjamin and Honesty. I failed Benjamin, but I won't shirk my duty with Honesty."

"Isn't that her husband's duty?"

"Mayhap, but I must stay with her in case he fails to be a faithful husband. I don't completely trust Sir Robert with her welfare after the way he broke their engagement over a year ago. He might have married her, but if he changes his mind again, she won't have me to turn to."

Miles stood staring at her, his brown eyes not reflecting any of the warmth that usually flowed from them. He let out a roar.

She'd never seen him so angry. Fear hardened her stomach. "I must fulfill my vow to my mother."

"You've lost your wits."

Her chin trembled, and she ducked behind a dresser. He was behaving as her father would.

He held his hands out, palms facing her in a placating gesture. "My pardon. I didn't mean to frighten you. I would never hurt you." His voice calmed, and he backed away a few steps.

She took a few breaths to calm herself. He was nothing like her father. She knew that. The fear began to dissolve.

"Your mother did not mean for your responsibility to continue after your sister found a husband." The muscle in his cheek twitched, betraying the calm in his tone. "Is it Jamestown? Do you hate the colony so much you would forego my love to stay in London?"

"'Tis not Jamestown. I never thought I would long for a place so primitive, but I do. I desire nothing more than to live there with you."

"Then why won't you return with me?" His voice now had a pleading tone.

"I can't do it." Her voice broke along with her heart. "I can't break my vow."

"What about the vows you made to me?"

"I meant those vows. Mayhap, I'll see Honesty is cared for, and in a year, I'll be able to return to you, but I can't depart until I'm sure."

"We'll talk of this again, but know I'll do everything I can to get you on that ship."

Elizabella swallowed back the lump in her throat. If only she could make him understand. "In the meanwhile, your father awaits our care."

Chapter Thirty-Five

Jamestown

Hugh sat at the table across from Hannah, her stomach enlarged from his baby growing within. He didn't speak, and Hannah kept her peace, waiting for him. He'd told her as soon as he'd returned that he had tidings, but how could he let her know how much danger they were in, how much danger the whole colony was in? At least Miles and Elizabella were safe in London. *Lord, convince them to stay there.*

"How bad is it?" Hannah asked. She placed her hand on his.

"Bad." His voice cracked. He took a deep breath and let it out. Then he told her what the chief had demanded from him. "I've been considering what to do on the way home, and I've made my decision."

Fear showed in her gaze. "What have you decided?"

"First, I'll inform the council. I'll try to get together as many of the supplies as Opechancanough demands. The hoes and axes are dear to every planter who has one, but the promise of peace talks will enlist their help."

"God shall provide."

Hugh swallowed. "A mirror? How can even God provide that when there isn't a piece of polished glass in all of Jamestown?"

Tears formed in Hannah's eyes. "Mayhap if you give him some of what he requested before the six months are over, he'll give you time to get the rest. A supply ship is due to arrive before then. We can order what we need for the next shipment. If he could give you a year..."

He couldn't bring himself to tell her the truth. Wupun and Kimi made their demands impossible on purpose. Wupun preferred his death to the bounty she demanded. "We'll do what we can, but we need to prepare."

"Prepare?" Hannah squeezed Hugh's hand. "How do we do that?"

"You're right about the supply ship coming some time before May. By then, I'll have together what I can, and I'll know what I need to order, but I'll have to sell the servants to provide payment. The ship's captain won't wait until I harvest my next crop." He paused, knowing how Hannah would react when he told her the rest. "When the ship leaves, you'll be on it."

Hannah gasped. "Nay, I won't leave you." She pulled her hand away and rested it on her stomach.

"You have no choice." Hugh swallowed hard, wishing there was another way. "It's my duty to protect you and our child. Everyone on this plantation will be in danger. As your husband, I'm ordering you to go.

When you get to London, you can find refuge at my brother's estate. If you can't find him or he's already left, I'll give you some names of others who'll open their doors to you when they hear you're my wife."

Hannah stood with her back to him. "You expect to be killed." It wasn't a question, only a statement of fact.

"Aye." Hugh wished he'd hadn't vowed to never lie to her.

Hannah turned toward him, tears pouring down her cheeks. "I shan't give up that easily. We still have a God who does miracles. Aren't I proof of that? Mayhap, God intended this to start the peace talks."

For the first time since he'd met with the chief, hope started to rise in Hugh, but he tried hard to tamp it down. If God saved him, so be it, but if not, he would give his life for the colony and make sure Hannah and the babe were far away from the danger it held.

~~~~~

London

It had been a week since they'd moved into his father's house to care for him. The nurse, Miles, and Elizabella took turns sitting at his bedside. Elizabella had helped in so many ways, and Miles appreciated it, but they hadn't talked about her staying in London since the conversation last week. Mayhap she was reconsidering.

Miles' father slept as he sat at his bedside and prayed God would give him one more chance to convince his father to accept Christ's forgiveness. Every time he'd brought it up, his father would scoff and change the subject.

A heaviness rested on Miles, making him feel as if he were weighted down with boulders. A year ago, if someone had told him he would grieve at his father's bedside like this, he would have called the man a lunatic, but now, a profound sadness at his father's impending death overtook him.

Father flitted his eyes open. "You're still here." His voice sounded so weak.

"Aye."

"It shouldn't..." He coughed and hacked up blood. "...be much longer."

Miles took a wet cloth from the basin on the dresser and wiped up the blood. "Father, I must speak with you."

"What are you about this time? Can't a man die in peace?"

"You're not dying in peace."

Father turned his head away.

"Every time I've tried to converse with you about this, you've dismissed it, but I won't be scorned this time."

"Say what you must."

Miles lifted his eyes to the ceiling and said a silent prayer. "First, I'm sorry for what I said before I left for Jamestown. I was wrong, and I regret it. I ask your pardon."
~~~~~

"Is that all?" Father's voice was so weak Miles could barely hear him. "Staying with me at the end like this more than makes up for it. I forgive you."

Miles nodded. "Thank ye, but I have more to say. It's not too late to ask God's pardon. Jesus forgave the thief on the cross while the thief was dying. If you turn to Him, He'll forgive you and welcome you into Heaven to be with Him for eternity."

Father started a coughing fit again, and Miles held a bowl under his chin as he coughed up blood. When the attack had subsided, Father glared at him. "Know this. I'll curse God with my dying breath." He gasped for air and cried out in pain.

A moment later, he was dead.

Miles bent his head to his father's chest. He knew there wouldn't be a heartbeat, but he had to try. He sat back in his chair. He'd just watched his father go to an eternity in Hades. He'd tried, but it had done no good. Father had made the same decision he'd made his entire life, to show disdain for his God.

His heart ached for the father he had once despised. Sobs came out of him from deep inside his gut, and he didn't think he'd ever stop.

A hand rested on his shoulder, and he looked up. Elizabella eyes were closed, and her mouth formed silent words. She was praying for him. It brought him more comfort than she would ever know. He wiped his face and took her into his arms where she belonged.

"He... He forgave me before he died." Miles cleared his throat. "And I forgave him."

"'Tis a comfort."

"Nay. He died in his sins."

"I'm so sorry." Elizabella placed a hand on his chest and gazed at him, tears filling her eyes. "Why don't we go to the kitchen? I have some stew cooking in the fireplace."

Miles pulled away and turned toward his father. "I'm not hungry. There is much to be done. I need to prepare the body and go to the church to let the vicar know." His thoughts were sluggish and tangled together. "I suppose I should inform His Royal Highness King James."

"There's time for that. First, you must keep up your strength. You've barely eaten anything since we arrived here."

His wife took him by the hand and led him to the kitchen. He didn't have the strength to refuse her, so he did as she bid. She placed two bowls of stew on the table and they sat across from each other.

He ate by rote, not really tasting the food. Neither said anything until the stew was eaten.

Elizabella placed her hand on his. "I know only one way to bring comfort in such a tragedy. Husband, we should take this time to read God's Word and pray. Then we can set about doing what must be done."

Miles nodded.

~~~~~

After the burial, Elizabella took a walk with Miles through the streets of London. She tried to remember how she felt about the city before Jamestown, but it was no use. It was crowded and dirty. As they passed the butcher's, the stench of rotting meat assaulted her. She longed for the untamed beauty of the colony. If only she could go back.

They wandered into St. James Park, and Miles motioned for them to sit on a nearby bench.

"I have need to discuss something with you." Miles' jaw twitched.

Elizabella placed her hand in his. "You can converse with me about anything. You know that."

He squeezed her hand. "I've arranged for us to stay with Lord Robert and Lady Honesty for the next couple of weeks. It will give you an opportunity to spend time with your sister."

"Thank ye." Her stomach tightened. He was troubled. This conversation wasn't about moving in with her sister.

"When I met with my father's banker yesterday, I found out my father had left me a sizable sum. I'm putting his house up for sale and giving the Worthington estate to my father's manager. It's only fair since he has been running the properties for at least twenty years. The sale from the house should assist him, and King James has approved my giving my title as Duke of Worthington to him."

"A sound plan." She watched a squirrel carry a nut into a hole burrowed in a nearby oak tree while she waited for him to continue.

"With the gold and supplies we're taking back to Jamestown, I should be able to pay the Burgess for the copper they provided and mayhap make a new bargain with Chief Opechancanough to satisfy him and get him to release Hugh from his debt."

A jittery feeling rose in her stomach. So that was what he was about. He planned to return to Jamestown.

He wiped his hand across his mouth. "I've purchased the journey for both of us on the *Marmaduke*. It's leaving in two weeks. It'll take that long to purchase the supplies and have them delivered to the ship."

Elizabella pulled her hand out of his grasp and stood to her feet. "Why both of us? I already informed you I can't leave my sister for at least a year. You said you wouldn't force me to go."

"I won't." He let out a heavy sigh. "I was hoping you'd reconsidered, but if you won't go, then I'll stay."

She sat back down beside him. "You can't. You must help your brother now that you have the means to do so."

"You're my wife. I can't leave you." Now, Miles stood and began pacing.

Tears filled her eyes, and she blinked to keep from shedding them.
~~~~~

"You have no choice. Your brother needs you."

Miles sat and placed his hands on her shoulders. "If I go, you must go with me."

"I can't." A tear wet her cheek. "My sister needs me."

"Nay, she is a grown woman with a husband. You're being absurd. Come home with me."

She shook her head.

Miles took her in his arms. "I'm not giving up. I have two weeks to convince you of your folly."

Elizabella sobbed on his shoulder. As much as she wanted him to succeed, she wouldn't leave her sister. She couldn't break her vow to her mother.

Chapter Thirty-Six

Two weeks later

Miles placed his hand on the doorknob and paused. "The *Marmaduke* departs at noon. For the last time, please come with me."

"I cannot."

In two large strides, he crossed the guest room to Elizabella and took her in his arms. He kissed her so passionately, her resolve almost faltered.

"I'll be there in a year, mayhap six months," she said.

"Ah, my love, how do you know what the year holds? If you stay, this may be the last time we hold each other. Do you want to take that chance?"

"Only the Lord can know that." She squared her shoulders, determined not to let him sway her from what she knew was right. It was difficult when all she wanted to do was run away with him. "I love you, but I'm staying here for now."

Miles headed to the door. "If you come to your senses, I shall see you there. If not..." He walked out.

Elizabella watched him go and felt her heart sink. After what had happened to Benjamin, she couldn't leave Honesty no matter how much she wanted to. *Lord, give me strength to fulfill my promise, and give me peace through this.*

She ran to the window and watched him get into the carriage. Her knees wobbled, and she sat on the bed. It had become her habit to pray when she was distraught. The Lord would sweep over her with a sweet peace even if the problem didn't go away, but that didn't happen this time. There would be no peace for this ache in her soul, and she knew not why God didn't answer.

Honesty came into the entranceway and sat beside her on the bed. "Miles says he's sailing today. Why aren't you with him?"

"Miles," Elizabella said thickly. "I can't go with him."

Honesty took hold of her hand. "Didn't he want you to sail?"

"Aye." A sob escaped her throat. "I told him my place was here."

Honesty's mouth dropped open. "Why?"

Elizabella waved her off. "I made a vow to Mother to take care of you."

"I'm married. I would miss you, but I have a husband to care for my needs. I no longer need an older sister brooding over me."

"You don't understand. It's my fault Benjamin is dead. I can't desert you as well."

Honesty shook her head. "Your fault? How could his death possibly be your fault?"

"He woke from a bad dream. When I went into his room, he begged me to leave the lantern lit. He must have knocked it over in his sleep. If I hadn't given in to him, he'd be alive."

"Elizabella, I can't believe you've carried that burden for so many years. No wonder you hovered over me so, but it simply is not true."

She looked up at her sister, trying to understand her words. "God has forgiven me, and it was an accident, but the fault was mine."

"Nay." Honesty squeezed her hand. "Do you really not remember what happened?"

"How could I forget?" Elizabella's head throbbed. "The lantern started the fire that killed Benjamin."

Honesty let out a gusty sigh. "The magistrate declared the fault was not yours."

"Aye." Elizabella rubbed her temples. "When he took you into the back room, you told him it was an accident."

"He declared it an accident, but he said you were not at fault in any way." Honesty gazed into her eyes. "It's time I told you what I told the judge, since you don't seem to remember what happened."

"I know not what you're about."

"I also woke that night after you returned to bed," Honesty said. "Father came in late, drunk as usual, and staggered down the hall making a noisy racket. I cried out, and you told me to go back to my slumber. If anyone knocked over the lantern, it was him."

"But..." She rubbed her eyes to try to alleviate the pounding in her head. "'Twas me, not him. Didn't you hear his foul words? I killed my brother. He even spoke against me at the trial."

Honesty let out a heavy sigh. "He was a mean drunk. He said those things to hurt you and take the blame off himself. The judge declared it an accident caused by Father." She took hold of Elizabella's hand. "You tried to save him. You did your best to take care of us both. Benjamin's death was not your fault, and your obligation to me ended when I married Robert. Go with my blessing."

"Nay, I don't believe it. You're deceiving me to convince me to sail. If Father had awakened us coming into the house, I would have remembered." Elizabella cried out from the sharp pain in her head. *Lord, help me remember.*

<div align="center">~~~~~</div>

Elizabella woke with a start. Father was drunk again, and he came stumbling up the stairs, singing a tune too vile for her sister's tender ears. She hurriedly rushed to the hall, hoping she could keep him from waking her siblings.

"Father, please," she whispered. "Everyone's asleep."

"Nay," Father stammered. "See the light from my room? Benji's awake."

"He's sound asleep. I lit the lantern because he had a bad dream."

Father leaned against her, almost tipping her over. "Do you think we're made of gold, girl? We can't afford oil to keep the lantern lit all night. Have some sense about you."

Her stomach tightened. "It won't happen again."

He let go and slapped her across her face. "See it doesn't."

She drew her hand to her cheek. "I'm sorry."

His words slurred. "I don't know why the boy can't sleep in your room."

She knew he wouldn't remember what he said tomorrow. He was the one who said Benji was too old to sleep with the girls. He said the boy didn't need a nursemaid to turn him into a pansy. But she was tired and afraid and would do anything to settle Father down. "I'll see to it in the morning."

"If only God had given you some brains." Father headed to his room.

"Don't forget to turn out the lantern."

Father waved his hand and walked into the room.

Elizabella made her way back to her bed.

"Why does he always have to be so mean?" Honesty said.

"Shhhh. It's all right now. Go back to sleep."

~~~~~

Elizabella swooned.

She awoke to a horrible smell that made her cough. She sat up and coughed a few more time. Honesty and Sir Robert were hovering over her with a bottle of smelling salts.

"Get that foul smell away from me," she said.

"Thank the Lord you're all right." Honesty patted her hand. "Do you remember what happened?"

"I remember." Elizabella shook her head, trying to clear the fog. "I had a headache, and then I saw a vision of Father coming home." It all became clear. "I didn't start the fire." A bark of laughter escaped. "It wasn't my fault."

"That's what I've been trying to tell you." Honesty clasped Robert's hand. "I'm a married woman with a baby on the way. I love you, Sister, but I don't need you to nursemaid me anymore."

Elizabella suddenly realized what Honesty said. "A baby?"

Robert smiled. "My wife is at least four months along."

"Why didn't you tell me?" Elizabella asked.

"And do you want to stay to help me give birth?" Honesty crossed her arms. "I have a midwife. You need to sail with your husband."

"Miles!" Elizabella stood. "The ship is sailing at noon. I must get to the wharf."

"Fredrick," Robert called.

The butler, who Elizabella hadn't seen until that moment, came out
~~~~~

from where he'd been standing against the wall. "Aye, my lord."

"Get a carriage ready posthaste." Robert turned to Elizabella. "We must hurry. It's nearly noon now."

They all rushed to get Elizabella's belongings together and darted to the carriage. By the time they left the house, it was ready, and a driver sat ready to steer the horses. Elizabella, Honesty, and Robert climbed into the carriage.

Robert stuck his head out the window. "Drive us to the docks, and make haste about it."

The carriage took off at greater speed than Elizabella would have thought possible. "I don't know how to say goodbye."

Honesty took her hands. "I'm grateful to you for everything you've done for me. You've been more than a sister. I'll always love you for it."

Elizabella embraced her. "You can repay me by being content with the life you've chosen."

"I am," Honesty said.

The carriage came to an abrupt stop.

Robert stuck his head out the window. "Why are we stopping?"

The carriage driver pointed to a cart of chickens turned over in the road. "It'll be a while before we can go any farther."

A dread came over Elizabella, and she closed her eyes tight. "What am I to do? The ship sails soon." She looked up. The sun was high in the sky. "He'll leave without me."

Robert got out of the carriage and looked around. "How far from the wharf?"

"Just over the bridge and a couple of furlongs," the carriage driver said.

He pointed to a man with an empty man-powered cart sitting on the side of the road. "Send that carter with the trunk." Robert opened the door of the carriage. "Honesty, say your farewells here. I'll travel with your sister on foot. If we reach the ship in time, I'll delay them until you arrive with her trunk."

Elizabella embraced her sister one last time, wiped her face, and got out of the carriage. She turned to Robert and swallowed hard. "We'll never make it in time."

"If we walk," Robert said. "Hoist your skirts, take my hand, and we'll make a run for it."

Chapter Thirty-Seven

Miles looked out over the dock. He'd kept the captain from setting sail until he took one last look around. The captain wasn't happy about it, but he didn't care. After all, he was paying for this voyage. He wanted to give Elizabella every chance to change her mind.

His shoulders slumped. How would he manage to go through life without Elizabella? *Lord, why are You taking away everyone I love?* A sadness covered him like a blanket. "The Lord giveth, and the Lord taketh away. Blessed be the Name of the Lord." He surrendered himself to the truth. She wasn't coming.

He walked up the gangplank and nodded to the captain.

The first mate barked out orders. "Aboard, aboard ship. Cast off."

The sailors started pulling up the gangplank.

Miles' mind was in a fog. Would he ever see her again?

He gazed over the dock one last time. A man and woman were running toward the ship. The woman wore a navy-blue cloak like Elizabella's. Could it be her?

"Toss oars."

As they drew closer, he saw it really was her, and Robert accompanied her, but they would never make it in time. "Stop!" He ran to the captain. "Stop, lower the gangplank."

The captain's brow furrowed. "Now, see here. You have no right."

Miles wanted to shake the man. "I've commissioned this ship. You'll obey my orders. Lower the gangplank. Now!"

The captain nodded to the first mate, and the men worked together to lower the plank. As soon as it was down, Miles ran off the ship and toward Elizabella.

When they reached each other, he took her in his arms and spun her around. He kissed her so fervently he was concerned he might break her lips, but he couldn't help himself.

Someone cleared his throat. Miles looked up. Robert stood there with a large smile on his face.

Miles let go of Elizabella and shook Robert's hand powerfully. "Thank ye, Sir Robert, for getting her here in time."

"You're most welcome, Sir Miles," Robert said. "Perchance we'll visit you in Jamestown one day."

"Not 'sir' anymore," Miles said. "I gave up my title. I'm a simple Jamestown planter."

Robert nodded. As soon as the cart arrived and the trunk was loaded on board, Miles led Elizabella up the gangplank. As the sailors prepared to sail, he gazed at her face. "What changed your mind?"

Elizabella let out a laugh. "The Lord showed me the truth about the fire. I was never to blame. I'll tell you all about it on the journey home."

~~~~~

February 1621

Miles held Elizabella's hand as the ship moored on James River at their plantation. Since he'd commissioned the ship and there was so much to unload, it made sense to order the captain to dock on his land.

They'd managed the trip in three months, so he wasn't surprised nobody was outside to greet him. In late February, it was too early to start getting the land ready for planting.

He led Elizabella to Hugh's home. Hopefully, his brother wasn't at the fort or out hunting. He would need every man to help him unload before the ship headed to the fort. He knocked.

Hugh answered the door with a flintlock pistol in his hand. "Miles?"

Miles raised his eyebrow. He'd never known his brother to be so cautious. "I'm home, Brother, and I brought my new wife."

Hugh shook his hand vigorously and then gave him a bear hug. "I'm so happy for both of you." He glanced at Elizabella's growing stomach. "It looks as if we are both expecting children."

"Hannah?" Miles said. "Good tidings indeed."

"We must talk." Hugh cleared his throat. "Alone."

Elizabella nodded. "I'll go inside and greet Hannah."

Hugh didn't say any more until the door closed. "You must sail back to London and take Elizabella and Hannah with you."

Miles wiped his hand over his mouth. "I knew something was wrong when you greeted me with a pistol in your hand. You haven't even asked about Father."

Hugh turned his back and took a few steps away. "Is Father well?"

"He's dead."

Hugh jerked toward Miles, his face ashen.

Miles stepped tentatively toward his brother and hugged him, then stepped back. "He wasn't executed. The king declared him innocent of all charges, but his stomach stopped working. I was there when he died."

"Thank ye for going." Hugh wiped the tears off his face. "It is some comfort to know he wasn't alone."

"We made peace with each other." Miles decided not to tell him the rest, at least not now. There would be time for that later. "You were distressed before I told you about Father. What's wrong?"

Hugh's Adam's apple bulged. "Chief Opechancanough has informed me that Suleta's younger sister, Kimi, is betrothed. I am to provide a wedding gift by May, and my commitment to them is done. They also
~~~~~

vowed to enter peace talks with the council if I succeed."

"That's wonderful news, Brother." Something was wrong. Hugh's whole body matched his drooping expression. "Why did you want me to take the women away from the colony?"

"The wedding gift is impossible to obtain. He asked for a variety of farm tools, iron pots, and a number of other things I won't be able to provide until I can order them from a supply ship. Even then, we don't have the funds to pay for it, and if we did, it will take at least a year. He demands these things by May or I'm to turn myself in to the Powhatan where I'll be executed."

"Executed?" A knot formed in the pit of Miles' stomach. His thoughts swirled so fast he couldn't get hold of one. "You're the one who needs to leave Jamestown. I've chartered a ship. You and Hannah can sail tonight."

Hugh placed his hand on Miles' shoulder. "I won't leave. If I don't return to the village, with or without the bounty, the Powhatan shall attack the colony. He gave me this impossible task as an excuse to murder me, but I won't run away and leave innocent men, women, and children at his mercy."

One of the thoughts in Miles' head came to the forefront. "Father left me a fortune. I decided to buy some supplies. They're on the ship now, ready to be unloaded. What do you need?"

Hugh rubbed his chin. "I've already obtained ten beaver pelts, two iron pots, an axe, scissors, a barrel of rum, and a musket, but I still need two hoes, another iron ax, half a dozen woven blankets, a pair of scissors, another barrel of rum, and some glass beads."

Miles couldn't help the smiles that spread over his face. "I've brought with me at least a dozen of the axes, hoes, pots, and an array of glass beads for trading. We also purchased a couple of extra pairs of scissors for Elizabella. She insisted I was crazy for buying them, said she didn't need that many. She can easily weave five blankets in time, and with the bounty I have, we'll be able to get another barrel of rum from the fort."

Hugh let out a gusty laugh and fell to his knees. "Thank ye, Brother. You have rescued me again."

"Not I." Miles sat on the ground beside his brother. "When I found how much gold Father had left me, the Lord put the thought in my mind to bring a bounty to the New World to help you get out of your agreement with the Powhatan and to provide the plantation with needed tools. I'm happy I obeyed."

Hugh's smile started to fade, and his forehead furrowed. "Wait, it won't work. Kimi asked for something else I know you wouldn't think to get. You must sail to London with the women. There's nothing else for it."

Miles placed his hand on Hugh's back. *Lord, help my brother.* "What wouldn't I have thought of?"

"A mirror," Hugh said in a mournful tone. "Even if I deliver everything else, Kimi wants a mirror. She was insistent on it."

Miles let out a belly laugh and dropped to his knees on the ground.

"What are you about?" Hugh asked. "Did you not hear what I said? The Powhatan will kill me unless they get their precious mirror."

Miles tried to calm his merriment. Finally, he was able to speak. "Brother, when I was buying all of this bounty, I saw a looking glass in the window of a merchant's shop and thought how nice it would be if our wives had mirrors to look at themselves. I brought two. I suppose our wives can share one."

Now Hugh started laughing.

"The Lord knew what you needed and provided more than enough."

~~~~

May 1621

Elizabella stepped outside with her husband at her side as they walked to the well to fetch water, something they did every morning together. She set her hand on her growing stomach where their son or daughter kicked with the force of one of the king's horses. It wouldn't be long now. Hannah already had birthed a healthy baby boy, and she hoped to do the same, but a healthy girl would be a blessing as well.

It was spring, and the men were in the fields getting the land ready for planting. She couldn't help thinking about this time a year ago when the trees were blossoming. She had been in such despair. Now, the sight filled her with joy.

Miles took her in his arms. "Any regrets?"

"Not a one. It's good to be home."

Then he kissed her.

The End
~~~~

ABOUT THE AUTHOR

In her spare time, Tamera Lynn Kraft loves to watch classic movies, drink quality teas, and ride on roller coasters, but not while drinking tea. She does drink tea while being managing editor for Mt Zion Ridge Press, a traditional Christian publishing company and writing. LOST IN THE STORM, RED SKY OVER AMERICA, and ALICE'S NOTIONS are among her published works, some of which have won awards.

Tamera has been married for a very long time to the love of her life, Rick, and has adult children she's proud of and some adorable and smart grandchildren. She is the leader of a ministry called Revival Fire for Kids. She has written children's church curriculum, including Building Foundations, and is a recipient of the 2007 National Children's Leaders Association Shepherd's Cup for lifetime achievement in children's ministry. Visit her website at *http://tameralynnkraft.net* or use this URL code.

Other Books By Tamera Lynn Kraft

RED SKY OVER AMERICA
LOST IN THE STORM
FORKS IN THE ROAD
SOLDIER'S HEART
ALICE'S NOTIONS
RESURRECTION OF HOPE

9 781955 838481